A Grey Matter

Natasha Scholey

WYDION

ISBN 978 0 9873894 2 8

Gwydion Books, PO Box 391, Stirling, SA, 5152, Australia

A Grey Matter

Doctor Brodie looked at Jacks—astounded, as if trying to discover whether her words were in jest. Her face, however, was stone and revealed nothing.

'Jacqueline …' he began, but Jacks broke in again.

'How the hell did she get hold of a blade? What do you do, hand them out for good behaviour?' She was ranting and knew it, but she felt so strongly the after-effects of the situation.

The doctor's voice was quiet and steady. 'We don't know how she got the razor, Jacqueline, but really you shouldn't concern yourself; just try to put it out of your mind.' It was a ridiculous thing to say, but he had spoken without thinking.

'PUT IT OUT OF MY MIND!' she hollered. 'FOR GOD'S SAKE, IT SHOULDN'T HAVE BEEN PUT IN THERE IN THE FIRST PLACE! How could you have allowed this to happen? She was supposed to be in your care.'

She stared at him bitterly, expecting him to shirk responsibility, instead his shoulders sagged and he bowed his head, as if he felt the burden her words had placed upon him.

'Do you think that I wanted it to happen?' His voice sounded strange, lacking its usual control. 'Do you think I enjoyed watching that woman mutilate herself?'

Also by Natasha E Scholey

Gifts from the gods come at a price...

Knightfall
Book One of The CODM Prophecy

When Kirsten receives a P.E. detention, it feels as though life can't get any worse. However, that's just the beginning of her troubles. From the moment she hears about the killer on the news, she becomes fixated with him. It's as though she knows him, although she can't recall from where. Clearly, he knows her too, having killed his way across half of Europe to find her.

The Police thinks she's crazy; the killer thinks she's some missing princess from another world and she ... well she would rather crawl in a hole and pretend that none of it's happening. Unfortunately for her, that's not an option.

Destined to return power to the ancient gods, she sets out on a quest to find the lost shards of the Anarkhane stone. With unlikely help from fairies, dragons, a priest and a police inspector, she seeks to fulfil her destiny, not because she really wants to, but because she has no choice. She can neither return home or exist in Maldahl, for once the Lord Katahl discovers who she is, he will do everything in his power to prevent the CODM prophecy from coming to pass, stopping at nothing to blot her out of existence

King's Gambit
Book Two of The CODM Prophecy

Torn between duty and desire, she stands to lose everything she holds dear.

Following an argument with her father, Princess Exzalander disguises herself as a servant and runs away with the King's entourage in effort to consult secretly with her friend, the wizard Ardahl.

Had the dragons not attacked then all would have gone to plan. Had the dragons not attacked then she would have made it to the palace in safety. She would not have been abandoned to the will of a power hungry and depraved Counsellor who seizes the opportunity to take advantage of her, his true object of desire—the crown.

For Lesley

Acknowledgements

Thanks to Michaela Scholey, Nicos Kyriacou and Giuseppe Morrone for your initial proof reads and comments. Many thanks to Dr Stephen Wills for allowing me to bounce medical jargon off.

Biography

Author of the CODM Prophecy series, Natasha was born in Coventry, England. She is a graduate of both Brunel University and Roehampton University.

Over the years, Natasha has had a varied career including the performance arts, various managerial roles and teaching. She has maintained a keen interest in science and ancient to medieval history and often includes an aspect of these within her writing.

She lives in the Northern Beaches of Sydney, Australia, with her forensic pathologist partner.

Grey Matter:

Greyish tissue of the brain found mainly in the cortex, involved in muscle control and sensory perceptions, including, hearing, seeing, emotions and memory.

Prologue

'Who's dead?' Jacks exclaimed, as she answered the telephone. The sense of foreboding she felt had been growing all day. She hoped her mother would laugh and say, nobody.

The woman sounded exhausted as she made her reply. 'Patrick. I phoned earlier but no one was in.' She sniffed deeply to gain control over her wavering voice as the tears began. 'The funeral's a week Wednesday if you can make it ... are you all right?'

Jacks paused briefly; her reply seemed quiet and distant, as if the words came from somewhere else. 'Yeah, I'm fine, I ... thanks for letting me know, mum. I'll ring you tomorrow; I need to be alone right now.'

Replacing the receiver, she walked calmly to her room. The mirror faced her as she opened the door and she stared at her reflection for a while.

'What a day!' she said, aloud, running her fingers through her hair.

As she approached the bed, her body slumped; she untied her laces, slipped off her boots and drew her knees in to her chest. Hours seemed to pass before she burst into tears.

'Oh God no. Please ... no.

Chapter One

Put your hand in my heart,
Pull out the pain,
Reach into my soul,
Make me whole again.

Fill the empty cup,
Remove the vacant chair,
Let me be with the stars
And find you there.

Allow me to grieve,
But think of you with joy.
Let me be alone,
But never leave me.

Cut open my heart
Let my blood drown the earth,
Let flowers grow where your body lies,
Above all, let me live again,
But live without you,
Let me love you
And my love always be with you.

'It feels like a scream trapped inside—trapped in a little box,' Jacks said, in a hoarse whisper. She banged her chest with a clenched hand. 'It's trying to escape, but every time it thinks it's found a voice, it discovers another box and another and another.' Her voice rose to a miserable crescendo, disturbing to hear. There was a hint of tears in her words and yet no tears came.

'Cry if you need to,' Polly said calmly.

'Cry!' Jacks repeated the word as if it was wholly alien to her, but the look in her eyes convinced Polly that nothing could be further from the truth. Her tears were spent; she had no more left to give. She was a hollow shell, deprived of all warmth and joy, anger and sunshine. Her world consisted of hues of black and grey, mingling to create a strange abstract painting. All that remained to Jacks was her emptiness and loneliness, which consumed her entire being.

'Tell me about Patrick, Jacks.'

Jacks winced, her glazed eyes staring dreamily as she searched her memory. She saw the suitcase as she clicked the latches shut and remembered how she had refused to accept that he was gone. She recalled running to the dresser and rummaging through the drawer until her hands grasped the cold silver frame …

She smiled.

Re-opening the case, she placed the photograph of Patrick gently on the top. 'Something isn't right,' she said, as she stared at him beaming up at her. The clothes surrounding the frame were all black. It looked like a tiny star twinkling in a midnight sky. She began to unpack her belongings.

Black, black and more black, piled onto the bed. Jacks gazed down at herself and sighed.

Black.

She glanced at the photograph next to the mountain of black attire. Patrick's eyes glinted and his smile seemed to mock the depressing garb. Her eyebrow rose as she shook her head and laughed; she guffawed. The mourning period was over.

Picking up the photograph, she kissed it and began to pack more suitable clothing for the record summer temperatures that had been predicted.

As she left the house, she blinked in the sunlight; it was the first time she had ventured outside since the news of Patrick's death. She felt shaky and weak as she perched on the doorstep trying to force herself to remember what she had been doing for the past week or so. It seemed a blur. She breathed in the morning air, feeling newly awakened—inspired. It felt as though Patrick was with her, all around her. She knew that it would sound trite if she told anyone, but it was true nonetheless; she would celebrate Patrick's life through his death. He was everywhere, but most of all in her heart …

'Jacks, do you not want to talk about Patrick?

'Not really,' Jacks replied. 'He's not the reason I'm here, is he?'

Polly appeared different somehow, more real than she had previously in Jacks' wandering mind. Before, she had seemed like a shadow, just a voice in her head, but now that Jacks refused to speak about Patrick, Polly gained substance—a reward for focusing on what was required.

She took a deep breath and began to speak, not caring what the woman would say or what notes she would write; each word she spoke made her world seem more substantial and less like a bad dream. She wanted to be normal again, more than anything …

Five weeks earlier:

Jacks sat outside the local supermarket in the blistering heat, with her mother and a ton of shopping, waiting for the taxi to arrive. Her mother had taken lessons after her father left and was actually an accomplished driver, but she had given up when she started seeing Blake, saying it was pointless both of them having a car. Jacks was more convinced it was Blake's wish to dominate that had led to the decline in her mother's freedom.

She felt parched. Reaching for the bottle of Pepsi, which was conveniently sticking out of the one of the bags, she tipped it back and gulped eagerly; the bottle stuck to her tongue, giving way with a pop. Replacing the cap, she handed the bottle to her mother. The woman had lit up and was puffing away happily beside her; Jacks turned away in silent disgust and sat staring at nothing in particular.

Feet passed—hundreds of pairs of feet, the sight of which combined with the effect of the sun, made her drowsy. She shook herself and looked up. Approaching, was an employee; he was tall with dark hair and Jacks suddenly realised that she had been aware of him, if only subconsciously, for some time. He looked strangely familiar to her. She did not have time to ponder the riddle, however, as two hoots from the taxi knocked the thought from her mind. She bounded forward with the trolley and helped the driver load the bags into the trunk.

In the days that followed, Jacks found it increasingly difficult to concentrate. Her work seemed nothing more than a pile of good intentions whose services would no longer be required. She had started several angles on her project for work, none of which seemed to inspire her any longer. The week was spent reading, thinking, and hiding from the sun. Her sleep patterns were erratic and her dreams, strange ...

She was in a fourth floor office. Paperwork lay scattered, most of which had been screwed up and discarded. A journalist was bickering with her sister over some legal matter. Some of his colleagues entered and Jacks climbed onto the window ledge. The man tried to calm her down, but she decided to jump. It seemed the only sensible decision to make; any other would bring pain too much to bear.

A man in a uniform entered, his face remarkably like her own. His legs were missing, and he wore a monocle neatly fixed in front of his left eye. Floating over, he urged her not to jump. She remembered thinking that he resembled greatly, a subject in an Otto Dix painting,

Looking down, she saw the blood as it spread outwards across her white cotton pyjamas and she allowed herself to fall.

Her eyes opened. Patrick stood at the foot of her bed. Her heart raced and she shook herself. He was gone—just a bi-product of a waking dream.

Jacks found it difficult to adapt back to the Sydney summer heat, struggling to reacclimatize after her extended stay in England. She took to staying indoors, as was her wont, retreating to the back of the duplex, where it was a little cooler.

The waste paper bin overflowed with a selection of rejected set designs and she sat, cross-legged in the enormous armchair, the director's creative vision doing nothing to inspire her thoughts. She began to scribble themes from the play, but her attention wandered and she realised she was no longer focused on work at all …

She nodded into waking, not realising she had dozed off. Looking down, she had repeatedly scribbled the name Patrick, as if not to do so, was to forget his very existence. She felt parched and shaky; her head ached and all she wanted to do was to crawl into bed and not emerge until she felt normal again. Screwing up the paper, she tossed it onto the overflowing bin, feeling immediately a little restored.

When her mother requested a helping hand with the shopping again, Jacks realised it was the first time she had been outside in a whole week. She winced as the sunlight stung her eyes and held them closed while she took in a deep breath of air.

The store's air conditioning was down, causing her to loiter about the freezer section, relishing the cold while her mother shopped. On joining the queue, she noticed the man she had seen the week before. She eyed him more carefully, noting how good-looking he was. *I know him from somewhere,* she thought, *but where?*

For some reason he made her think of her sister's fiancé, but he certainly looked nothing like Mark. *I never forget a face … of course, four years ago at my sister's engagement party. He's a friend of Mark's. He must have made quite an impression on me,* she considered. *I'm not renowned for remembering names. After all, I'm the woman who declared with complete conviction that my MD was called Norman Bates.*

Claude—yes, I remember well enough. I'd not been able to take my eyes off him all night. I never expected to see him again, yet here he is, pacing up and down the shop floor, looking more gorgeous than ever.

'Oh bugger,' she muttered under her breath, as the butterflies did tiny loop the loops in her stomach. Hurriedly packing the shopping, she made her exit.

On arriving home, she found her sister drinking tea and chatting.

'Hi Trude,' she hollered through to the living room.

'Yeright?' said Trudi, in her broad West Midlands accent she had managed to retain, despite having emigrated over a decade ago. 'Where've ya bin?'

'Coles,' Jacks replied, as she jumped into an armchair, her sweaty skin sticking at once to the leather.

'Did ya see Claude?'

Jacks' heart missed a beat. *Why do I feel like I've just entered a poor episode of 'The Twilight Zone'?* she thought. *Come on, Jacks, she's waiting for an answer.*

'Claude?' She gave a puzzled look.

'Yeah, Mark's mate, don't ya remember 'im? Ee woz at me engagement partee,' Trudi said, with a frown.

'Oh right,' Jacks exclaimed. 'I thought I saw someone who looked familiar.' Jacks stared awkwardly at the floor. *Play it cool, Jacks, play it cool,* she thought, *you're overacting and they'll suss.*

Luckily for Jacks, the subject was soon changed. Although Jacks knew she was off the hook, she felt a tug of regret. She *wanted* to talk about Claude. She wanted to find out anything she could about him.

Jacks was well known for having the appetite of three large men, or to put it in more traditional terms; she ate like a pig. She sat and stared at her plate, half expecting the food to disappear without aid. Closing her eyes, she let out a sigh and opened them again; the food was still there, getting cold. She looked up and saw the dog patiently eyeing her plate. Standing up, she wondered if she could make it past her mother.

'Not hungry?' her mother said, without taking her eyes away from the television.

Jacks shook her head. 'Sorry,' she said, with an apologetic smile. Even so simple an effort felt exhausting.

She wearily scraped the contents of her plate into the dog's bowl and watched for a moment as he gulped it down, before making her way up the stairs to her room. *How different the old room looks now,* she thought, *so bare.* When she lived there, she had so many posters and pictures tacked up, that the colour of the walls could only be guessed.

She reeled forward, unable to see. Catching her balance in time and lowering herself onto the bed, her vision seemed invaded by a million tiny insects, buzzing and fluttering.

What's wrong with me? she wondered. *I haven't eaten,* another voice in her head seemed to suggest. *No, no, no, no. I know what's wrong; it's him, isn't it?* She laughed a huge bellowing laugh that came deep from within. Kicking her feet on the bed, she turned over, burying her head in the pillow and screamed. She felt sixteen again—a love-struck teenager.

The day had been exceptionally hot, which drifted into a hazy evening, inviting Jacks to sit outside sipping ice tea. She watched her mother with admiration as she fetched in the laundry. Her mother was a handsome woman of forty-one, with a medium build. She seemed to live her life in summer and was aglow with the warmth of that season, appearing at her best when in the admiring company of others. It was that glow which set their appearances so far apart; Jacks enjoyed peace and solitude and was more comfortable running carelessly through blankets of fallen leaves and hiding in the shadows of sleeping trees.

'Are you going out tonight?' her mother asked.

The question was means to a conversation rather than a genuine enquiry. Jacks did not socialise with anyone at night. She felt uncomfortable in public and did not trust easily. Perhaps what her mother had meant was, *'you should go out.'* She knew that she should, but she was not able to yet.

'How about you?' she said, after a moment.

'Blake and I are just popping up to Coles,' her mother replied. 'But apart from that, I'm not going out.'

'Coles ...' Jacks wriggled, feeling like a child being told it is going to the park. 'Can I come?' she asked, trying to sound casual, as if it really didn't matter either way, when in fact it felt more like life and death.

Her mother walked back to the house, a pile of washing cradled in her arms. 'Yeah sure,' she shouted back.

Jacks jumped to her feet and dashed after her. 'What shall I wear? What shall I wear?' she chanted under her breath, as she leapt up the stairs taking three at a time.

'Are you ready to go?' her mother called.

Jacks looked down at herself. *Denim shorts and a skinny-rib,* she thought. *I guess this is what I'm wearing'.* She took to the stairs again, a little more carefully.

Blake decided to go away and meet them later.

'*Good,*' Jacks thought. She slipped on her sunglasses and made ready to enter the store.

Her mother stepped by a notice board reading 'Singles Night.'

Jacks laughed harshly. 'A singles night in a supermarket! What a thoroughly ridiculous notion, what a brainless idea, what a ...'

'Why don't you go?' her mother suggested, at the very moment they passed Claude.

'What!' Jacks screeched, a little too loudly.

Claude's glance shot towards her.

Great, she thought, *just bloody great. Thanks mum. I'll tell you what you can do with the idea; you and the idea can go to hell, that's what.*

She felt her skin burning and she spoke a little quieter, but she hoped loud enough for Claude to hear. 'Mum, I may be single, but I'm not desperate.' Whether the comment did more harm than good, it was too early to tell.

In the half hour that followed, they sauntered casually around the store. Every time they reached the end of an aisle, Jacks would catch a glimpse of Claude and would linger for a while. By the time they reached the checkout, he was walking up and down shop floor, collecting baskets as he went. With her sunglasses on, she was able to watch him to her heart's content, while he strode about, his walk displaying confidence and authority; yet there was something else she noticed, a shyness and quiet, which she found even more enticing.

They packed the goods into the trolley and Jacks wheeled them over to the cigarette counter where her mother had joined the queue.

Jacks frowned. *I thought she was going to give up,* she thought. *That'll be the day! How can a woman who cares so much about her physical appearance have such a disregard for her health?*

Just at that moment, Claude walked past.

'He's good looking, isn't he?' her mother said, loud and clear.

Great, bloody typical, mother. Why don't you say it a little louder? Jacks thought bitterly. 'Who?' she asked, trying to sound bewildered.

'Claude,' her mother replied, as he passed them again.

It was one of those moments when an overwhelming desire to be consumed by some great natural phenomenon arose—earthquake, flood—Jacks wasn't picky. She grew nervous, unaware whether Claude was standing close by to hear the answer to her mother's question. She took in a large breath, held it, and decided to ignore her mother's nosiness, letting the breath out in an annoyed hiss.

'Mum, we're late,' she said, 'Blake will be waiting.' She knew that the mention of her mother's controlling husband would be enough to deter the woman from further interference into her private life.

Her mother's smug look faded and she took over steering the trolley, muttering, 'Oh hell,' as she made for the exit.

Jacks made it back to her mother's house, before sunset. She sat outside, staring out at the rooftops with their golden halos. Her hair seemed on fire as it caught the sun's final rays. It was not just her hair—she was aflame. She sat perfectly still and yet every part of her was dancing. Finally, she comprehended what her subconscious had known all along. She was in love and she felt marvellous.

Chapter Two

The clock chimes,
A spider on the curtain scuttles
Toward the open window in search of air.
The musty room seems darkened by my sadness,
Is it the humidity or my own aura of self-pity and
gloom that chokes the atmosphere?
As I gaze out of the window,
The sun dazzles me with its golden brilliance,
It seems that all that lies between the light and I, is
a pane of glass.
Oh that I was that spider and could embrace the
sun through the open window,
But we have doors for such things ...
Is it really that easy?
Do I only have to make the effort?
Turn the handle and step out into ...
Into the wide world.
Perhaps all said and done I had best remain
Here in my easy chair,
And let others lose themselves out there,
Out there where I know life is cruel.
Let others be fooled by the inviting, yet deceptive,
warmth of the sun,
I choose to wear my veil of truth and bitter
acceptance.

'Engaged,' Jacks repeated, scarcely aloud. Beads of sweat began to form on her forehead. Shivering, she wondered what had happened. She couldn't see, as spots formed before her eyes, engulfing the world around her. She became aware of a noise, dim at first.

What is it? she thought. *My heartbeat,* she realised. It was pounding, accelerating, and through that thumping sound, she became aware of a voice, distant at first and then it became closer and clearer. Her sister.

Trudi's talking to me and hasn't noticed that I've been on another planet for, how long has it been? Minutes, maybe hours, Jacks thought, as she drifted into yet another little corner of her mind.

'Jacks, are you even listening to me?' Trudi's voice was abrupt and displayed more than a hint of annoyance.

'I'm sorry, will you excuse me a minute.' She rose and crossed the kitchen, trying to appear composed, knowing that Trudi was watching her intently, suspicious, perhaps worried, especially after the extremely formal manner in which Jacks had addressed her.

She shut and locked the bathroom door, resting her forehead against it as she did so. Staring blankly at the carpet, she noticed how shabby and damp it was. *What is the point in having a carpeted bathroom anyhow?* she thought, *It's bound to get in a mess after a while.*

At that precise, tiny moment, she forgot why she was there and became confused. The memory returned like a shuttling train, which rammed into her headlong. She gasped for air, and a feeling of nausea began to grow; clutching at her ribs, she vomited.

'Are you okay?' Trudi's voice sailed through from the kitchen.

'Yeah fine,' Jacks said shakily. She reached for the toilet tissue. 'I've been sick,' she exclaimed, whilst trying to mop up the carpet.

At least she might consider pulling it up now, was the only thought Jacks dared let enter her head. The word "engaged" she locked up behind a little prison door, and knew it would have to remain there until she could be alone.

Later that evening, Jacks sat cross-legged, as if meditating, but she was far from being relaxed. She felt as one does on waking from a bad dream, yet was wide-awake and the nightmare continued.

How could this have happened? How? she wondered. *I'm the woman everyone turns to for advice because I'm always so in control ... control, that's what's needed.*

'For God's sake, Jacks, pull yourself together,' she said aloud, and then burst into tears.

* * * * *

It was the morning of her sister's wedding. Jacks walked down the aisle, a bridesmaid. 'Where is Trude?' she asked. 'Surely she should be up front.'

Glancing down, she saw that she was wearing Trudi's wedding gown; it hung off her like the skin off an old man. She looked up and saw the vicar as he stood waiting at the altar—the same vicar who had married her mother to Blake.

This can't be right, she thought.

Two children were being naughty and the vicar came and handcuffed them to railings, which had appeared from nowhere. It was at that moment Jacks noticed the enormous toad sitting on a pew. He was bright green with large yellow spots that looked as though a careless child had painted them on.

She waded through piles of legal documents toward the exit, disturbed that she had taken the place of Trudi. On leaving the church, Jacks wandered alone, through streets that seemed familiar and yet she knew she had never visited them before.

She awoke.

Her eyes were reluctant to open.

What time is it? she wondered.

Reaching over, she squinted at the clock. Five a.m. and the morning sun shone as brightly as if it was midday. Her skin glistened with sweat and she stripped the duvet away to allow her body some air. Lying gently back, she listened to the chorus of butcherbirds and currawongs outside, feeling calm and relaxed, almost as if the day before had been a dream after all. She knew it was merely an illusion, however; she always felt at peace after crying herself to sleep.

She closed her eyes; although her clock read 5:10, her senses were aware of the sunlight flooding the room, and refused to believe that it was time to sleep again.

'Great,' she muttered, realising that she was to lie there for an hour or so, during which time thoughts of Claude would creep up on her. *Engaged to a woman he's only known a few months, he's either very foolish or madly in love,* Jacks thought. Neither label appealed to her very much. *What am I supposed to do? I can't simply fall out of love at the drop of a hat.*

Jacks thought back to how happy she had been at the mere mention of him. Now, she felt guilty for having those feelings about someone else's man. She knew that the moral thing to do would be, leave well alone, but wondered if she could find the self -restraint to be able to do it.

No.

She knew that for all her good intentions, she would find herself back in his presence and it was pointless trying to kid herself.

If only I could make him notice me. If he grew accustomed to seeing me then maybe he might have second thoughts about his marriage, she thought hopefully, and then on realising what she had planned, she grew cold. *What am I doing?* she asked herself. *Am I seriously considering trying to break up someone's engagement?* She felt ashamed. *This is what it boils down to, let's face it, I'd never attract him in the first place, but if I did, could I live with myself with what I'd done?*

All choices seemed ill and she felt trapped, with nowhere to turn and no one to turn to. Her thoughts strayed back to Claude, wondering if she really loved him so much that she was prepared to sacrifice her morals. She had always lived by such a strict code of rules, and breaking up someone's relationship had been right at the top of the list of taboos.

I only have to remember the state of mum after dad ran off, she thought. *Can I really put someone through that pain? One thing's for sure, if do make a play for Claude, I'll have to keep it from mum. It's none of her business anyway; I'm not a child anymore.* She laughed ironically. *I may not be a child, but I'm sure as hell acting like one—a stubborn child who refuses to obey some simple ground rules.*

'Oh to hell with it,' she said quietly. *I'm going to see him. Nothing will come of it I know, but I also know that I don't want to spend the rest of my life wondering "what if?"* It's going to be a painful experience, but I'm too stubborn to give up. I'm aware that there is only the slightest chance of success, but I don't care, I've got to go for it, because I'll probably go through life without feeling this way about anyone again.

Another sleepless night had taken its toll on Jacks. Dark rings crowned her eyes and no matter how much make-up she applied, she could not quite disguise them. Her hair looked lank and lifeless, and no style seemed to want to go right.

Why is it that whenever you want to look stunning, everything goes wrong? she thought, while separating her long black curls.

She arrived at Coles by eleven-thirty and felt far from comfortable.

What did Taylor say? Oh yes, look him straight in the eyes and smile. However, her friend had also ranted on about how beautiful Jacks' eyes were. She smiled sardonically, well aware that on that particular morning, her eyes appeared so black that could have been through ten bouts with Jeff Fenech.

Oh well, here goes, she thought, as she pulled off her sunglasses and stepped nervously forward.

He was not standing where she was expecting him to be—where he usually was.

Plan A) out of the window, she thought, *there will be no eye contact today.*

She caught a glimpse of him at last, standing at the customer service desk. She glanced out of the corner of her eye, without actually shifting her eyes in his direction. It was an excellent trick to be able to do, and lately Jacks had become an expert at it.

She felt giddy and sick as she entered and walked past him; passing close for a second it felt as though their two souls had touched, their auras temporarily mingled. She felt a surge of heat that shot down her spine and distributed a tingling sensation to every part of her body. It was over in an instant and Jacks thought she saw him glance after her.

She attempted a sexy saunter toward the milk. Why milk? Simply habit and she thought of all those shopping trips with her father as a child. She gave a poignant chuckle as she headed off toward health and beauty, considering how all shoppers had an individual route that they stuck to ritualistically. Her smile broadened as she thought of her mother's routine, fading as she became aware of a man staring strangely at her. She moved quickly on, remembering her reason for being there.

Placing the "next customer please" bridge onto the conveyer belt, she plonked down the bottle of hair conditioner whose blurb stated that using it would prevent further bad hair days. *It's worth a try*, she figured.

A wave of tiredness travelled throughout her body, and she yawned. Claude saw her.

Oh well, that was the object of the exercise, was it not? she thought, and immediately looked down. When she glanced up again, he had gone. She yawned once more and made her way to the adjacent cafe.

The cashier gazed for a moment at the two flat whites, Pepsi and a glass of orange juice.

'Fifteen dollars sixty please,' she reeled off in that polite voice which Jacks hated; it lacked sincerity. The girl had been told to smile and be polite no matter who the customer. As she handed over the money, Jacks thought she caught a nervous gleam in the girl's eye. Why? Perhaps it was her first day and she was nervous, or could it be that Jacks had four drinks on her tray and not a companion in sight? She grinned, unable to resist trying to look as maniacal as possible.

It was after four hours of sitting in that café when Jacks realised ironically, the cashier had been quite correct in her assessment—she *was* crazy. The best part of her day had been spent sat at a table, just to be near a man who did not even know she existed, a man she did not have the courage to even look at.

How utterly ridiculous the whole situation is, she thought. *I have never chased after a man before, never. I have never let a man get the better of me and yet amazingly enough here I am, an utter wreck. There is nothing I wouldn't do for him, and that frightens me.*

Rising from her seat, her buttocks were numb and her bladder heavy. She wondered how many drinks she had consumed and decided it was probably too many.

That evening, the rains started. The water did not fall so much as plummet from the sky. Jacks wandered the familiar streets, trying to centre her thoughts and make sense of her situation. Her emotion and deep melancholy was too much for any logic to take hold and she began to murmur to herself.

As she turned the key in the lock, the strangest sensation came over her. It was as though she was suddenly detached from the situation that she had been so bent upon; it was unreal. Cold fear crept upon her, crawling across her skin and along the length of her body. She felt as though she was freefalling and reached out with her mind to grip something, anything to stop herself from falling into the abyss.

What's happening to me? she thought, and heard her voice repeat the words aloud. Just as suddenly as the sensation had arisen, it was gone, forgotten almost immediately and the inner anguish took over once more. The only thing recalled was a pang of loss at the thought of Patrick, and the guilt that followed as she realised she had not thought of him in so long. It was as though Claude had stolen him from her, making her feel more wretched than ever.

The skies rang out with storms, seeming to mimic her inner turmoil. Sleep was long in coming that night; when it finally arrived, her dreams were strange. The most bizarre being, yet another vision about her sister's approaching wedding.

She ran down flights of stairs, trying to escape from a gunman and found herself at the church. Parked outside were five black limousines. The sky darkened with heavy thunderclouds. It rained, and yet no one was getting wet. Hundreds of people filled the street, dressed in black.

They can't be going to Trude's wedding, Jacks thought. *They must be holding a funeral beforehand.* She grew annoyed, knowing the morbidity of such a thing would upset her sister. Gazing up, she followed the line of the cathedral as it loomed like some gothic megalith. The sky darkened further and a deep rumble of a thunderstorm approached.

It being a funeral, the obligatory tears and false sentiment were exchanged. Trudi stood beside her, a sensible navy blue dress hung off her too pale skin. Jack glanced down, noticing the wedding ring on her waxy hand. Trudi smiled. No one else noticed the deceased talking to Jacks. They didn't notice anything was wrong. Everyone accepted the situation and she felt the heat of anger rise within her.

'You haven't met Claude, have you?' Trudi said. 'He was just telling me how jealous he is of your hair.'

Jacks smiled awkwardly and then with the derision that had gotten her into trouble on more than one occasion, she stated loudly, 'Well Claude would look more than a little ridiculous with my hair now, wouldn't he?'

He was stood behind her she knew it. She turned to face him. He was in mourning dress.

She woke up.

4:45

Later that day Jacks found herself next door to Coles again, sitting in the familiar café, chewing mindlessly at a paper Pepsi cup. She watched as shoppers went about their daily business, quite unaware of anyone but themselves it seemed. A little girl sat at the next table and eyed Jacks curiously. Jacks felt sorry for the child, who knew little of the world and of life, and how cruel it could be.

One day, she thought, as she returned the girl's glance. *One day you'll fall in love; you'll think that it is the greatest moment of your life; everything that went before will seem meaningless. The man you fall for will be perfection in your eyes, and do you know what, little girl?* Her face hardened. *He won't even know you* exist. *He's probably already found the woman of his dreams, he'll be engaged—married even, and you'll be alone, left alone to contemplate your folly—that moment of weakness when you gave your heart to a pipe dream.*

She sipped her drink, frowning. *Perhaps I'm being cynical,* she thought. *Maybe somewhere fairy tales do exist. Yes, I'm sure they do, and I stand on the edge of the book, looking down at its pretty pages, but to me it will only ever be a book, nothing more. I could tear out a page and stick it on my wall in effort to feel closer to that world, but it will not be the same; nothing will ever be the same again. I don't exist in the fairy-tale, but the horror, where there is a lot of pain and screaming and the heroine dies slowly.*

She tightened her jaw with a feeling of bitterness, noticing that the girl was no longer looking at her.

Where is he anyhow? she thought. In the two hours that she had sat there, she had only caught a glimpse of him. Now he was gone. *Lunch perhaps?* she pondered, and then her paranoia got the better of her. *Has he seen me and is avoiding me? He couldn't get away fast enough, could he?*

She glanced at her watch again. 13:12 Taylor had agreed to meet her at half past one, so she would have to sit and wait until then. 'There's no point in staying all afternoon if he isn't here,' she huffed under her breath.

In front of the cafe was a big flower stall. Jacks

had never been that fond of flowers, it was always the thought behind them she had found appealing. *Now how long has it been?* Jacks thought. The last man to buy her flowers had been her second boyfriend. That seemed so long ago. *In ten or twenty year's time it will seem even longer,* she mused. *No one will ever buy me flowers again, will they?*

Jacks failed to notice a woman standing at her table.

'Hello,' a familiar voice said.

She turned her head. There, stood the athletic figure of Taylor.

'Sorry, I was miles away,' Jacks said wearily.

Taylor took the seat next to her and leaned in conspicuously.

'Where is he then?' she asked.

'Who knows,' spoke a voice that Jacks scarcely recognised as her own. 'Shall we go?' she said, rising. The feeling in her legs had gone, from sitting too long in one position. She made her way unsteadily to the carpark. Turning, her eyes made one final search for Claude and then she left.

Taylor and Jacks walked aimlessly. Taylor had problems of her own and Jacks, although she wanted to help in any way she could, felt as though she was no use to anyone. She was wary about giving advice at the best of time, considering it a dangerous gift to bestow; she had always tried to make people see both sides of every coin rather than forcing an opinion on them that might backfire later.

She grew depressed and her stomach began to churn. They reached a bridge over the road and stood looking over the edge. Jacks watched the HGVs speeding along and wondered how instant death would be if she decided to jump. The sickness in her stomach grew.

She screamed—a scream louder and longer than any she had ever screamed before.

Taylor laughed. 'Do you feel better for that?' she asked.

Jacks shrugged and rested her arms on the bridge. The feeling had not gone away, but was more apparent than ever. Her mouth quivered and her eyes brimmed with tears. She laid her head on her arms and wept. Her body shook as she did so, and to Jacks it felt as though the whole bridge foundation shook too.

Taylor rested a comforting hand on her shoulder and Jacks looked up. Tears stung her eyes and she blinked them away. Up the road, a long red and white lorry zoomed; painted on its side, in large red letters, was Coles. Jacks laughed harshly, the sound being so insincere that it made Taylor uncomfortable.

'Come on,' Taylor said. 'I'll race you to the quay.'

Running in the scorching heat was utter lunacy,

and it left Jacks gazing longingly at the green, blue water, wishing she could swim in it. She and Taylor sat at its edge and reminisced about times when they used to dangle their feet into its cool depths. It had seemed so much clearer then, like many things, Jacks figured, as she reached for her sunglasses, which were balanced precariously on her head.

Her hand failed to take hold of them and knocked them off; for a moment, there was a ridiculous juggling scene and then, sploosh; they hit the water. They watched and laughed hysterically as the glasses submerged—lost forever.

Jacks exclaimed that it had been an omen. She had owned the sunglasses since the age of fourteen. She bought them not long after she had fallen in love for the first and last time, until now. She saw their watery grave as a cleansing action—getting rid of the past to make way for new things. They were the mirrored glasses she had so often used to hide her eyes from Claude. She would be able to hide no longer.

'Strange are the twists of fate,' she remarked, and then laughed again.

On arriving home, Jacks' sister informed her that her mother had been discussing her.

'She said you fancy Claude. I stuck up for ya though and told her that you think he's a goof.'

Jacks smiled nervously and Taylor turned away, too afraid to laugh.

'Thanks Trude,' Jacks said. 'What else has she been saying?'

'That you're always miserable and you never go out and that you're going to be lonely for the rest of your life.'

Jacks felt her capillaries open and her face flushed. So intense was the heat of her anger, she thought she might explode. She walked stiffly through to the dining room, Trudi's voice trailing after her.

'She thinks you're up at Coles now as well.'

'WHAT THE HELL DOES SHE KNOW ABOUT HOW I FEEL? AND WHAT DOES SHE CARE?' Jacks roared. 'She's just worried about what people will say when they realise that her daughter refuses to fit into an outdated social construct. I won't get married to the first Neanderthal who comes along. I won't have children, get taken for granted, smacked around ...' *Why am I so angry?* she thought. *Mum is only concerned.* 'I wish she'd keep her nose out of my business,' she muttered. *Perhaps I'm angry because I know she's correct on all accounts.*

'Hello Jacks, where've you been?' her mother's voice called from the kitchen.

'GO TO HELL!' Jacks snapped. Leaving the house, she slammed the door behind her, immediately feeling guilty for the way she had spoken, but she couldn't go back; she had to calm down first.

She found herself walking the familiar path back to the harbour and sat staring at her reflection in the water. Her pallor took on the greyness of fear.

I've lost control, she thought. *The one thing I've always had in abundance and it had been torn away from me.* She threw a twig into the water, in a gesture of bitterness, and watched her reflection distort slightly then return. She got up. *I've got to do something,* she thought. *I've got to try before it's too late.*

She made her way back to Coles and watched as the cars left one by one, convinced that each one of them contained Claude. People stared at her strangely. *Why am I sat here? That is what they all want to know,* she thought, and then paranoia took hold and she began to convince herself that everyone knew exactly why she was there. They were tutting, shaking their heads and laughing at her. *Is Claude laughing too?* she wondered. *I'm driving him further and further away.* She sat with her head in her hands. *I'm losing my mind and there's not a damn thing I or anyone else can do about it.*

She felt a hot veil against her cheeks and an intense pain deep inside. The tears fell freely from her eyes and dropped into her lap. Nothing could quench the feeling of intolerable loneliness that had set upon her. She felt like one of the twigs she had thrown absent minded into the water, carried along with no control over its destination. As she sat comparing her life to that twig, she realised she *did* had a vague idea where she was going. It loomed up ahead, a tunnel so long and dark that it could have been another dimension, a world within a world—her mind perhaps.

She had been able to stand a great deal of pain in her life, yet realised now that pain was merely a state of mind; it was how to control mental anguish that she could not handle.

I now know what real pain is, she thought. *I have to face it every hour of every day, and it never ceases. I have to cope with the feeling of being torn apart from within, being eaten alive by a parasitic disease called love.*

Shivering, she looked about her; the sun had almost set. As she watched its final rays sink beyond the horizon, she realised it had set forever; only by some miracle would it shine for her again.

Chapter Three

Long walks in the rain,
Important decisions to be made,
Puddles filled with fallen leaves
And painful regrets.

My heart as heavy as thunderclouds,
Mocking voices in the trees,
Past mistakes and chances lost,
Drift by me on the breeze.

Dreams of what could be,
Even now is it too late?
To reach out and touch the sun,
But the whispering wind tells of a different fate.

'I don't know why I'm here.' Jacks said, and shifted forward in an effort to leave. *What can this woman do?* she thought. *She has no potion or magic she can perform. No one can cure me; no one can retrieve me from the abyss into which I have stumbled quite unintentionally.*

She wanted to leave, but could not move. She thought she could feel herself rise to her feet. The room darkened and she seemed to be wading through deep water.

I must be near the door now; I must, she thought. Her legs ached with weariness of someone who had seen many more years than she. She became vaguely aware that someone was touching her arm and fought to clear her eyes of the mist that seemed to envelop them. She felt as though she was falling ever deeper.

The darkness grew brighter, so bright that it burned. *What is going on?* she thought. *Am I dead?* The light continued to pierce until the silhouette of a man came into view. The light surrounded him like a Kirlian aura and she became gradually aware that he was speaking to her.

What is he saying? she thought. *Something about being sane ... no ...*

'Can you tell me your name?'

'My name,' Jacks considered. *I have a name—an identity—somewhere,* she thought.

The man repeated the question, but she could

not answer, not yet. *What happened?* she wondered. She tried to grasp for a memory, any memory …

She was five years old and sat on the grass at home, her bottom lip thrust out as far as it would go, sulking because of an argument she had had with her father …

No, that was years ago, she realised. *My father is gone and I wasn't sitting on the grass, but on a couch. I was in some counsellor's office …* 'Polly,' she said quietly.

The man repeated it. She did not have the strength, or will, to correct the misunderstanding. Closing her eyes, she began to dream …

Fields stretched for miles, fields of flowers, all colours, shapes and sizes. Her vision zoomed in to focus on a small red poppy, beautiful and delicately swaying in the breeze. Looking about, she realised that the fields of flowers had turned into people thousands, millions even. Panicking, her eyes searched once more for the poppy, but it was lost in the sea of people; that delicate flower, which had appeared so perfect and unique, now suffocated in the prevailing mass. Desperately she searched, but was unable to find herself again.

She awoke in a cold sweat. *What time is it?* she wondered. *Where am I?*

Outside it was dark and the moon was riding high. It shone with a hypnotic glow, but there was a coldness about it, which made her shiver. The bed she lay in was hard and the sheets felt starched. The room was hot and had a smell to it that caused Jacks to panic. *That smell,* she thought, *I know that smell* …

Her head swerved clumsily from side to side as she surveyed the room. To her right stood a small wooden cabinet on top of which was a clear plastic jug of water and a beaker, which looked as though it would have been at home in a school canteen. Beside the items, pink chrysanthemums sat slowly dying in a plastic vase. There was a railing system about the bed, from which a drab coloured curtain hung, drawn to the left. The floor was uncarpeted and made Jacks recall a sound—the squeaking of rubber striking rubber, as flat, sensible shoes, strode up and down corridors. On the windowsill, a cartoon cat on a Get Well Soon card grinned down at her, daring her to remember.

Hospital, she concluded. *How did I get here?* She fought to make sense of the situation, remembering the man, and the light. Reaching back further into her mind, she recalled the image of Polly, but why she had been with the counsellor in the first place, remained a mystery to her.

She sat up with difficulty, feeling strangely weary. As far as she could tell she had suffered no broken bones; everything seemed intact.

Why do I feel like this? she thought. Her body felt tender and drained as one does after being violently sick. She grew frightened, wondering what had occurred in Polly's office. She considered the possibility that she may have accidentally knocked herself out. *Perhaps I have amnesia.* Her mind raced and she became angry with herself. *What have I forgotten, what?* Her jaws clenched until the action proved too fatiguing. She heard a high-pitched whistling in her ears and the room seemed bathed in white light; everything was dancing.

When Jacks arrived slowly to consciousness again, she saw it was daytime. Her eyes struggled to focus on the image at her bedside. It was her mother.

'She's awake!' exclaimed a voice from the other side of the bed. There sat her sister, gazing anxiously down at her.

'How do you feel, Jacqueline?' her mother asked.

The woman's voice filled with mixed emotion—fear, joy and possibly anger. Jacks considered if she might be imagining it.

'What happened?' she asked hoarsely, trying to sit up. It was at that point Jacks realised she had been moved to a ward, other beds were symmetrically situated about her, their occupants disinterested in her presence.

A nurse entered smiling; she plumped up Jacks' pillows in order to make it easier to maintain a sitting position. The woman's broad smile reminded Jacks of something, a dim vision of a girl who held her hand out to receive money for Pepsi in a paper cup …

No. It was gone.

Jacks looked at her mother, waiting for an answer to her question. The woman's eyes refused to meet her own.

'You collapsed,' she said.

There was a moment's pause during which the atmosphere became so tense that it took Jacks' breath.

'You were suffering from…' Her mother paused again. 'Nervous exhaustion.'

Jacks noticed the worried glance she shot to her sister. She turned to Trudi, whose eyes fixed firmly on the bed. *Why can nobody face me?* she thought. *Nervous exhaustion? What kind of dim-witted explanation is that? Nervous exhaustion is the result of severe anxiety. What do I have to be anxious about? They're hiding something, but what?*

Nobody spoke.

'Thanks for the flowers,' Jacks said, assuming they had brought them. Who are the cards from?' Her throat was sore and she felt the need for a drink.

Trudi passed her the cards with an unsure smile. Jacks eyed them suspiciously wondering why there were only two. She looked at them each in turn. They appeared solemn and serious as if they were attending a funeral. *Is that it?* she thought. *Is that what they're keeping from me? Am I dying?* She stared hard at them and relaxed slightly. It was something else; she saw it in her mother most of all. If she did not know better, she might have said that her mother was ashamed.

She began to feel nervous; no one was giving her any answers. Tired and parched, she reached for the jug of water, but her strength left her. Her mother took over and poured the water into the beaker.

'I'll bring you up some pop tomorrow,' she said, handing Jacks the drink.

Jacks received it gratefully and pressed it to her lips, her mind grappling with another image; she remembered biting a paper cup in her mouth. *I was sat in a cafe,* she thought, *looking for someone ... who?* She took a sip of the water and forced herself to think, convincing herself that it was imperative that she remember clearly.

'Are you okay?' Trudi asked, 'You look miles away.'

Jacks looked at Trudi with a puzzled expression. *I was close then, very close* she thought. Her eyes dropped to Trudi's hands, they were sweating and she played nervously with a ring on her left hand—a wedding ring.

The wedding! she thought. *Trudi's wedding, why is it so important?* Reaching back in her mind, Jacks tried to recall every detail ...

It was a fine September morning, crisp and cool. The house filled with voices, panicking, laughing, excited voices of the bride and her bridesmaids as they busied themselves to be ready on time.

Jacks stared long at her reflection. At first glance, she looked quite pretty in her long green dress. Small white flowers wove into the mop of curls on her head. Through the make-up she was aware of the dark rings encircling her eyes—black rings caused by a deep weariness, beyond the result of insomnia. Under her blusher, she knew that her skin was ghost-like. That is how she felt; she was a wraith, merely a pale shadow of what she had been.

The Mercedes beeped its horn. She grabbed her bouquet, hitched her skirts, ran down the stairs and they were off.

As the party stood waiting to go in, Jacks noticeably shook.

'What are you so nervous about?' Trudi laughed. 'I'm the one getting married.'

Jacks gave a shrug. 'Why indeed?' she thought.

The organ sounded and they began to walk slowly toward the altar. Jacks spotted Claude immediately, but refused to look directly at him, determined to remain composed. The procession seemed to take forever and she silently willed the organist to play a little faster.

Breathing gently, her features were of stone; not a flicker of emotion shone out. Claude turned smiling at the bride, but catching Jacks' glance, a look of recognition and horror beset his features; his head snapped 'round to face front like a soldier called to attention. Every muscle froze. His head turned again, the movement slow and subtler. It was obvious he hadn't been able to believe his eyes. Turning again, he leaned over and whispered to his fiancée …

Remembering was like dropping into a pool of ice from a great height. Try as she might, Jacks could not shake the image in her mind. She saw Claude's face so clearly, it was as if she could simply reach out and touch him. She knew he was not there, but he seemed so real. *What's wrong with my sense of reasoning?* she thought.

'Oh my God, what ward am I in?' she demanded.

Her mother looked at her blankly as if she had misunderstood the question.

'**Answer me**!' Jacks screamed, and threw her glass to the floor. She was surprised at her sudden burst of strength, but frightened by her lack of control.

Her mother began to cry and Trudi glared at Jacks, her eyes full of bitterness.

'You're in the psychiatric ward,' she said. 'You've had a breakdown.'

Jacks heard the words over and over again in her mind. She attempted to appear stable, as if to convince them that she was perfectly fine, but considered that she would fool no one after her little outburst. *That is why I sensed anger in mum's voice,* she thought, *she's angry with me for being so weak.* A wave of guilt washed over her and she began to cry.

'I'm so sorry,' she said. 'What a disappointment I must seem.'

Her mother rose to her feet and Trudi followed example.

'I think it's about time we were leaving,' she said. 'We'll see you soon I expect, take good care of yourself.' She kissed Jacks on the forehead.

Without knowing why, Jacks shuddered. She felt that there was something else she was forgetting, but her mind refused to focus properly.

They were gone.

A nurse approached and picked up the beaker. 'I'll fetch you another one, shall I?' she said, in a friendly tone.

'Please nurse,' Jacks said, 'how long do I have to stay here?'

The woman smiled again. 'Well I know there's a specialist coming to speak with you tomorrow so we'll have to wait and see what he says. I shouldn't think you'll be here that long now though. The worst is over.'

She went away and did not return with the glass for her. In the woman's stead appeared an ancient looking doctor, his well-trimmed white beard giving the appearance of an old goat. He set a clean beaker down and offered a smile.

'Well Jacqueline, how do you feel eh?' his voice cracked.

'I don't know.' She paused to consider. She felt strangely weary as though she was waiting for the effects of an anaesthetic to wear off. 'I don't feel depressed anymore. I know I was a mess before, but I feel better now,' she said, while puzzling this new riddle.

The doctor peered at her like an owl through his tiny gold-rimmed spectacles. 'Indeed?' he said. 'Well that is a positive sign. I'm sure you will be out of here in no time, no time at all.' His voice was comical; he paused after every few words and sounded as though he might fall asleep at any moment.

Jacks tried to smile. 'I hope so,' she said. 'I need to make one huge apology to Claude.' She could not believe how detached she felt from him. It was as though her mind, sensing the danger it was in, had shut down for a while to completely remove any emotion concerning him, as surely as a surgeon would cut out cancerous tissue.

'Claude eh?' chirped the doctor, 'who's he then?'

Jacks was surprised at his not knowing; she assumed that he would have been mentioned in her records.

'He's the reason I'm here,' she said sheepishly.

The doctor drew down his great bushy eyebrows so that they framed his glasses perfectly. 'Mm well it doesn't say that here,' he said. He scribbled a few notes on her file. 'So who is he then, a boyfriend of yours?'

Jacks shook her head slowly, marvelling at how calm she felt; there was barely a trace of her former feelings for Claude. 'He's a man I met when I went to stay with mum for the summer.'

The doctor interrupted her. 'Home from where, Miss Chase?'

'From London. I like to spend a couple of months back in Sydney each year, especially when the weather's so grim back at home,' she answered. 'Anyway I went a bit crazy over Claude, obviously, and things got a bit out of hand. But I really do think I'm over him now.'

The goat-like doctor frowned and pursed his lips, as though he was about to chew cud. His old hands scribbled frantically, making Jacks nervous; she wondered why he was writing it all down, deciding that if it had not been important enough information to begin with, she hardly wanted it made public news now.

She still felt thirsty. Her parched mouth made talking difficult. Reaching out for the jug of water, she again found herself too weak to complete the action. The doctor ceased writing, poured a drink and passed it to her. She leaned forward awkwardly and gulped at the water, ignoring the fact that it tasted as though it had washed dishes. Staring at the file in his aged hands, she wondered what the man had written about her. As if sensing her curiosity, the doctor snatched it up.

'Well yes, erm, I shall leave you to er, rest now,' he said. 'That's it, you drink plenty of water, you need to replenish your fluids now you're off the er, drip, that's it. Well goodnight, Miss Chase.'

He nodded and Jacks watched him hobble off, wondering whether he was two-thirds short of a barrel himself. *I'm certain he's senile,* she thought. *I'm sure they wouldn't let him perform any kind of surgery.*

The glass was empty; she stretched out and placed it back on the cabinet. She was still thirsty, but knew she could not reach the jug. She failed to understand why her body felt so drained. During the hours that followed Jacks spent her time observing the other patients.

Opposite, was Clarissa who had postnatal depression; Jacks thought it entirely unfair that the woman had been placed on the psychiatric ward. To Jacks' right, an attempted suicide spent all her time asleep. *Drugged up to her eyeballs most likely,* Jacks thought. A large woman called Bertha, who had been committed after assaulting a ferry passenger, continually raised her voice and was presently singing bawdy songs. At the far end, a young girl sat crouched, clutching a teddy bear, as she rocked backward and forward. An old woman opposite Bertha, clapped along to the songs, humming tunelessly. To Jacks' left lay a woman receiving treatment for Schizophrenia; she appeared to be listening to voices situated directly beside her.

I don't belong here, Jacks thought, *surely they must see that.*

The nurses attempted to calm down another rousing chorus and there came a clatter of plates as the evening meal was served.

Plastic plates, Jacks noticed. *They obviously don't trust us with anything breakable.* The dinner plonked onto her plate, was an unidentifiable puree. She gazed uneasily at it, wondering if she were to vomit at that moment, if anyone would be able to tell the difference.

The nurse helped her into a sitting position, plumping up the pillows behind her. Jacks scooped the mush onto her spoon and swallowed. Her face contorted; it tasted worse than it looked. Although pureed, it felt heavy as it went down. Her stomach felt completely empty. She attempted a few more mouthfuls then had to give up.

Bertha stopped singing and was swearing about the food. She threw the plate at the staff and yelled.

'You eat it bitches!'

The nurse attempted to calm her, and the woman who had been singing along, continued to copy Bertha.

'Wheeee,' she said, as she threw her food.

It struck the senior nurse on the rear and a chorus of laughter broke out across the ward. The girl with the teddy bear sniggered behind her toy, and one of the nurses bit down hard on her lower lip, to prevent herself from laughing aloud. However, the food-covered nurse was not amused.

While the commotion took place at the far end of the ward, a nurse Jacks had not seen before arrived and removed her food. She returned shortly afterwards with a bowl of chocolate ice-cream.

'Here we are,' she said, 'since you have been so good.'

Jacks' eyes widened and she smiled with gratitude. 'Thanks,' she said, looking up at the nurse who was already walking back through the doors.

The ice-cream tasted heavenly. The cold soothed her throat and the taste of chocolate helped relax her amid the chaos of the ward.

A doctor entered to help administer a sedative to the raucous woman. On seeing him, Bertha became obscene and told him where she would really like pricking with his needle. At that point, the staff member who had only just managed to remain composed before, giggled childishly. The senior nurse glared, causing her to bite her lip again.

The ward was almost silent once Bertha drifted off. The doctor paced back with the food-covered nurse, following close at his heels. He stopped suddenly, noticing Jacks for the first time. She gave him an unsure smile. He did not speak to her; he simply looked, for what seemed like forever to Jacks, then read her notes briefly, replacing them with a huff before walking out. Jacks found herself annoyed by the man's discourtesy.

'Well hello to you too,' she said, through gritted teeth. She stared outside the doors. The nurse and the doctor could plainly be seen conversing and she was fairly sure that they were talking about her. She leaned toward them, aching to know what was being said.

The voice of another staff member broke her concentration.

'Everything all right?' she asked, in a friendly tone.

'Yeah I guess so,' Jacks replied, turning away.

'Did Doctor Hoffman say anything useful to you?' she enquired, while taking her bed down.

'Which one's that?' asked Jacks, hoping she would not have to resort to bitching about the arrogant git she had just encountered.

'The one that looks like a gnarly old wizard,'

the nurse said, with a grin.

Jacks laughed. 'No, he seemed far more interested in taking notes,' she said.

'Oh well, he enjoys that; it gives him a sense of purpose. I'm glad you played along with him. It'll make his day if he thinks someone thought he was a real doctor.'

The nurse carefully poured Jacks another glass of water.

She was stunned. 'You mean he's a bloody patient!' she spluttered. 'Oh my God!'

The nurse laughed heartily. 'Ha, I had you going, didn't I? Of course he's a real doctor; I know it's hard to believe to look at him.'

Jacks smiled with relief, although secretly she had not found the jape amusing in the slightest.

The medication trolley was wheeled onto the ward. She had no idea what pills she was taking, but she swallowed them anyhow. The lights went out and the senior nurse bade them goodnight. She lay for a while staring up at the high ceiling. The woman opposite began to cry softly; it was horrible to hear her suffering. Jacks drew the covers over her head to try to blot out the sound. The girl with the stuffed toy began to sing.

'Hush little baby, don't you cry...'

Her soft voice lulled Jacks into slumber.

Jacks awoke in the hours before dawn; a sound

had disturbed her unconscious and finally roused her. She could hear loud snoring, which seemed to vibrate the walls. Turning on her side, she tried to find a more comfortable position, and started. Someone was at her bedside. Jacks squinted in order to focus in the dim light. It was the nurse who had brought her the ice-cream earlier. She must have noticed that Jacks' eyes were open because she spoke.

'I've just re-filled your water in case you get thirsty,' she whispered, and then left.

Jacks closed her eyes, but could no longer sleep. The feeling was creeping up on her once again, as though there was something of vital importance she was forgetting, and whatever it might be, remained trapped just out of reach of her conscious memory. She lay on her back, trying to force the thoughts out, but it made her confused and tired.

The snoring had ceased, the sun was beginning to rise, a couple of patients were already awake and talked quietly to each other, or themselves.

Today, Jacks decided, *I'm going home today.* She reached for the glass of water and drank slowly. A voice from her left made her jump.

'Careful, they're after you; I should know; they've been after me for years. But don't you worry; the trick is to stay one step ahead. I know their little game. I can hear em see, so they can't get me. Listen, there they are again.' She looked blankly at an empty space beside her bed. The teddy bear girl scampered. It was then that Jacks observed that she was not a little girl at all, but an old woman.

If I stay in this place much longer, I will go crazy, she thought. She considered how beneficial it was for the patients to be cooped up together in such a way. They were all different cases and had individual needs. Jacks failed to see how such needs could be met by placing them all together and leaving them to their own devices for most of the day.

The public don't care, as long as they don't have to see them; out of sight out of mind, she thought, and it made her feel sick. *These people had been rejected and neglected by society.*

The familiar sound of the drug trolley rattled onto the ward and a soft Irish voice echoed,

'Morning ladies.' A couple of the patients replied, another grunted; the old women hid behind her bear and Bertha slept on. Jacks continued to sip her water until she drained the glass. She eyed the two tablets as the nurse poured her another beaker of water.

'What are these?' Jacks ventured. The nurse looked at her as if the question had been completely out of the ordinary.

'Don't you worry, pet; they'll do you good. If you're still curious later I'll get a doctor to talk to you, all right?'

She spoke in a way that convinced Jacks that the woman had not the least intention of answering her question. Jacks received the pills and gulped them down with the water.

'Now, have you managed to go to the toilet yet?' the nurse asked.

Jacks realised that she had not been since she arrived there. 'No,' she answered. 'But I think I could.'

'Good,' said the Irishwoman. 'It shouldn't be too difficult considering the amount of water you've been drinking. I'll fetch you a bedpan, shall I?'

Jacks found it annoying that the nurse had asked, since she was going to fetch the pan regardless of whether Jacks said yes or no. Although kindly meant, it was such an attitude that led Jacks to believe that as a patient, especially a mental patient, she had waved her rights; she was no longer permitted to think and act for herself.

A while later, the nurse returned, bedpan in hand. There was a scraping sound as the nurse drew the curtains around the bed. Jacks strained to lift her abdomen high enough so that the nurse could slip the pan beneath her. She wondered why her limbs felt so leaden. A short time passed before she was able to urinate. It was a strange sensation; it felt as though her urethra was not functioning properly at first. She seemed to go on a long while, and for a moment, she was worried that the pan might overflow. Her bladder pained her slightly, but she decided not to mention it, not wanting to give them any reason to keep her there.

The nurse covered the bedpan with a white paper towel and took it away. She returned with a bowl of water and an assortment of toiletries.

'You read my mind,' Jacks said, who had been thinking how grimy she felt. The wash was extremely refreshing, and on completion of cleaning her teeth, she felt almost human again.

'Thank-you,' she said brightly. 'Could you pour me another glass of water please?'

'Gosh you have drunk a lot this morning, haven't you? You'll be wanting a bedpan again if you don't slow down.' The woman smiled as she poured the water then gathered the wash things and left.

Jacks drank again, wondering why she was so thirsty. The nurse had left the curtains closed, which offered her a little more privacy—a brief escape from her surreal companions. The curtains gave her something new to stare at. Before long, every flower and pattern had imprinted on her mind; she could close her eyes and envisage them in perfect detail.

She listened to the sounds outside her little space, feeling glad not to have to face it for a while.

Separated in such a way, she pretended that her predicament was not real, until Bertha awoke and demanded a fry-up for breakfast.

'Hey you in there,' came the voice of the schizophrenic next to her. 'They want to take you away; I wouldn't let them if I were you. The man said not to.'

'Be quiet Martha,' barked the voice of the senior nurse from the previous night. She drew the curtains partially with a brisk movement. 'Good morning, Miss Chase, I trust you slept well.' Her formal manner lacked sincerity and it was obvious she did not care for an answer.

Jacks disliked the woman, finding her cold and snobbish. *The patients are here to be cared for,* she thought. *It is unfortunate that such a word doesn't seem to enter the woman's vocabulary.*

'I must say, your uniform cleaned up a treat, didn't it, Sister?' Jacks said.

There was a giggle from outside the cubicle and a voice whispered a little too loudly. A guffaw of a laugh rang out across the ward.

The woman glared. 'I keep a spare in case of emergencies,' she said, with such a tight-lipped expression that Jacks was surprised the woman could speak at all. 'This is Doctor Brodie,' she said. 'He's here to talk to you about your removal from here.' Turning swiftly away, she ordered the nurse to accompany her.

In stepped a man whom Jacks supposed to be in his late twenties. He didn't look much like a doctor; he reminded Jacks of a concert pianist, with his hair neatly combed back and tucked behind his ears and yet long enough to slip into a frenzied dance on reaching the more difficult and passionate passages of music. His posture was unusually erect. *Perfect for sitting at the piano*, she mused

'Hello Jacqueline,' he said, 'May I?' He gestured to the chair to the side of her bed.

Jacks nodded, finding herself amused by his antiquated manners. He held her notes in his hands and glanced over them briefly.

'Jacqueline, have you any idea why you are here?' he asked, in such a uniform manner, that his voice seemed to exceed his years.

'I was told I'd had a breakdown, but I don't really remember what happened.'

As he showed no sign of interrupting her, she assumed he required an elaboration.

'I know I was depressed,' she continued. 'I remember doing something really stupid.'

She paused to look at him, hoping he had no desire to hear about the events that had just popped into her mind; again, he made no signal to stop her.

'I was obsessed with a man,' she was reluctant to make casual use of the word love. I followed him home. I knocked on his front door; I don't remember what I said.' She paused again, feeling guilty and embarrassed because of her pathetic behaviour. 'I know that a policeman dragged me away and I tried to cling to the door.' There was another long pause and Jacks began to chew the inside of her mouth. 'I remember Polly, who was some kind of counsellor I was seeing; sitting in her office is the last thing I recollect before waking up and finding myself here.' The feeling crept up on her again, a niggling little voice in her head telling her that not all was as it should be. A shiver ran down her spine and she immediately shook it off.

The doctor was looking closely at her. He had not written any notes, but seemed more interested in observing her every word and gesture.

Jacks felt uncomfortable by his silence and resisted the urge to fidget.

'So when can I go home?' she asked.

'I'm afraid it will be a while yet, Jacqueline,' he replied.

Jacks was wounded, unable to understand; she felt perfectly fine.

'I need to be sure that you can come to terms with your situation before I consider your discharge,' he said.

The way in which he had spoken, made Jacks feel like a prisoner rather than a patient.

'But I *have* come to terms with everything,' she protested. 'I made a stupid mistake and behaved abominably I know, but all those feelings are gone now.' She tried to calm herself. She felt flushed and so reached for the final bit of water remaining in the jug, lacking most of its contents it was light enough for her to pour. She took a few sips and tried to clear her head. *He can't possibly warrant me staying here,* she thought. *There are hundreds of people who need this bed more than I do. Why doesn't he just refer me to my GP?*

'How long do you think that you've been in hospital?' he asked evenly.

Jacks considered the question. She knew that she had been unconscious when they brought her in and so guessed that she could have been there a day or two before she was fully awake.

'About three to four days altogether I expect,' she said, after a time.

He crossed his legs and leaned forward, resting his chin on his hand. His eyes bore into her so deeply that she felt everything she did was being analysed and interpreted as a sign of insanity.

'So,' he said, 'it will surprise you to learn that you've been hospitalised for almost five months.'

Jacks was not sure she had heard him correctly, and wondered if he might be joking.

'Five months!' she exclaimed, 'but it can't be … I only remember just over a day and I …' she trailed off, too shocked to offer anything but silence. Her head ached and she felt thirstier than ever.

'Jacqueline, you have been in a coma. You were involved in a traffic accident in which you received substantial head trauma. You were lucky to survive at all.'

She was astounded, wondering why she had she not been informed of as much before. 'But they said I'd had a breakdown,' was all she managed to say.

'From what I can see from your notes, you had. However, that is not the reason you were brought here. Had you been receiving the proper care for your condition, the accident may never have occurred.'

His eyes continued to analyse as Jacks became visibly distressed.

'It states in your notes that you stepped in front of a lorry; whether it was intentional or because you were unaware of your actions at that time, only *you* have the answer to, and we must help you to recall the truth.'

Jacks found the news shocking, but the last thing she wanted to do was to be seen losing control. For some reason the news had set off warning bells in her head, and the situation seemed inexplicably dangerous to her.

She attempted to piece together what had happened. 'So the accident occurred when I left that woman's office?' she ventured.

'What woman?' the doctor replied, lifting his

head briefly before returning it to rest on his hand.

'Polly, the counsellor I just told you about,' Jacks said, getting annoyed.

'There was no counsellor, Jacqueline and there was no Claude. Claude does not exist; he must have been created by your unconscious during the coma, probably to whitewash your recent disappointments.'

Her head throbbed. 'I don't understand,' she said. 'What are you talking about?' She was agitated and made no attempt to hide the fact.

'I know that no one has discussed this with you as yet, but it is best that you are told during the early stages of your treatment, so that you may better come to terms with your true situation.' He uncrossed his legs and placed his hands on his knees.

'What!' Jacks said. She was growing more annoyed by the second, by every single word that escaped the doctor's lips. *He is so vague*, she thought, *as if he has all the answers, but is reluctant to relinquish more than one at a time.*

'I understand you took it pretty hard when you failed your HSCs, Jacqueline,' the doctor said, seeming to ignore the change in her temper.

Jacks winced and let out a conceited snort. 'Don't be ridiculous, of course I didn't fail, I wouldn't have been permitted to read for my degree unless I passed them.' A surge of heat began to increase until every limb felt ready to strike out.

'You don't have a degree, Jacqueline. You scored so low, that you didn't even receive an ATAR. You couldn't have gone to university, even if you'd wanted to.' His words came slowly and calmly, as if she was too stupid to comprehend them.

She was burning hot and clearly envisioned herself punching Doctor Brodie in the face.

She breathed deeply. 'Are you deliberately trying to make me angry?' she asked. 'Is this some sort of test to see how long I can cope before I snap?' Her voice flecked with violent intonation and she glared at the doctor.

He withdrew slightly, sensing her dangerous mood.

'If this upsets you, Jacqueline I am sorry, but I do believe that the truth is not so deeply buried in your mind, so stop lying to yourself. You must embrace reality, even when it is not to your liking, and you must let go of these adolescent fantasies.'

The man is serious, she thought. *He believes what he is saying is right.* She was furious. *Who in hell told him all this crap and why?* She made an effort to calm herself. *Mustn't have the jumped up, patronising bastard thinking I've lost control.*

The doctor watched her closely, waiting like a patient spider for a response to his comments. A flicker of a smile lifted the corner of her mouth and she repressed it instantly, but her eyes could not disguise their twinkle as she challenged him.

'If I didn't take a degree then why have I been living in London for the past five years? I suppose you're going to tell me that I simply upped and left the country, my home, in a fit of despair. In which case why do I have memories of my time there? My friends and the tutors?' She was becoming increasingly excited. *Got him,* she thought. *Now he'll have to admit he's made a mistake … why is he staring at me so sympathetically and shaking his head like a bloody car mascot?*

'Jacqueline, please try to understand that this is a world that you have created for yourself to protect …'

'WHAT!' Jacks broke in with indignant disbelief. 'So now you're telling me that the past five years of my life have been a bloody lie!' she shouted.

The doctor glanced past her and nodded his head. Two men appeared at her bedside. 'Now try to calm yourself,' Doctor Brodie said, as they restrained her.

She screamed. 'Get your fucking hands off me, you bastards!'

Thrashing about violently, caused their grip to tighten and Jacks felt a sharp pain in her arm. Tears stung her eyes and she caught the voice of the doctor,

'We'll talk again later.'

The ringing increased in her ears and the darkness fell white about her.

Chapter Four

Reality is fleeting,
The heart cries out with a voice of silence,
What is reality anyway?
But another prison for the mind,
Merely a word without true meaning,
Left to rattle about within an empty shell.

The sun beat down on Jacks and, although her eyes were closed, she knew that about her the flowers were an explosion of colour. The birds were singing softly and she felt the warmth of the fleecy tartan rug beneath her reclining body. A shadow crossed her closed eyes, as if a cloud had passed overhead, blotting out the light of the sun. She shivered. The singing had ceased and the air grew chill.

Opening her eyes, she discovered that snow had settled gently about her and the glistening white veil shrouded the garden's summer glory. The flowers looked beautiful, yet disturbing, in their frozen state. All was quiet and still; it was as though a moment in time had stopped and been subjected to such an extreme temperature in order to keep it intact in effort to preserve its beauty.

More snow began to fall. Ahead, Jacks thought she could see a figure lying motionless on the sunlounger. She stood up, somewhat stiffly. Underfoot, felt warm and she noticed the snow did not fall there. Cautiously she took a step off the rug. The cold greeted her like a host of icy hands groping at her exposed flesh. After she had ventured several steps forward, she glanced back, considering a return to the warmth, but the rug was no longer there; in its stead, stood a hospital bed. Horrified, Jacks turned away and made for the figure on the sunlounger.

It was Patrick.

A thin coverlet of snow lay upon him and he made no movement, seeming as frozen in time as the rest of the garden. She reached out slowly to her dead friend; flakes of snow settled on her bare skin and melted instantly. She paused, glancing back at the hospital bed; it seemed so far away and even more uninviting than the rest of the cold, inhospitable place. Turning back to Patrick, she started, her heart pounding in her chest. He stood before her, his eyes open, looking like some terrifying snowman.

Her eyes flickered open, and for seconds she retained the nightmare image of her dead friend. Her breath came in short gasps then gradually began to slow, until she inhaled a great gulp of air and released it with a heavy sigh. She shivered, and a bead of cold sweat trickled down her cheek. Reaching up, she wiped it away and tried to steady her breath to alleviate the feeling of nausea.

As the panic sensations passed, she looked about her to see she was in a room of her own. It was then that she realised she had been moved while she had slept.

Outside, she could hear the hustle and bustle of everyday hospital life—nurses as they paced like soldiers up and down the wards, clangs, bangs, lowered voices whispering conspiratorially. Memories of why she was there came flooding back to her waking mind and she felt reality was no better than the nightmare. Wondering what had incited them to remove her from the public ward, she remembered the forcibly administered sedative.

Bastards, she thought. *They had no right to treat me like that, and where the hell does that doctor get off telling me all that bullshit! I don't live in London indeed and Claude doesn't exist. He's the reason I'm in this mess.*

She tried to picture Claude's face ... nothing.

That's strange, she thought, *I can't remember what he looks like.* She concentrated ... still nothing. Her glance shot about the room, as if the walls would reveal the knowledge she sought. *Was he tall, short, fair, dark? Oh my God, what's going on? Perhaps my mind has tried to blot him out because the memory would prove too painful at present,* she considered without conviction. Jacks worked herself into a state and was visibly startled when Doctor Brodie entered the room.

'Good morning, Jacqueline,' he said. 'I trust you are feeling a little calmer today.'

Jacks attempted to ignore his condescending tone and stared past him. During the very short time in which she had known him, she already utterly despised him. She felt he could not possibly give the answers to her multitude of questions. *I need to get out,* she thought, *to prove I exist outside my subconscious mind.*

'Can I go home?' she asked coldly.

'That depends on where your home is, Jacqueline,' he replied.

Why couldn't he just say yes or no? she thought. 'My home's in London.'

As soon as she said it, she realised it was a mistake. He sat shaking his head and frowning.

'I don't understand why you refuse to believe me,' she said. 'Why don't you phone my friends? They will tell you ... or my employer. I can prove that I have a life there. A thought suddenly occurred to Jacks and she felt foolish for not having thought of it before. 'Even better, why don't you just ask my mother? She'll tell you.'

'Jacqueline, I have consulted with your mother many times since you were first admitted into our care; she knows as well as I do, that you have never at any time lived in London.'

Jacks felt betrayed. *He's lying*, she thought.

'Jacqueline, what sort of work do you suppose that you do?' he asked

'I'm a set designer. At the moment I'm being employed by the Royal Shakespeare Company, although I would have undoubtedly lost my contract if I've been here as long as you say.' Her stare challenged him. *I dislike him intently,* she thought. *He's so self assured, so annoying and so very wrong about everything.*

He gave a cynical laugh, causing Jacks to

cringe.

'Do you not think that is a rather large responsibility for someone of your age and,' he coughed in way of an apology, 'capabilities.'

Jacks felt her muscles tighten. 'Yes of course it's a big responsibility,' she said. 'But I fail to see what age has to do with it. Besides, you can scarcely criticise me, you're not much older than I am; isn't being a patronising bastard freshly graduated from his medical degree a lot of responsibility for someone *your age?'*

She was quite pleased with her snide remark; Doctor Brodie, however, was not amused.

'Jacqueline, I am a full fifteen years your senior. I have been a consultant for almost a year. Prior to that, I spent four and half years working as a registrar. I wouldn't say that I'm *fresh* from university.' His tone flecked with hurt pride.

Jacks was genuinely surprised. 'Fifteen years?' she queried. 'No way! You don't look forty to me.' She hoped her remark did not sound too much like a compliment.

His eyebrow rose slightly. 'I'm not. I'm just turned thirty-three,' he said. 'Jacqueline, how old are you?' his voice had returned to the good old analysing, monotonous, I'm a doctor, you're a nobody tone.

Jacks was confused and made no attempt to hide the fact. 'I'm twenty-five,' she replied. 'It should be written in my records surely.' She made a gesture toward the file he held.

'Jacqueline, you are eighteen years of age. So I put it to you again, surely you can see that a famous and reputable theatre company is not going to hire a teenager to design for them when they can have the pick of the best in that field.'

She was stunned. 'Why are you doing this?' she asked. 'Why are you telling all these lies? I don't understand; is it some sort of test?' She felt drained.

The doctor took her hands suddenly in his, in effort to gain her complete attention.

'Jacqueline, it is you who are lying; you're lying to yourself. You must come to terms with who you really are. You must let me help you.'

His voice was different; it sounded strong and sincere. Jacks could no longer look at him and drew away.

'You stuck a needle in me!' she said stubbornly

'Your behaviour was threatening and you needed to calm down.' His voice softened. 'I did it for your own safety as well as others.'

'I was angry that's all,' Jacks protested. 'I think that I acted perfectly normal given the way you've been treating me; you're trying to make out that I'm some sort of violent maniac.' She held his gaze, wondering why he did not react.

'Just a moment,' he said, and walked to the door. He tapped on the glass and seconds later, a man entered. She recognised him as one of the men who had restrained her previously. It was easy to see why he had been employed in such a capacity; He was *huge.*

'Do you recognise this man, Jacqueline?' asked the doctor.

She nodded. 'Yeah,' she said, 'he's one of the hired help you very kindly got to hold me down yesterday.'

The doctor looked at her in disbelief.

'You don't remember what you did to him, do you?' he asked.

She looked blankly at the man. He had a black eye, split lip, and various scratch marks across his face. Her heart began to thump; her confused face darted its attention back to Doctor Brodie.

'Yes Jacqueline,' he affirmed, 'you attacked him when he tried to calm you down.'

'He didn't try to calm me down,' she said. 'He pinned me to the bed, and you know bloody well that I didn't do that to him!' She marvelled at the audacity of the man and the composed manner he presented his accusation.

'Thank-you John,' Doctor Brodie said, and gestured to the door.

Taking his cue, the man left.

'Why do you think you were moved here, Jacqueline?'

'I didn't do it, I'd remember if I had,' she almost

whispered.

The doctor smiled knowingly. 'I have to attend to another patient now. Try to be positive and think over what I have told you,' he said, and without giving her a chance to respond, he was gone.

Jacks considered his parting words and spoke aloud, 'Well that's a contradiction in terms.'

She tried to concentrate, attempting to recall every detail of the previous struggle. *I didn't do it. I didn't*, she thought. *How could I? The two men were so strong I could scarcely move my head.* She sighed, her thoughts shifting. *I'm not eighteen, how can I be? If I were still eighteen, then it would be 2004.* Jacks considered for a moment, an idea forming in her mind.

She swung her legs around, a movement that proved to be extremely difficult. Her body felt heavy and as her feet touched the ground, she instantly collapsed. She felt weak and her legs were not functioning properly. Her body failed to respond as she tried to pull herself up with her arms. She tried to avoid becoming upset, knowing that she could not have damaged her spine because she had the sensation of feeling in her legs, along with seemingly limited movement. After several attempts to get back into bed, she gave up and lay on the floor in despair, feeling useless and feeble.

Hours passed and cold settled in her defeated body, feeding hungrily on all the warmth that remained in her motionless limbs.

She remained in a crumpled heap beside the bed when the nurse finally discovered her. The woman shouted for assistance.

Jacks felt shaky and peeped through half closed eyes in time to see John approaching. Strong arms lifted her almost effortlessly back into the bed. Her eyelids felt heavy and she had difficulty keeping them open. The nurse took her hand and felt her pulse.

'Is she all right?' came a deep, resonant voice.

'I don't know, John,' the woman replied.

A thermometer was thrust into Jacks' mouth. Her head was swimming.

There was something I was trying to do, she thought, *something I needed to know ... something important.*

As the nurse bent down to remove the thermometer, Jacks gripped her arm. The woman started.

'What year is it?' Jacks moaned.

John was there in an instant, removing her grasp with ease.

'Why is she asking that?' queried the nurse, in a disturbed tone.

'I'll get the doctor,' John said. 'Don't go near her; she's dangerous.'

Jacks felt faint and sick; her breathing was shallow and came in short gasps; her head was pounding. 'Please,' she whispered hoarsely. 'What year is it? I must know.'

'Calm yourself, Miss Chase, the doctor's on his way.' The nurse tried to sound soothing, but there was a hint of fear in her voice. Being left alone with Jacks obviously made her uncomfortable.

'Please tell me,' Jacks pleaded, with a pitiful wail.

Doctor Brodie entered and nodded to the nurse in signal for her to leave. She remained, however, until the doctor dismissed her again.

'Thank-you nurse; that will be all.'

She turned and walked toward the door. As she pulled the handle, she glanced back to Jacks. 'It's 2011,' she said quietly and left.

Jacks face lifted and she snivelled pathetically. 'You see I can't possibly be eighteen. I was born in 1986 ... I'm twenty ... five ...' She was having difficulty speaking. Her eyes rolled open to see the doctor frowning with concern.

Putting his hand to Jacks' forehead, his brow furrowed further. He saw her glazed look and smiled gently. 'I can't leave you for five minutes, can I? I suppose that you were trying to walk out of here to escape from the evil doctor who treats you so abhorrently.' He laughed.

Jacks failed to find amusement. She felt on the verge of losing consciousness. 'You're ... not ... funny,' she whispered as she slipped away.

'Jacqueline,' the doctor said, shaking her gently. The word echoed for a while in her unconscious before dispersing into nothing.

Darkness enveloped her like a great cloak, woven from the fabric of night. Voices reached out but were lost, as if sound could not wholly penetrate the prevailing density of darkness. The feeling of falling was growing gradually as time passed and her body felt as though it was being subjected to extremes of both hot and cold.

Despite the fact that she could not see anything, she knew that all about her everything was spinning. Her head began to throb. The pain seemed to reach a crescendo and the surroundings span so fast, that darkness transformed to white—dazzling bright. Her throbbing head seemed to create its own sound as it pounded ... a voice.

'She's coming 'round,' it said.

The lights in the room made her waking eyes sore. She squinted.

'How are you feeling?' the voice asked.

'Like death,' Jacks replied, looking more than a little dazed.

'You're not dead, I'm glad to say, although we were a little worried. You're fever was so high that we thought you might slip back into a coma.'

'What's going on? Why am I here? Jacks struggled to get her words out. Every muscle seemed to ache. It felt as though she could distinguish each nerve ending in her body by the pain, which issued forth.

'You collapsed, but you're all right now. You've contracted swine flu. That is why you feel rather poorly at present. Quite a few of the patients have caught it and we have been trying to keep it isolated. Anyway, now we know what's wrong with you, I think we should get you back to your room and let you sleep it off.'

'But why am I here? I've been put in a psychiatric ward, why? Please tell them they've made a mistake. I'm ...' Her voice trailed off, as if speaking was too exhausting in her fragile state.

'Don't trouble yourself,' said the nurse, 'I'm sure we'll have you better in no time. Now you have a good rest and try to get rid of that nasty flu bug.'

Jacks did not reply; her entire being felt alien to her. Closing her eyes, she fell into a fitful state of semi-consciousness. She awoke soon after to discover herself back in her room. She felt tired, but could not fall asleep again. Feelings of helplessness swept over her like a tidal wave, battering down all defences. She could not think coherently, feeling too frail and depressed. She simply lay zombie-like until a nurse came in, trying to persuade her to eat and drink. The food, she could not face, but she managed to take a few sips of water.

Later that evening, Doctor Brodie paid her a visit. He wore a mid-length woollen coat over his usual suit and Jacks assumed he was on his way home.

'I just thought I'd pop in to see how you are doing, Jacqueline,' he said brightly. 'God, you had us all scared there for a minute.'

'Yeah I bet I did,' Jacks said, attempting sarcasm. 'Can't anyone give me something for this? I feel like crap.'

'We've got you on anti-virals,' he said, 'but the best thing you can do is sleep. Keep drinking plenty of water, and for God's sake do not go trying to walk again whatever you do. You have just come out of a prolonged coma and you're going to need physiotherapy before you can go gallivanting around, pestering the staff with your outlandish questions. Anyway,' he clapped his hands, 'I can see that you desire my immediate absence, so I shall avaunt.' He made a melodramatic gesture with his arms. 'I'll see you in a couple of days. Bye Jacqueline.' He smiled and was gone.

Jacks experienced a tug of regret as he left her. She felt intolerably lonely. Every minute dragged to make hourly existence torturous. The fever attacked again, her breathing became erratic and still sleep did not come.

Three days passed in that way. She ate nothing. The fever broke, but the sleeplessness still afflicted her.

So this is insanity, she mused. *No escape from these four walls. At least my dreams offered a temporary release, but this … this is Hell.'*

She began to close her eyes; a figure came into view at the edge of her vision, standing at the foot of her bed. On opening her eyes fully, she saw no one. She shook her head, as if to shake out the cobwebs of prolonged waking, then closed her eyes once more.

A strange sensation crept slowly over her. A tingling, which began at the feet and worked its way upward; the hair on her arms stood on end as goose pimples formed. She held her breath, sensing the presence of someone. Her eyes shot open.

There stood Patrick, his grim features fixed on her face. She seemed to forget to feel frightened and stared back in curious wonder.

Neither spoke, and when Jacks dared to blink, he was gone. She remained motionless, marvelling at how real her delusion had been.

The sound of metallic objects crashing to the floor awoke Jacks. *I must have fallen asleep after all,* she thought, *through sheer exhaustion I shouldn't wonder.* She recalled her vision of Patrick and wondered whether she had been delusional or had merely had a dream. The heaviness had lifted from her limbs and, as far she could tell, her temperature seemed to have regulated itself back to normal. She felt much more like her old self after her rest, or at least as much as she imagined her old self to be.

There was another crash from outside the room and voices rose up in an argument of some sort. It was a woman and a man; the woman was screeching like a banshee; the man seemed to be trying to calm her down, but his voice rose in effort to display authority. It was not working. More voices joined the throng, and then a yell resounded painfully.

Jacks pried herself up into a sitting position in an effort to see through the window at the top of her door. A man's head suddenly struck the glass, as if he had been pushed violently backward. Jacks jumped slightly; she wanted to see what was happening and she felt helpless and a little frightened, being aware that her legs wouldn't function well enough to stand, let alone get out of the way of any trouble.

There was a shrill cry from the woman. 'Stay away from me!' she yelled.

Suddenly the door opened and the woman stepped in. She looked terrifying; her face was ashen and drawn, her hair a mass of rats' tails; her eyes were sunken and dark purple rings encircled them. The nightdress she wore was drenched in the blood that oozed from a vertical slit in each wrist. Blood trailed across the floor as the woman approached.

Jacks was horrified; she backed away, unable to tear her gaze away from the grisly sight. Every drop of blood that fell to the ground formulated a sound in Jacks traumatised mind.

Pitter, patter, pitter, patter—like a leaking tap.

The woman held her mangled wrists outstretched toward Jacks. She winced as the blood dripped across the crisp, white hospital sheets.

'See what they did?' the woman screamed.

Jacks was frozen, her mouth drawn back and her eyes wide. She could not respond; the nightmarish sight did not seem real to her.

John appeared in the doorway along with another male staff member. He had a slash across his cheek, from which blood issued. The two men made a grab for the woman and she kicked, growling like a wild animal cornered. Blood spattered across Jacks' face and she let out a cry of revulsion, quite unintentionally, and wiped it away as though contact with it was deeply offensive.

The outline of Doctor Brodie stood in the doorway and Jacks wondered how long he had been present. He entered the room followed by a nurse with a stretcher on a trolley. The crazed woman was growing weaker and Doctor Brodie took the opportunity to administer a sedative. She looked Jacks in the eye.

'He's a killer,' she said, 'don't listen to him.'

For that brief moment, the woman did not seem mad at all, but so utterly sane that it sent a cold shiver down Jacks' spine. The woman grew limp in their arms and the nurses immediately set to the task of stopping the bleeding.

Jacks finally forced her gaze away from the scene. Her pulse was racing, but she barely perceived it. She looked at Doctor Brodie who watched her, as if gauging whether or not to order Thorazine to go.

'I'm sorry you had to witness that, Jacqueline,' he said. ' It should never have happened.'

In a way, she was glad to hear him say as much; for a moment, she had feared that he might attribute the entire incident as being part of her mind, probably because she associated Doctor Brodie with denial with a capital D.

The nurses, having speedily dressed the woman's wounds, supervised orderlies as they lifted her gently onto the stretcher and made ready to take her away for treatment.

'Make sure you see to that cut, John,' the doctor said, with professional nonchalance. 'It looks as though you may need stitches.'

'Certainly will, sir,' John replied, wincing through the pain.

They were gone.

Jacks watched as the door swung closed. All was quiet once more, almost as if the whole event had been no more than a dream. Her gaze retracted slightly, catching sight of the blood on the floor and her bed. She stared, her mouth feeling parched.

Doctor Brodie sat on the edge of her bed and moved to take her pulse. She flinched backward, her eyes flashing dangerously at him. He lifted his hands, palm upwards, to show he was no threat.

'Jacqueline, can you hear me?' he asked.

Jacks' jaw tightened and she nodded quickly. 'Yes,' she rasped through pallid lips. Her hands shook uncontrollably and her body twitched as she stared back at the blood.

'Jacqueline, I think you're suffering from shock. Will you allow me to take your pulse?'

Jacks' head turned to the doctor, but her eyes remained with the blood a while, before meeting his. She nodded slowly in agreement to his request.

Tentatively, he took her wrist and she looked immediately back to the darkening stains on the bedspread. The doctor raised his hand lightly to her forehead; copious perspiration had broken out on her pale skin. The doctor frowned. Rising, he pressed a buzzer above her head and then moved to the end of the bed. With a swift jerk, he raised it at her feet. Jacks continued shaking.

'It's all right, Jacqueline; it'll be all right.'

She barely perceived his voice, remaining

focused on the river of blood that threatened to sweep away her room, drowning her in the process. It seemed to be spreading, crawling up the bed-sheets to consume her. She could not blink for fear of what might appear if she did.

There were voices beside her, speaking quietly, and then the blood moved suddenly. She gasped and looked up. A nurse had torn away the bed-sheet. Glancing nervously about, she saw Doctor Brodie observing another nurse prepare a drip.

Her gaze shifted back to the bed, failing to notice how thin and frail her legs were. The nurse flicked a clean sheet over and tucked it in briskly, followed by some blankets. So imprinted on her retina was the ghastly sight of the blood, that it still seemed to be there.

'Jacqueline,' said a soft and familiar voice beside her. 'We're going to hook you up to a saline drip, which will make you feel better.'

The nurse on the other side took her temperature.

'You're going to feel a little pain in your hand.'

The needle went in, but Jacks barely perceived it; she watched intently to ensure that the blood stayed away. She risked blinking at last, making her eyes water.

Gradually, she felt warmth returning to her limbs. Her breathing became more regular and her body visibly relaxed. She looked at the sheets, then the newly washed floor. She rolled her head toward the doctor. The nurses, having completed their tasks, had flitted away soundless as fairies.

Doctor Brodie let out a sigh and smiled warmly. 'My, what a dramatic little life you lead,' he said.

Jacks raised an eyebrow, but felt too feeble for a repartee. She glanced up at the drip, then to the ugly tube protruding from her hand and grimaced. Doctor Brodie chuckled at her expression.

'I take it that you are feeling better,' he said, while walking around the bed. He took her pulse again. 'Ah that's more like it.' He smiled. 'How about your bout of flu, have you managed to shake off the worst of it yet?'

Jacks looked at him quizzically. 'Does that sort of thing happen to *all* your patients?' she asked.

His smile faded. 'Of course not,' he said. 'That was an unfortunate incident and I'm very sorry that you were a party to it ...'

Jacks broke in. 'No believe me, I'm not sorry. I'm glad I got the opportunity to see what really goes on around here. I'd rather know what you've got in store for me now; I don't like surprises, but I guess you just discovered that,' she remarked dryly.

Doctor Brodie looked at Jacks—astounded, as if trying to discover whether her words were in jest. Her face, however, was stone and revealed nothing.

'Jacqueline ...' he began, but Jacks broke in again.

'How the hell did she get hold of a blade? What do you do, hand them out for good behaviour?' She was ranting and knew it, but she felt so strongly the after-effects of the situation.

The doctor's voice was quiet and steady. 'We don't know how she got the razor, Jacqueline, but really you shouldn't concern yourself; just try to put it out of your mind.' It was a ridiculous thing to say, but he had spoken without thinking.

'PUT IT OUT OF MY MIND!' she hollered. 'FOR GOD'S SAKE, IT SHOULDN'T HAVE BEEN PUT IN THERE IN THE FIRST PLACE! How could you have allowed this to happen? She was supposed to be in your care.'

She stared at him bitterly, expecting him to shirk responsibility, instead his shoulders sagged and he bowed his head, as if he felt the burden her words had placed upon him.

'Do you think that I wanted it to happen?' His voice sounded strange, lacking its usual control. 'Do you think I enjoyed watching that woman mutilate herself?'

She stared in disbelief. *How the mighty has fallen,* she thought, with tremendous satisfaction. It was good to know that he was human after all, prone to making mistakes and feeling guilt. She contemplated his new behaviour and her features hardened. *He may be acting,* she thought, *so I'll feel sorry for him and so be willing to forget the incident.*

Her voice cut with a spiteful edge. 'I suppose tomorrow, you will say this was simply part of my delusional mind, or even better, you'll say that *I* attacked that women and I should be sedated again.'

The doctor's posture changed instantly, his head flicked up. 'Jacqueline, you're being paranoid. Can you not see that?'

Jacks did not answer; she smiled snidely with her tongue thrust into her cheek, and shook her head.

'We're not persecuting you,' he said. 'No one is.'

Oh it's we *now, is it?* she thought.

'Do you honestly believe that I would try to pass this incident off as part of your condition?' he asked. 'Because if you do, then I must inform you that it opens a new part of your state of mind of which we had been unaware. You're displaying the symptoms of paranoid anxiety.'

Jacks was livid. 'I don't believe this! You're threatening me!' she said, in disbelief. 'What the hell do you expect me to think of you? Every time you speak to me, you wipe another piece of my existence away. I'm not paranoid; I'm just on my guard against *you*!' She felt like a sulking child and looked away, realising how hypocritical her words sounded.

'Oh well, if it's just me you have the problem with,' he said, rising, 'perhaps I should find another consultant to take your case.' It was his turn to behave like a child.

Jacks heard the door swing open and close as he left the room, knowing he would have slammed it if he could.

She huffed in frustration, feeling stupid; she had sounded off out of embarrassment and her feeling of helplessness. She knew a change of doctor would not change their insistence that her life was a lie.

Chapter Five

There must be something else to life,
Something more than the daily routine,
If only I could break free and find it …
And as I reach for freedom the reins they do
tighten, constrict, and I am snapped back into
orderly shape.
If only I could find the strength to shatter the prison
bars,
To break through the initial barrier,
So that I might find my true self and run naked and
free,
Rather than tread the gloomy paths of the present.
Every day darkens,
The weight grows heavier, every step I take,
But I make no advance and seem rather to be
walking backward into a never-ending void.
My world is grey, cold, without feeling.
Everything around me seems to be drowning in a
constant deepening water.

Staring blankly at the magnolia walls, Jacks thought how out of place they looked in her clinically clean abode. She tried to think of Claude.

Although she could remember details of the events, she was unable to visualise them. *It all seemed so real,* she thought. *How could it possibly have been a dream? I have years worth of memories of life in London. How could they be crammed into a few months of sleep? I even remember falling asleep and dreaming during the coma. Why would my mind create an existence, complete in detail and routine? Why would it create a completely new birth date leading me to believe that I'm seven years older than I'm supposed to be? It's just not possible.*

She sighed and felt that she did not know herself at all. Being eighteen was so many years ago to her, she had forgotten what it was like. *I was still a child back then,* she thought, sighing again. *Does that mean I grew up while I was sleeping? That's ridiculous!*

Jacks heard Doctor Brodie's voice outside her room and strained to interpret what he was saying. He seemed to be talking to John about the man's injury. She lay back, waiting for him to come in to see her, but he didn't. After bidding John goodnight, he walked off. Jacks felt hurt and tried to shrug off the feeling with stubborn indignation. She realised he had been the closest thing she had to a friend. *Even if he is a pain in the arse,* she thought. Now she had scorned him and driven him away. *Does this mean that I am willing to accept that what he's been saying to me is the truth?* She felt as though she was going around in circles, tangled up in her own personal paradox.

Caught up in her thoughts, she failed to hear the door handle turn. She looked up with surprise and eagerness, expecting to see the face of Doctor Brodie. It was not the doctor, however, but Nurse Cadeaux, who had assisted her earlier. The empty feeling afflicted Jacks again.

'Hello there,' the nurse said, in her Queensland accent. 'I've brought you something to eat.'

Jacks realised she had not eaten for days. She did not feel hungry, however. The nurse plonked the meal on a tray in front of her, and the homely smell from the steaming bowl of soup invaded her nostrils.

'I brought you something light, in case you hadn't much of an appetite,' she said, with a smile.

Jacks stared at the soup, feeling compelled to at least try it, as Nurse Cadeaux was being so nice. It was rich in flavour and Jacks savoured the warmth it yielded to her as she swallowed it. *The food has certainly improved since I've been moved from the main ward,* she thought.

'I'm just going to remove this drip for you,' said the nurse.

Jacks felt a cold sensation as the needle was drawn out, then the pain from the bruising issued as the woman firmly pressed down the dressing.

'You're going to start your physio tomorrow,' she said, setting a clean jug of water down.

Jacks had a mouthful of food and so smiled back politely. *Good,* she thought, *I shall finally be on my way to being mobile again. Then I'm out of here!* She placed the spoon down and huffed. 'I'm sorry, I can't eat any more,' she said, feeling bloated.

'That's all right, it'll take a while before you get your appetite back fully I should think.' The nurse smiled and removed the tray.

Jacks started a conversation quickly to prevent the nurse from leaving straight away. She wanted to avoid being left alone, feeling unable to face it again.

'When do you think that I'll be fit enough to go home?' she asked.

Setting down the tray, Nurse Cadeaux seated herself. 'Well, you've got to complete your physio of course,' she said, 'and beyond that it's Doctor Brodie's decision.'

'Do you think I'm mad?' Jacks asked.

The woman raised her eyebrows and sighed. 'That's a big question, and I'm sure you understand when I tell you that I'm not going to answer it. At any rate, I'm not qualified to answer it. In my opinion, we're all a bit mad, some more than others of course; but you seem okay to me. I know you've had your little outbursts, but I would too I expect if I was cooped up in here day in day out.'

Jacks smiled. It was good to feel that someone was on her side and trying to understand where she was coming from. 'Thank-you,' she said. 'So do you believe that my mind could create a new existence while I was asleep?'

'You do like your complex questions, don't you? As I said, I'm not a psychiatrist, just think of me as general dogsbody; but I don't see why your mind couldn't create in the way you say. When we sleep, we dream, and in our dreams we can invent anything from a day in the life to a completely new world. Remember as well, that the subconscious is far more powerful than our conscious mind, and there is still so much that we have to learn about its capabilities.'

Jacks took an instant liking to the woman. She had a down to earth approach to everything, which made the most complicated situations seem clear-cut, and her easygoing manner made the most stressful situation appear trivial. She decided to change the subject as Nurse Cadeaux had given her a lot to think about.

'How's the woman who tried to kill herself earlier? Did she die?' Jacks asked, feeling she could have put the question a little more tactfully.

'Meg? Well she's in a critical condition at

present I'm afraid. They've given her a transfusion, so we'll just have to hope she pulls through.' Nurse Cadeaux bowed her head, obviously feeling sorry for the woman.

It's nice to know someone cares, Jacks thought. 'How long has Meg been here?'

Nurse Cadeaux thought for a moment. 'I don't rightly know—longer than me; I've only been an enrolled nurse for a short time, but I worked here in another capacity for almost eight years. Meg was transferred here after a fire in her home. She would have burned to death if the fire-fighters hadn't got her out.'

'Is that what sent her mad?' Jacks asked.

'I know her husband committed suicide before that, but as to the cause, I really wouldn't know. I just look after people once they arrive.'

Jacks nodded sadly. The woman's story was vague and she felt sure that the nurse knew more than she was letting on, but Jacks was reluctant to dig deeper.

'What have you been told about why I'm here?' she asked, seizing the opportunity for secondary information. The nurse appeared pleased that she wanted to talk.

'I was told you'd been suffering from what seemed like a neurotic depression, but it manifested into a psychosis; or in English.' She smiled. 'You were feeling emotional and low and these sensations were persistent and severe, but then your behaviour became illogical and abnormal, until finally you stepped in front of a lorry, almost killing yourself. You spent five months on a life support machine, and when you woke, you were sent to us here. Does that fill in any blanks for you?'

'Kind of,' Jacks replied, amazed by the candid manner of the woman. 'But why was I depressed in the first place? Doctor Brodie said that when I was eighteen, I scored so low on my exams that I couldn't go to uni. He said that I couldn't handle failure, so it sent me off the rails.'

'Jacks, you're still only eighteen now, you're speaking as though this is the distant past. It wasn't that long ago, even if it seems like it to you, and I think it's perfectly normal to feel low after a setback. The trick is to try again or let it go.'

'But I can remember how well I did,' Jacks said. 'I went out for a drink with my friends and then we went to a party at Rick's house and danced 'til three in the morning.'

Nurse Cadeaux interrupted her.

'And that is why you're here,' she said. 'You've answered your own question. You remember things that never happened. You've blanked out the truth; our job is to sort out that jumbled noggin of yours and help piece back together your real life so that you can return to it.'

Her voice was so kind and soothing that Jacks,

for the first time, felt ready to accept what Doctor Brodie had told her as the truth.

'You're right,' she found herself saying. 'I just wish I didn't feel so vulnerable and lost.' She had not tried to express her feelings before and regretted doing so now.

Nurse Cadeaux gave her a knowing smile.

'These feelings are perfectly natural,' she said. 'Your innermost thoughts are in the process of being stripped bare, and your privacy has been put up for investigation. You've been through a frightening ordeal and you're lost and confused; but you'll find it easier if you remember that people are here to help you.'

There was a noise as the door clicked shut. Jacks jumped, looking at Nurse Cadeaux in alarm.

'I left it open I expect,' she said dismissively.

Jacks remained suspicious, however; she knew that the only way in which the door would stay open was if it was held open, which meant that someone had been eavesdropping. They were silent for a short time and then a thought struck Jacks that she had wanted to know, but had been reluctant to ask the doctor.

'Why have my family not been to visit, nurse? I saw them when I first awoke, but no one has been since.' She felt lonely as she said it and Nurse Cadeaux's eyes answered with pity.

'The consultant and your mother agreed that it

would be best if she did not see you while you are undergoing treatment, because of what happened that night.'

Jacks was not happy; by consultant, she assumed the nurse meant that Doctor Brodie was disallowing her visitors. 'What happened? What are you talking about?' she asked, in annoyance. She wondered why no one had informed her of as much before.

'You attacked your mother, or so I was led to believe,' nurse Cadeaux replied. 'Apparently you were screaming and swearing and they had to drag you off her.' She frowned, as if finding it difficult to believe Jacks had no recollection of such an occurrence. 'Your mother agreed to stop her visits, so she doesn't upset you further.'

Jacks did not know how to react to the new disclosure. She didn't remember anything of the sort occurring. She felt sick at the thought that she could even be capable of doing such a thing as attacking her own mother.

Nurse Cadeaux stood up and began tucking Jacks in.

'I think we've talked enough for one day,' she said. 'You look done in, and Nurse Wong will be telling you off for monopolising my attention if you're not careful.' She stopped and looked at Jacks, who was lost in thought. 'Would you like me to give you something to help you sleep? It's been a rough day,' she ended kindly, trying to draw Jacks from her dark brooding.

'No, I'll be fine, thanks.'

Jacks glanced at the nurse, who in turn seemed satisfied that she would indeed be all right. Drawing the curtains, she bade Jacks goodnight.

The curtains were thin and light still invaded the room, until the sun finally sank about half an hour later. As the room darkened, Jacks noticed the light that streamed in from the corridor through the window in the door directly opposite. The nearest point of which highlighted the end of her bed.

She felt warm and realised that she still had three blankets covering her. Sitting up, she stripped two of them away, letting them fall to the floor.

Despite her recent discoveries, she felt relaxed and peaceful. She was extremely tired and the only thing that entered her mind was she had a new friend. Her breathing grew deeper and it took little time to lull herself to sleep.

Her dreams were a temporary remission, and she drifted lightly to the sound of her own breathing, before the rhythm changed into the tinkling of tiny drops of water. She sighed and sat up finding herself on the edge of a small lake, surrounding which, willow trees cast hazily their yellow blossom on the surface, like a crown of confetti.

She ran her hand through the pleasantly warm

water and smiled at the music it made. Laying back, staring into the boughs of the tree, she continued to run her hand through the water. The blossom rained down and she breathed in its pungent fragrance as the flowers landed delicately on her resting body.

Closing her eyes, she absorbed the sounds about her; the trickling as the water seeped through her fingers and the tapping as it fell from an unseen source.

The air grew suddenly chill and the dripping increased in volume, reminding Jacks of something; it was the same sound the blood from Meg's injured wrists had made as it struck the floor.

The scent of the flowers grew sickly and Jacks sat up, startled by her change in perception. The lake was stained red, stagnant from the flowers rotting on its surface. She removed her hand from the water in disgust, recoiling as blood trickled down her white flesh, in mockery of Meg's wounds. Her gaze dropped to the rotting flowers upon her body where maggots crawled and writhed.

Jumping to her feet, she yelled as she brushed them off, her voice ending in a repulsed gargle. The blood still stained her arm and she rubbed at it in effort to remove the mark.

A low rasping laugh sounded that made her forget all else and she turned to face its maker.

Meg stood before her.

'They killed you too,' she said. Outstretching her arms, she displayed her terrible injuries as she had done previously. This time, however, the blood was coagulated and the lacerations were festering. Maggots crawled from her wrists and fell to the ground, squirming at her feet.

The rank odour of rottenness caused Jacks to gag. She turned to run and stumbled over the willow; the now uprooted tree, was in the final stages of decay. Horrified, she tried to cry out and thrashed about in effort to get to her feet to escape the choking madness.

She awoke suddenly to the darkness of her room. Sweat fell from her brow and trickled down her cheek before meeting with her pallid lips. Her tongue made contact with the perspiration. Its salt-like taste reminded Jacks of blood, and she could not shake the terror she felt. As another drop of sweat ran down her face, she cried out quietly.

Flashbacks of Meg appeared, and try as she might, Jacks could not make them go away. She stared at the pool of light in front of her and realised that it illuminated the exact spot where Meg's blood had spilt. She began to visualise it, spreading and creeping toward her, as though it had a life of its own and wished to contaminate her with its tainted foulness.

She kept closing her eyes tight then reopening them, to see if the vision would disappear.

Her breathing was short and heavy as she wiped the sweat from her brow. She dare not allow herself to catch a glimpse of it on her fingertips, for fear of seeing blood there. She reached for the buzzer, which Doctor Brodie had used; it was high up and way out of her grasp. Facing forward once more, she pushed herself into sitting position, trying to take her weight on one arm, whilst making a second attempt to reach up for the buzzer.

She froze.

Someone stood beside her.

Her glance strayed upwards and met the eyes of Patrick frowning down at her. His face looked deathly white and his eyes large and dark, as though his pupils dilated so much that his true eye colour was indiscernible.

Jacks opened her mouth as if to scream, but only a squeak emerged. Her hand fell back to the bed as her body paralysed with fear. Patrick reached over and pressed the panic button.

There was a tormenting moment, during which they stared at one another, before the lights in her room flickered on and Nurse Cadeaux entered. Jacks' eyes flashed back to her bedside, but Patrick was gone. She gazed wide-eyed at the nurse, gasping for air and beginning to hyperventilate. Nurse Cadeaux ran to her side and took her hand.

'What is it?' she tried to determine. 'What's

wrong, Jacks?'

Jacks attempted to reply, but gulped air so fast that she sounded like an over excited sea lion. The nurse dashed out and returned almost immediately, carrying a paper sanitary bag.

'Here, breathe into this,' she said.

Scrunching up the end, she handed the bag to Jacks, who did as the nurse instructed.

'Try to breathe slower if you can.'

The light-headed feeling began to clear from Jacks' head. She looked again to her bedside; there was no one there. The feeling of terror had left her system and seemed wholly illogical in the light of the room.

She removed the bag from her lips, but could not bring herself to discuss the events with Nurse Cadeaux. The nurse had been the only person who seemed to think she was reasonably sane; she did not want to shatter that bond unless entirely necessary.

'I'm sorry,' Jacks ventured, 'I had a bad dream; it shook me up a bit I guess.'

The nurse appeared satisfied with the explanation; it was after all, plausible that anyone present when Meg burst into the room would suffer from a nightmare or two.

'I'll pop and get you a sedative, shall I?' the nurse said.

Jacks sighed out a huge backlog of tension as

the woman made her exit. She stared to her side. *It seemed so real,* she thought. *As long as I can remain aware that they are hallucinations, I know I'm still sane. It's the moment I lose insight and convince myself they're real that I really have to worry.*

The EN entered, producing a tiny syringe. Jacks looked away as the drug was administered.

'There,' Nurse Cadeaux said, 'that should help you rest a little easier.'

She sat beside Jacks and gently stroked her hair. Jacks imagined it to be the sort of thing a mother would do, although she could not recall her own mother ever doing as much. Her eyelids felt heavy and she slept.

Her dreams were long in coming …

She found herself in a children's playground, but the image was grey and vague. She concentrated on keeping her focus on the empty swings, in effort to deter her mind away from the fact that surrounding the island was a sea of blood.

Jacks woke late. Her body felt drowsy and tired. Looking about her, she saw that the curtains were open and sunlight flooded her room. Beside her were an apple, two slices of toast and a cup of tea—the latter of which were both cold. Jacks drank the cold tea, grateful for a change from water. She guessed that it must have been Nurse Cadeaux's doing. Just as she finished her second piece of toast,

Nurse Daily entered with a washbowl.

After Jacks' wash, Nurse Daily helped her change into a pair of loose fit pyjamas, and handed her a soft brush to tidy her hair, which felt greasy and matted. While the nurse tidied her tray, she mentioned Jacks' nightmare.

'No more bad dreams I trust,' she stated.

Jacks shook her head, reluctant to enter into a discussion on the matter. She felt cold, and remembering the presence of Patrick at her bedside, tried to convince herself it had been part of her dream

'I shall leave you now. I hope you're feeling fit because you'll be starting your physio in a while.' The woman gave a brisk smile then left.

Jacks was barely paying attention; she had had an idea. She attempted to reach the buzzer by balancing on one arm as she had done in the night. She stretched and strained, but still it remained a couple of inches out of reach. There was no possible way that she could have pressed the buzzer to alert the nurse. As she continued to strain, the physiotherapist walked in.

Seeing Jacks in her odd posture, he commented, 'You've started without me I see.'

Jacks slumped immediately to the bed, feeling uneasy about her discovery. She looked up at the man and froze, as recognition hit her like a speeding train.

It was Claude.

Chapter Six

Voices on the air sing a sad song,
Regardless of my pain,
Your life goes on.
Why do I love you?
I guess I'll never know.

Jacks' jaw dropped. She remained speechless as she stared in wonder at the man who was supposed to be a figment of her imagination. She had just begun to think of him as such and now there he stood, smiling at her as if there had been no animosity between them.

'Claude,' she managed at last. She stuttered several inaudible sounds and then said, 'I was told you didn't exist; they said you were in my mind.' Her voice was wavering and she did not know whether to be angry or happy.

The man's smile faded and he seemed distinctly uncomfortable, looking as though he was considering calling for assistance.

'My name's not Claude,' he ventured a little nervously. 'I'm called Andy.'

Jacks failed to hear his words; she was in complete awe over the vision. She began to disbelieve his existence and stared at him in paralysed wonder. Memories of her encounters with him flooded back with the colour, which until that moment they had lacked. She shook her head violently and looked up again.

Her face had changed; she appeared distressed, feeling that he was yet another hallucination. Seeing her state, the man called for help. The senior nurse on duty entered shortly after and approached Jacks, who immediately looked down at the bed-covers.

'What's wrong, Jacqueline, are you able to tell me?' asked the woman sternly.

Jacks risked an upward glance expecting Claude to have vanished and turned away again on seeing him there.

'She seemed to think my name is Claude,' the man said.

Jacks winced. She was trying to block out the sight and sound of him, determined not to admit he was real; but on the nurse's reply to him, she looked slowly upward.

'Did you ... can you see him?' she stammered.

'Jacqueline, this is Andy, your physiotherapist,' said the woman, her voice displaying no sign of emotion.

'But he's Claude,' Jacks whispered, unable to take her eyes away from him.

'Come now, Jacqueline,' she said as if scolding a young child. 'Stop this silly nonsense. You know perfectly well that this Claude person does not exist, and if you insist on harassing Andy then you will find yourself minus a physiotherapist. Now we wouldn't want that, would we?'

Jacks bit her lip and tried to take in the senior nurse's words. Everything seemed out of focus, but she attempted to appear normal, even though she knew how absurd it would seem.

'It's nice to meet you ... Andy.' She had difficulty forming the words. 'I'm very sorry for my outburst, it's just that you look just like someone I know,' she corrected herself quickly. 'Like someone I had a dream about.' Jacks felt every utterance a strain; she did not know what to believe anymore. By saying what she had, felt like admitting she was insane.

The senior nurse remained for part of the physio session, until she felt satisfied that there would be no more problems. Jacks felt acutely embarrassed as the Claude look-alike proceeded to massage the backs of her legs. Andy was an easy-going, friendly man who did not seem a bit deterred by Jacks' peculiar behaviour.

'So who is this Claude then?' he asked, whilst finishing the massage.

Jacks felt uncomfortable. *It's bad enough having a life that's a complete lie,* she thought, *but now it seems those lies have sent their own doppelganger to torment my fragile mind.*

'He's not real,' Jacks said.

She swallowed hard, trying to clear the tenseness from her throat. Andy turned her back over and began lifting her legs.

'If he doesn't exist, how can I look like him?' he quizzed.

It seemed apparent to Jacks, that Andy would not stop asking his annoying questions until she had told her tale. She cleared her throat with an uncomfortable cough.

'Claude was created by my subconscious mind while I was in a coma. He's a dream, contrived to give me a sense of catharsis over my other problems existing at the time.'

'How could you have other problems while you were in a coma? When you're unconscious, daily worries cease to be an issue surely,' Andy said, with a twinkle in his eye.

Jacks had never considered such a thing before; if what Andy said was true then it only seemed to make the whole manifestation even more baffling.

'So who was he then?' continued Andy, 'Superhero? Lover?'

His voice had a mocking tone, to which Jacks did not take kindly.

'He was a man I fell in love with, but he didn't love me. He was engaged ...' she trailed off, not wanting to continue further. She felt annoyed at how he had made light of her whole situation.

Andy moved closer, his face was serious, but his eyes shone with laughter. 'So does this mean that you're in love with me? Shucks and we've only known each other less than an hour.' He laughed. 'That's good going even by my standards.'

Jacks was annoyed. Her jaw tightened and her lips twisted as she snapped back at him. 'I'm not in love with Claude. He isn't real—remember? And neither were my feelings for him; they were manufactured by my mind.'

Andy stopped laughing, realising that he had upset her. 'I'm sorry,' he said. 'That was a bit insensitive, wasn't it?'

Jacks raised a solitary eyebrow. 'That's all right, I'm getting used to it. It's like someone else 'round here I know,' she said, thinking of Doctor Brodie.

Andy's eyes gleamed with restrained mirth. 'Not another imaginary person, is it?' he asked

She glanced up at him and laughed, although she did so to humour him; she felt far from happy. His statement had served to remind her of Patrick's visitation and the bell that she could not possibly have pressed. She fell silent for a while, attempting to force the thought to the back of her mind; there were other questions she wanted answering first.

'How do you think it's possible that you can look exactly like a dream?' she asked.

He shrugged. 'It's a mystery I guess.'

'It's just not possible.'

He glanced at his watch. 'Anyway, I must be off. I'll see you tomorrow, and hopefully we might start the session minus your freaky antics.'

Jacks smiled snidely at him and he was gone. She stared after him a while, her teeth clenched. *Another day, another riddle,* she thought. *At least this proves without a doubt that Claude never existed, and therefore he couldn't have been the cause of my being here ... unless of course he has a twin that he is unaware*

121

of. She huffed and glanced up at the buzzer, focusing suspiciously on it for a while, as if by the power of thought alone she could make it ring.

'God help me,' she said aloud.

'Will a doctor do?'

Doctor Brodie entered, as she had been lost in thought. Jacks started and scowled at him, despite being secretly pleased by his unexpected arrival.

'I thought you'd given up my case,' she said.

Smiling, he pulled up a chair. 'No one else would have you,' he said, 'so I guess you're stuck with me.'

Jacks could not bring herself to be polite; she was glad to see him, but remained annoyed by his behaviour toward her.

'Cut the sarcasm,' she replied stubbornly. 'I've had enough from Andy, so I don't want any wise cracks from you as well.'

Doctor Brodie's eyes narrowed slightly, while considering for a moment who Andy might be, then realisation struck and he relaxed visibly.

She observed his reaction and added,

'Don't worry, I haven't had any *unauthorised* visitors, Mein Führer.'

Jacks thought she caught a look of hurt on his face, but it passed so quickly she could not be sure.

'I understand your dream sprang to life so to speak,' he said. 'Does that mean that you're now ready to admit that Claude was your own fantasy at last?'

She resented the sound of triumph in Doctor Brodie's voice. *Just because he's right, doesn't mean he has to gloat,* she thought.

'I'm not sure,' she said carefully, and watched with a spark of pleasure as the doctor was obviously taken aback. 'I've been considering that the accident was real, even if I don't remember it, after all it is quite normal not to remember such things as the shock would have prevented memory of the accident from being properly consolidated, would it not?' She did not wait for an answer. 'But it strikes me that *this* could be the dream, this whole place, this weird situation that I'm in. It certainly seems stranger than the reality I recall; so I may not have woken up yet.'

Jacks had spoken in jest, but regretted the words as soon as she said them; they only served to confuse her further. As ridiculous as it sounded initially, on second consideration it seemed credible to her.

'It would certainly explain Andy's appearance; that sort of thing happens in dreams.' She spoke quietly, as if considering every word carefully to measure its level of possibility.

Doctor Brodie stared back incredulously.

'It would make sense,' she protested. 'It is after all impossible for me to meet a man identical to that of a dream, but it is far more likely to *dream* of a man I don't know, who exists in reality.' She stopped abruptly; her head was beginning to ache. She felt as though she had created a paradox—or at least stumbled blindly into it.

The doctor crossed his legs calmly. 'So let me see if I understand you correctly,' he said. 'In order for you to explain the existence of a man who *doesn't* exist, you are willing to completely alter reality. You will allow your fantasies to dominate your mind and you reject the real world. Had you not even considered that you may have met Andy before, and his image had been imprinted on your mind, which in turn delivered his image to your unconscious for the creation of Claude?'

Jacks was startled by the anger in his voice.

'Surely I'd remember,' she mumbled.

'Probably not, considering that there has been *nothing* which you have told me about your life which is actually factual. It seems that you remember very little, let alone a face that you may have only glimpsed for an instant.'

His point was valid and Jacks knew it, but she was unwilling to tell him so; tightening her jaw, she sulked. She hated it when he embraced such an emotionless tone.

'I take it by your lack of response,' he said, 'that you do not discount what I have said as a possibility.'

Jacks shrugged. There was an uncomfortable

pause, during which she felt the doctor's penetrative gaze upon her.

'Jacqueline, why do you dislike me so much?'

The question came as a complete surprise to Jacks and she stuttered her reply. 'What makes you think I don't like you? I mean, do you not think that you are being a bit on the *paranoid* side?'

Doctor Brodie smiled to himself. 'Touché,' he replied. 'What I mean is, why do you feel as though you can't talk to me? I'm the one who is supposed to be helping you through this—that is what I'm here for after all, and yet you put up barriers and fence yourself in as if I'm an enemy force.'

Jacks was dumbfounded. His words suggested he had feelings to hurt and care to give

'I find it difficult to talk,' she said. She was tempted to tell him that she thought he was a pompous arse, which created a definite wall between her thinking of him as a confidante, but on reflection she felt that it would be the wrong thing to say.

'Well you didn't seem to be having difficulties talking last night,' he snapped. 'You poured your heart out to Nurse Cadeaux, so why should I be any different?'

Jacks realised who had been listening at the door the previous night, and she was infuriated.

'It was *you* who was eavesdropping,' she cried. 'How dare you! That was a private conversation.

You had no right to listen in.'

Doctor Brodie looked a little flushed; he had obviously not meant to reveal the fact that he had been privy to their conversation.

'It's well that I did so,' he said, 'how else would I be able to determine how you feel? You're certainly not going to tell *me*; all you ever do is argue with me.'

'Since when has it been any of your God-damned business how I feel?' she shouted, then fell into silence, realising what his last words had been and how, yet again, she had proved him right.

'Why can't you see that I am trying to help you?' He sounded upset. 'Why do you treat me like an opponent all the time?'

'Why do you act like one?' Jacks replied. She frowned, her jaw tightening.

'There you see,' he said, 'when you're not shouting at me, you give me those cut-off remarks which show you to be evasive. It's as though you make light of your situation.'

Jacks was astounded. 'Is that what you honestly think? Do you have any idea how it feels to be in this predicament? *Have you?* I try my best to be as light-hearted as possible, because it's the only way that I know how to cope. Do you know how it feels to wake up one day and discover that you don't know who you are, and that the person you thought you were, doesn't even exist? The life you had isn't real? Believe me, I do not make *light* of my situation. It's *you*—you're so damned ...' She screwed up her face, unable to find the words she wanted. Something seemed to click in her mind; a small piece of a mammoth jigsaw puzzle shifted into place. She finally retrieved a tiny piece of her memory, something that she knew to be so, even if she was unsure why.

'I find it difficult to talk to you because you're a man, and I don't want you to know my weaknesses; I don't want you to have any hold or control over me.' She spoke slowly, as if every word was an effort in itself. Falling silent again, she glared down at the bed, wondering if it had been foolish to reveal such a thing.

Doctor Brodie blinked in astonishment. 'Why do you feel that you have this problem with men, Jacqueline?' he asked slowly.

Jacks failed to notice the analytical tone return to his voice.

She shrugged. 'I don't know. It could have been my father's fault I suppose. He had an affair and left home when I was young; it certainly made me distrust men.' A buzzing began at the back of her mind, almost like white noise. The familiar sensation of things not being quite right began to saturate her being. 'Somewhere along the way I guess I developed this *hatred*.' She flinched at the severity of the word. 'My relationships have all been difficult; I always brought men down and tried to control them. It's funny really; I probably turned into what I disliked so much in them.' The more she spoke, the louder the sound in her mind became. She rubbed her temples in effort to disperse the strange sensation.

Doctor Brodie appeared satisfied with what she had said. 'Well that certainly seems to make a lot of sense,' he agreed. 'I just hope that you can try to let go of this hang-up you have. I know it's a lame thing to say but, we're not all the same as your father you know.'

Jacks looked at him with the beginnings of a smile. 'No, some of you are worse.'

To her surprise, he actually laughed.

'That is why I like you so much,' he said. 'I remember the day I met you, when you put that Nurse Practitioner in her place.'

Jacks smiled. 'I'd forgotten that,' she mused. 'Personally, I don't think my comment upset her as much as you laughing so loudly at what I said.' She chuckled, feeling a warmth inside that had been missing so often of late.

There was a knock at the door and Doctor Brodie held it open while an orderly wheeled in a chair.

'There you go, doc,' he said brightly.

'Thank-you Craig.'

'Will you need any help with lifting her?' Craig

asked, grinning at Jacks.

'No, I'll manage from here thank-you,' the doctor replied.

Craig gave a little wave and left.

Jacks eyed the wheelchair with nervous anticipation. 'Is that for me?' she asked.

Doctor Brodie nodded. 'Nurse Cadeaux seemed to think that it's not good for you being shut up in here, so what do you say to a stroll around the gardens?'

Jacks eagerly agreed; it seemed an age since she was first placed in her room, and those four walls were so familiar to her that she seemed unable to escape the image of them. The room had become her prison and the thought of reprieve, no matter how brief, instilled her with a joy that she could not remember ever experiencing before.

Doctor Brodie removed a bag from the seat of wheelchair and opening it, took out a maroon dressing gown and a pair of slippers.

'Thank-you,' Jacks said.

He handed her the slippers and she pushed herself around so that her feet were on the floor. She bent down awkwardly to attempt to put them on, but giddiness made her immediately sit back up. Holding a hand to her forehead, she waited for the stars to clear from her vision. Doctor Brodie knelt at her feet and placed the slippers on.

'How did you know what size to get?' she

asked.

He grinned mischievously. 'I asked the assistant for the largest size in the shop,'

'Well thank-you very much,' Jacks said, with a scowl.

'Oh come on, they're not exactly what you'd call dainty, are they?' the doctor said, rising.

'Did I say my name was Cinderella?' she said.

'One never knows with you,' Doctor Brodie retorted. 'You seem to have so many personalities.'

Jacks kicked at him, but missed as he stepped backward to avoid the blow.

'That's not funny,' she said sulkily. She cast the bathrobe loosely about her shoulders and attempted to stand.

Doctor Brodie dashed forward and caught her as she fell. Jacks felt her face flush as she pressed firmly against him, grasping tightly to prevent herself from collapsing. He lowered her gently back onto the bed.

'That was a bit silly now, wasn't it?' he said. 'You know you really should try not to be so quick to take offence. If you're going to dish out that quick wit of yours so often, then you have to expect a healthy repartee`.'

He fetched the wheelchair then approached Jacks, who was blushing badly.

'Put your arms around my neck and then try to stand,' he said, bending at the knees.

Jacks felt embarrassed as she wrapped her arms about him. She stood, and again her legs buckled beneath her. He clasped her tightly about the waist, and for a moment they seemed locked in a bizarre dance before he helped her into the chair. Crouching in front of her, he pulled the gown tightly about her like a concerned parent.

'Let's do this up, shall we?' he said. 'We don't want you getting cold.' He noticed her rosy pallor. 'I've never seen you blush before, what are you so embarrassed about, eh?'

'Nothing,' she snapped. 'I just hate being a bloody invalid that's all.' She felt satisfied with her reply; she had no intention of admitting it was his close proximity that had set her in a flurry.

Doctor Brodie flung a blanket over her. 'Just to be sure, we don't want you coming down ill again, do we?'

'I'm in bloody hospital, one doesn't get much more ill than that!' she complained

As he pushed her foreword, she fidgeted.

'I thought you were getting a nurse to take me out,' she said. 'Surely this is beneath a consultant such as yourself.'

'If you don't stop bantering with me, you won't go out at all, and as for taking you outside, I thought we might have a counselling session in the fresh air.'

He wheeled her awkwardly through the door,

as he held it open with his back. Jacks smiled to herself, believing she was getting the better of him.

On entering the hallway, she was surprised; she had expected it to look dingy and dull, yet it was anything but. It was whisper quiet and not nearly as busy as she had imagined. There was a desk to the right of her room, where Nurse Daily and another woman sat drinking coffee. They half-heartedly acknowledged the doctor and Jacks as they walked left toward the lifts. The ward consisted of a short corridor of private rooms.

Jacks wondered which floor Bertha and co. were on. The two wards did not seem to match somehow. The ward she had been on originally was noisy and hectic, with decor of miserable hues of grey and blue, not the sunny yellow of her present surroundings. Something else that occurred to Jacks was the fact that the whole ward consisted of private rooms. *A definite luxury as far as Medicare goes,* she thought. She wondered exactly where she was; she had never thought to ask before.

Jacks gradually realised something else that was strange; the odour of heavy-duty, top of a COSHH list, detergent was absent. She distinctly remembered the smell when she had first woken up, because it had disturbed her; now the air smelt of fresh lemons, as if the multi-purpose crap had been replaced by a more expensive alternative.

The lift bleeped happily, as the doors closed. It

was a sparkling elevator and looked more fitting to a hotel than a hospital. Doctor Brodie pressed for the ground floor.

'You're very quiet,' he said.

'Oh, I was just taking in the surroundings.'

She watched the floor numbers illuminate on their descent. The doctor leaned over and spoke gently in her ear.

'No doubt you're memorising each tiny detail in order to plan your escape route.'

The lift arrived at ground level. In case there had been any doubt of the fact, a polite computerised voice informed them as much and the doors slid silently open.

She felt dazzled by the glamorous lobby, bathed in sunlight that issued from the tall windows to the front of the building. *Talking elevators, fancy architecture; is this a hospital or a hotel?* she thought.

Doctor Brodie wheeled her out through the main entrance. A buzzer system controlled the doors, operated by a receptionist.

Jacks was immediately taken back by the rich green gardens. The sun glinted off the trees, making them sparkle like emeralds. She gazed up at the sky and caught her breath as dreamy clouds drifted gently along in a sea of purest blue. She breathed deeply the air, savouring for a moment the taste of freedom after her imprisonment.

Doctor Brodie came to rest to the rear of the building, beneath a great Turpentine tree. He pulled the wheelchair about to allow Jacks a wider view, and then sat on the bench beside her.

The sheer beauty of the surroundings astounded her; the gardens were luscious, well kept, and host to wide variety of flowers, all of which were arranged to co-ordinate perfectly with one another. The hospital itself, certainly from the back where one could not view the extension, was more like a mansion, with tall brick chimneys, which spoke of roaring fires of yesterdays, luxury, style and extravagant beauty. More than ever, Jacks could see that the original ward did not fit in at all with the aristocratic home.

'What are you thinking about, Jacqueline?' the doctor asked, in his professional capacity.

She looked up from her brooding. 'It's so beautiful,' she said. 'I never imagined it looked like this from the outside.'

'I had a feeling you would appreciate it,' he said. 'You should see the place in spring; the blossoms are a sight too spectacular to miss. Of course, the gardeners can't stand it; they say it's messy, all those petals scattered about, and they run around with their rakes and their brooms trying to gather them into neat piles so to discard them, usually by burning them. But nature will have its way, and by morning the ground is covered once more in its magical patchwork of colour to blanket the seeds of sleeping summer flowers.'

He stared absently, imagining the changing season. Jacks watched him, moved by his expression. She too could recall the magic of spring and remembered that it was her favourite season. She felt grateful to him for rekindling the image. She now felt that another piece of the jigsaw had been discovered and put into place, only this time the memory was joyous; it was the sheer love of nature in all its changing glory. Her eyes shined at him. He turned and met her gaze, smiling.

'You make me sad that it isn't spring,' she said. 'I know how dearly I love it, but I really can't recall the last time I saw it.'

'You were around for last spring I can assure you,' he said.

'I don't remember,' she said solemnly. 'I wish I could.'

'It will come back to you; you've just got to give it some time. What you will probably find is that images from further in your past will appear to you first and then work back roughly in time order to the accident. You may never recall the accident itself. As you rightly put, the last few moments would probably not have been adequately consolidated on the brain.'

'But when will I start to remember? So far all

that I'm sure of is that I have a problem with men and that I like the spring,' she said, waving her hand flamboyantly.

Doctor Brodie smiled supportively. 'Let's find the point where your memory disappears and try and work from there.'

Jacks leaned forward. 'Wait a minute, doctor; I don't think you understand me.' She looked anxiously at his questioning brow. 'That's it,' she said. 'They are my only recollections. There is *nothing* apart from that. I don't know who I am, and the things I do remember, never happened. Don't you see? I don't exist. My whole life is a blank.' She was getting upset; bowing her head, she fought to calm herself.

Doctor Brodie tilted his head downward to see her face.

'Surely you remember at least some of your childhood,' he said, 'you recognised your family after all.'

'I remember things, things that are supposed to have happened, and I'm sure you would assure me that they had, but,' she paused, struggling to retain control over her wavering voice. 'I know they didn't happen. I cannot explain it, but they're not memories, they're not me ... I don't exist.'

Doctor Brodie's brow furrowed with concern. 'Jacqueline, please tell me, do you feel as though you are invisible to the world around you, or that people are ...'

Jacks cut in. 'Doctor please, please don't. Stop trying to fit me into some neat little category; stop trying to label me. It's not that simple. You cannot tell me that psychiatric medicine is that black and white. I don't belong in the picture you're painting for me, and please,' she added, noting the change in his look, 'don't start on the paranoia thing again. I don't think that I am an important person and I don't think I'm being persecuted, all right? All I know is that since I woke up in hospital I've had this feeling that things are not how they should be. My memories are no more real to me than dreams; even my mother wasn't as she should be.' She snivelled, and a lone tear trickled down her cheek.

The doctor held one of her arms firmly in effort to pull her out of the gloom into which she had sunk.

'It's perfectly natural to feel a certain amount of disorientation after what you've been through, Jacqueline.'

'It's Jacks,' she said suddenly. 'My name is not Jacqueline, so kindly stop calling me it.' She gritted her teeth, having persuaded her tears to stop.

Doctor Brodie let his arm drop and stared blankly at her.

'If you wanted to be called Jacks you could have said so earlier; I only called you Jacqueline because that is the name on your records.'

'Well I hate it,' she said. Glaring at the grass, she wondered why she had bothered to talk to him. She could distinguish every blade separately, as if each had a unique quality that allowed them to be identified one from the other. She observed an ant crawling along a single leaf. The bout of heightened perception unnerved her, her awareness of such things making her feel even more insignificant.

'I know what we'll do,' the doctor said. 'I want you to recall something from your past, even from your dreams, that you can identify with now, something we know exists.'

Jacks looked confused; she did not understand what he meant.

'Take for instance, the R.S.C,' he prompted. 'In order for your mind to knit it into your dreams, you had to have had some knowledge of its existence.'

Jacks was intrigued and the lines smoothed from her wrinkled brow.

'It's my bet that you have an interest in the theatre, or at least Shakespeare,' he said eagerly.

'It's possible,' she conceded. 'I don't know.'

'Oh come now, Jacks.' He grasped her hands and looked directly at her. 'Take Hamlet for instance, you seem to fit his situation so well.' He paused to smile and then quoted. 'To be, or not to be—that is the question.'

His blue eyes pierced into hers and, at that

moment, it seemed to Jacks that he knew the secrets her mind hid from her. She became aware of a voice; remote it seemed at first.

'Whether 'tis nobler in the mind to suffer
The slings and arrows of outrageous fortune,
Or to take arms against a sea of troubles,
And by opposing end them? To die, to sleep-
No more.'

The voice was her own. It sounded strange— older and more resonant, as though part of her sleeping mind had awoken with a voice that added richness to the one she already possessed, and yet at the same time, it was cold. She listened carefully to the words as they escaped her lips and understood what the doctor had meant.

'To die, to sleep;
To sleep, perchance to dream ...'

Her eyes seemed to mist over and images flashed into her mind; Meg holding her bleeding wrists outstretched toward her, another flash and Patrick gestured as he opened the door to the hospital ward.

Bertha was crying like a baby; she lay in foetal position and looked weak enough to jump at her own shadow. The woman, who had thrown her food at the senior nurse, did so again, but as the bowl struck its target, Jacks could see it was blood. It spread like an inkblot across her blue starched uniform. Jacks turned away. The woman with postnatal depression was holding her baby and rocking it gently.

'I have given suck, and know how tender 'tis to love the babe that milks me ...'

On approaching, Jacks was horrified to see that the baby was dead. Bruising covered the child's face; clearly, it had been battered to death.

'Have you ever wanted children of your own?' the woman asked sweetly, without looking up.

Jacks failed to respond; she felt sickened by the sight, but a terrible compulsion forced her to remain.

'HERE, HAVE MINE,' the woman growled, and tossed the dead baby at Jacks, who stepped aside with an anguished cry and the baby hit the wall with a thud.

'I would while it was smiling in my face, have plucked my nipple from his boneless gums, and dashed the brains out, had I so sworn as you have done to this.'

Jacks cried as she turned away from the maddening sight. The schizophrenic Martha stood before her. Jacks shook her head, unable to take any more.

'Don't listen to em, Miss,' the woman said. 'They're all mad here you know.'

A doctor approached her—the same man who had failed to talk to Jacks the night she had awoke in the hospital ward.

'How lovely to see you again,' he said. 'I barely recognised you.' He took her hand and kissed it.

Martha's voice chimed. 'Do not forget; this visitation is but to whet thy almost blunted purpose.'

Jacks felt a hand on her arm. Her mouth quivered and she gasped with fright. The piercing blue eyes of Doctor Brodie came into focus.

'Are you all right, Jacks?' he asked.

She failed to respond, as if she wished to make sure he was real and not part of the terrible vision. She became gradually aware of the green backdrop of grass and trees. The sun had shifted and glinted off his blonde hair.

'Heh, what's the matter?' he asked, gently rubbing her arm. She did not know how to reply, so shaken was she by the new experience.

'What did I do?' she stammered. 'How long was I gone?'

'What do you mean *gone*?' Doctor Brodie asked. 'You quoted Hamlet and then you began to tremble.'

'How long was it before I started shaking?' she asked urgently.

'You started almost immediately after you finished speaking. Why? What's wrong? Has it made you remember something else?'

'I saw,' she paused, reluctant to reveal the details of the vision, 'terrible things. But I seemed to be there for a few minutes at least,' she said. 'It was no memory though; I suppose it may have been a hallucination. It was as though my mind, remembering the soliloquy, triggered something else.' She screwed up her face in frustration, unable to grasp or focus on what she wanted to say.

'It may have been a defence mechanism,' Doctor Brodie suggested. 'It could be too early for you to remember your past. Alternatively, it might be directly linked to a painful memory that you have. I could change your medication; it is possible that the Tricyclic I have you on is causing side effects such as hallucinations, but more importantly the confusion and sense of non-reality you've been experiencing. But tell me, Jacqueline,' he corrected himself, 'Jacks, what did you see?'

Her face darkened as she remembered the horrors of her vision. She looked into her lap and spoke quietly.

'I don't want to talk about it,' she said. 'I'm frightened that I might be psychotic. I can't believe that my mind could create such horrible things.' She looked directly at him. 'I notice that you don't interrupt me, doctor. Could it be that you agree with me? Nurse Cadeaux told me that I had developed a psychosis before the accident, so am I still psychotic, and if so, how bad is it?'

'Jacks, try to calm down. I'm sure you are over-reacting. Please remember that you've been through an awful lot. A coma is no easy thing to get over. A high percentage of people die on entering prolonged sleep as you did, and those who do wake are likely to suffer from extensive brain damage. You are lucky to be alive at all, and to be as intact as you are, physically and mentally, is a blessing. Remember that it will take time to adjust. You will feel disorientated and frightened for a while, and whatever you saw that disturbed you, could be little more than your mind off-loading waste imagery in order to pave the way for true memory.'

His voice was full of reassurance, but Jacks felt uneasy.

'Doctor, if any part of me can even *imagine* those atrocities then I know that I am a seriously disturbed individual; but it didn't feel like my imagination—it felt real. It was as though I didn't create it; it already existed.' She spoke quietly, knowing how crazy she sounded. 'It does prove one thing though.'

'And what is that, Jacks?' the doctor said, in a worried tone.

'It proves how years worth of experience could have been created in a short period of time while I was in a coma. The mind creates and absorbs images so much quicker than true time, and even though I seemed to be experiencing things in a normal time frame, they were actually being transmitted to me at a much quicker rate, and therefore accounts for why so little real time elapsed.'

Doctor Brodie gazed quizzically, making no reply.

'Doctor, can I see Bertha and Martha and everyone else from that ward please?' she asked. 'I just want to make sure that they're all okay.'

He frowned. 'Sorry Jacks, I don't know who you mean,' he said.

'The women from the ward I was in before I was moved to my room.'

A look of puzzlement followed by realisation, shone across his features and he ventured, 'Jacks I thought you knew.'

Her eyes narrowed suspiciously. 'Knew what?' she demanded.

'The ward to which you are referring is in a completely different hospital; we transferred you here while you were sleeping off the sedative I gave you; so I'm afraid I have no idea of the state and well-being of those patients. I'm sure I could find out, if it's that important to you.'

Jacks' gaze drifted toward the great building and she wondered why she had not realised as much sooner. There were so many discrepancies existing between the two places. She nodded her head slowly; her mind raced, as though her recent experience had unclogged a blockage in her thought patterns.

'This I take it is a private hospital, is it not?'

The doctor nodded in agreement.

'Then can you please tell me who is paying for me to be here? I don't have insurance and it sure as hell can't be my mother. She is a little on the poor side, least that is what my mind is allowing me to recall, disturbing as those memories are.'

Doctor Brodie's face faltered. 'I'd best be getting you back indoors,' he said. 'You've missed lunch, but I am sure we can arrange for you to have an early dinner or at least a snack to tide you over.' He began to wheel Jacks back to the house.

'I see,' she said, 'you want to get yourself to safety before I turn into Mr Hyde. Thanks for the vote of confidence.'

'Jacks, that's not it at all; I just feel that you've had enough for one day. You had quite a scare a moment ago and I want you to rest, besides you're not the only patient I have to see you know.'

The doors opened as the receptionist nodded to him through the glass.

'When will you allow me to see my family again, Doctor Brodie? There's so much I need to ask them. I'm sure they are the best people to help me restore my memory.'

The doctor stopped in the lobby and walked around the chair to face her. The receptionist eyed them curiously, attempting to hear what was being said.

'Jacks, it's not me who stopped your visitors. That was your mother's idea. She felt that you needed time to adjust to your predicament; personally I thought it was the wrong thing to do and I told her you would need as much support as you can get, but she insisted.'

She frowned. 'Doesn't that strike you as odd?' I mean it's not exactly motherly behaviour, is it? Still I suppose that sort of neglect can happen a lot in these situations.'

Doctor Brodie's eyes no longer focused on Jacks. He stood up silently and began to wheel her forward again. He stopped suddenly and tapped her shoulder.

'Bare with me; I'll be back in a while.'

He left her alone in her chair. She could hear him speaking to someone to her rear. Moments later, John returned to take her back to her room.

'Where's Doctor Brodie gone?' she enquired, curious what was going on.

'He had a few things to do,' John replied, 'but said he'll see you tomorrow.'

The lift doors opened to reveal the fourth floor and the voice politely informed its occupants. Jacks, trying to shake the disgruntled feeling that had settled upon her, decided to ask after Meg.

'She's going to be all right,' John informed her.

'Would I be allowed to see her?'

'I've got to take you to your room, that's what Doctor Brodie said. I'll let Meg know you asked after her though, and I'll ask Doctor Brodie if you can visit her tomorrow.'

There was such simplicity mixed with strong definition to his voice that Jacks knew it meant the subject was closed. John wheeled her into her room and pulled back the bed covers.

'May I ask you something, John?' Jacks said.

'What?'

'Could you tell me what happened when I attacked you? You see I don't remember at all.

John looked at her strangely and replied with a shrug.

'Doctor Brodie signalled to me that he needed help. I tried to hold you down, but you were really quick. You scratched my face, I grabbed your wrist and you punched me with your other hand. Bob held your legs and got a kick in the ribs for his troubles.' He noticed her worried expression and smiled genuinely. 'Don't worry; you come to expect that in my job.'

He lifted her out of the chair and placed her on the bed.

'I'm sorry,' she said, as she drew up the covers.

He shrugged, indicating to the stitches on his face as a result of Meg's razor attack. 'I've had worse,' he said.

'You've had a rough couple of weeks, that's for

sure.'

'As I said, miss, you get used to it.' He smiled and was gone.

Jacks wondered whether anyone could truly get used to continual abuse.

Later that day, Nurse Cadeaux arrived with her evening meal, she was, however, too busy to stop for a chat. Jacks was just becoming resigned to an evening of complete boredom when there came a quiet tap at the door. Glancing up from her brooding, she saw the face of Meg at the window and felt panic-struck as the woman entered the room.

Meg's appearance had altered drastically since their last encounter. Clean dressings neatly wrapped about her wrists; her hair was brushed neatly behind her ears; her eyes sat calm in her pale face. Her dry lips broke into a half smile as she sat beside Jacks.

'I was told that you wanted to see me,' she said.

Her voice was lower than is wont for a woman, but it was as smooth as honey, giving it an irresistible quality. How contrasting it was to the screeching harpy she had been previously.

Jacks smiled awkwardly. 'I just wanted to know if you were all right.' She tripped over her words, feeling how silly they were. *Of course she's not all right,* she thought. *She tried to kill herself.* 'Or at least feeling a little better … than you were.' She bit her tongue and decided to stay quiet, until she could think of something sensible to say.

Meg gave her a knowing look. 'There's no need to tread on eggshells; I know what I am, I know what I did. You can ask me what you want, and don't worry; I'm not going to attack you. I am very sorry that I frightened you; I heard that you were in a bit of a state. I didn't want to hurt anyone, I just wanted to die, and it should be my decision to make not theirs … the bastards.'

'But why do you want to die?' Jacks asked, finding it incredible how the woman could speak so calmly about her own death.

Meg met her eyes and Jacks felt disturbed by the depth they seemed to express, as though hundreds of years of cruel experience lay behind them, crammed into half a lifetime.

'I have no right to live, Jackie. I should have died years ago, as was my destiny. Your name is Jackie, isn't it?'

Jacks shook herself, amazed at the sudden contrast between the woman's two statements.

'Er, Jacks,' she said quickly.

Meg nodded to herself.

'I was told that you nearly died in a fire,' Jacks said. 'Do you think that was fated to be so then?'

'Someone has been doing their homework, haven't they?' Meg said, with a wry smile. 'Did they tell you why I was in that fire?'

Jacks shrugged. 'I assumed it was some sort of accident.'

'What else were you told about me?'

Jacks fidgeted, feeling reluctant to say anything that might upset the woman. 'I know that your husband died,' she said carefully.

Meg laughed harshly; it was a sound that made Jacks' spine tingle.

'Stop being so bloody diplomatic! Yes my husband died—he killed himself, and if he hadn't done it, then *I* would have killed him.

'You're probably too young to remember the Bankstown Murders. Three young girls were killed, all under the age of eight. My husband was a paedophile; he got his kicks from abusing children. He wasn't content in the end to enjoy their silent suffering; he wanted larger stimulation; he wanted to play God.

'It was Friday afternoon and I was meant to be working the late shift. I was feeling ill, however, and they sent me home. By the time I put my key in the door, it was four-forty. I noticed Frank's car in the driveway and was curious why he was there. As I closed the door, I thought I heard a noise. It was quiet, on the edge of hearing—a tiny whimper. It made my heart jump. I wasn't sure why. I wasn't even sure that I'd actually heard the sound.

'I crept up the stairs; that was when the

moaning began. It was the unmistakable love cry of my husband. He hadn't made that sound in years of our marriage, but I remembered his sound of satisfaction well enough. I remember my heart pounding and a heat burned every part of my body, except somewhere in the centre, where I felt ice cold—cold and strangely calm. I wondered how long he'd been having the affair. I felt as though my controlled anger made me linger at that door for hours. What else was there for me to do, but confront him? I opened the door slowly.

'Oddly, the first thing I noticed, on entering my bedroom, was the plastic sheet laid upon the floor. Frank was naked, kneeling over …' Meg paused, her eyes closed for a moment as if seeing the scene in her mind. She sighed as she continued. 'Kneeling over a little girl—a little girl with no clothes on. Her tiny hand reached toward him and her eyes were so big and wide, pleading with him tearfully. Then her arm fell and I knew somehow that she was dead. As the life force drained from her body, Frank cried out in ecstasy and came over her bloody corpse. I'd never satisfied him like that.

'He failed at first to notice I was stood in the doorway. I couldn't speak; it didn't seem real to me; I wanted it to be a dream. I felt sick, so sick. I watched as he rang out an old flannel in the bowl of water next to him, then he washed himself and began to wipe the semen from the girl's body. I remember thinking that it had been a long time since I had seen that flannel, and how strange it is that there are things you don't realise are missing until you find them. The weird haze that made me think such stupid things began to lift. I screamed with rage and ran toward him, hitting him about the head.

'His face changed from the satisfied craftsmen, proud of his work to the terrified and ashamed piece of shit that he was. He backed away, whimpering in the corner like a dog that's pissed on the carpet and knows it will be kicked for it. He started saying how sorry he was, in barely audible tones. I stooped to check the girl's pulse with narrow hope that she might still be alive, but her skin already appeared grey to me.

'Tears ran down my face, and I thought, as I think to this day, if only I hadn't hesitated, or if I'd decided to come home as soon as I became ill, then she'd still be alive. Why did I delay when I realised what was going on? Of course, the doctors assured me that I was in shock and that time would have seemed to slow down. It didn't seem like seconds to me; I felt like a sick voyeur who had been present for hours, watching and doing *nothing*.

'The little girl's name was Sarah. She went to the local elementary school. No one ever discovered how my husband had managed to entice her away before her mummy arrived to pick her up just moments after. Little Sarah was tortured for an hour and a half before Frank finally killed her; at the same time her parents searched the streets frantically for her, seeking information that might lead them to the discovery of their little girl.

'He hanged himself.

'I couldn't feel anything by then. How could I after eleven years of marriage, the love and passion declining year after year? Then the final discovery—that terrible moment … I should have known; why didn't I know? Everyone assumed I was in on it, even after I was cleared of any culpability. Sarah's parents blamed me for her death as though I had been the hand who had held the knife. Still, who else were they to direct their anger and grief toward, if not me? Frank was dead and could not receive their condemnation, so they had to make do with the next best person … me.

'I don't know how many people gathered there that night, weeks later. It seemed like the whole suburb, when the emergency services dragged me from my burning home. I smelt the flames of course, and I knew they were trying to kill me, but despite my fear, I felt that they were justified. How could I have been with him so long and not have known? I *must* have known. I was equally responsible and deserved to burn. Besides, what had I left to live for?

'The crowd screamed and mocked as I was put

in the ambulance. I remember crying for the first time since that fateful day. I was still crying three days later when they brought me here.

'Some days are worse than others; you were unlucky enough to catch me on a day when I'd managed to avoid taking those bloody tranquillisers. They'll be more careful from now on.' She looked tired. Her tale had taken its toll on her.

Silence followed, as Jacks mulled over Meg's tragic story in her mind. She was unsure how to react; she felt like crying.

Finally, she ventured, 'Surely you must know that it's not your fault. Those people tried to murder you. Wasn't anything done about it?'

'I didn't press charges,' Meg said. 'I didn't see any point.'

The door opened sharply and Nurse Cadeaux entered, looking annoyed.

'Meg,' she said, 'you had us worried; you know you're not supposed to be out of bed yet. Come on; let's get you back to your room.'

Meg struggled to her feet and the nurse supported her arm to help her. The woman was obviously exhausted, either because she was too weak to be out of bed or because re-living the past had drained her.

'I'll speak to you again maybe,' Meg said, in a manner that convinced Jacks that there was no maybe about it.

'Never fear the truth, Jacks,' she said. 'Sometimes it's all we have.'

Nurse Cadeaux smiled as she helped Meg out of the room. Jacks pondered for a moment, Meg's profound parting statement; she felt estranged, knowing that the truth was the main thing she was lacking.

Chapter Seven

"Those who dream by day are cognizant of many things that escape those who dream at night. In their gray visions they obtain glimpses of eternity, and thrill, in waking, to find that they have been upon the verge of the great secret."

Edgar Allen Poe

During her physio' session, Jacks was aware of the strength returning to her feeble legs. On returning to her room, she insisted on walking from the wheelchair to the bed. Andy supported her; the scent of his after-shave was so familiar to Jacks, she could taste the recollection even if she could not see it. She was lost in a swamp of memories, unformed, trapped behind frosted glass. She clung tightly to him as he began to dance her around the room in effort to relieve her dark, brooding expression and the distance from her eyes.

She laughed light-heartedly as he whirled her around, her feet leaving the ground. The pair looked like lovers embracing as Doctor Brodie entered. He paused. Andy saw him, but failed to acknowledge him.

'Good-morning, Jacks,' the doctor said. 'I trust your physio went well.'

Andy spoke for her.

'I'll have her up and about in no time,' he boasted, as he lowered her to the bed.

Doctor Brodie's face remained emotionless. 'I'm sure that when that day comes we can look forward to more dancing, but until then perhaps you could refrain from dragging my patient around as though she's a rag-doll. She has been quite ill and rattling her about can hardly be seen as beneficial to her health.'

The two men glared at one another, and it

seemed to Jacks that a silent battle took place between them, one to which she was not party. She repressed the urge to smile as she considered offering them a ruler.

'You are quite right of course, Doctor Brodie,' Andy challenged. 'But look at her.' He moved gracefully to Jacks' side, placing a hand on her shoulder. 'Her face is rosy and blooming. Tell me have you ever seen her look so beautiful? Still, I expect you know best in your professional capacity. I shall be off.'

He strutted like a cockerel toward the door. 'Bye gorgeous,' he said, and blew Jacks a kiss.

Jacks' face was scarlet as she met Doctor Brodie's seething expression.

'You were a little harsh on Andy, don't you think?' she said.

His jaw clenched visibly and Jacks could see a vein in his forehead throbbing, but his voice remained calm as a summer breeze.

'Have you any idea the extent of the damage that your brain incurred?' he said. 'Not only did you suffer haemorrhaging, but also you had an oedema; that was the reason you fell into your coma. These are both very serious conditions and we don't know as yet to what extent the damage remains. It is one thing doing gentle physiotherapy to aid your walking again, it is quite another to be frolicking around shaking up your cranium like a cocktail. Still, I expected you to take his side over mine,' he ended sulkily.

Jacks could not have looked more like a stubborn child if she crossed her arms and stuck out her bottom lip. 'It's nothing to do with taking sides,' she said. 'Simple manners are a virtue. I feel fine, and it was nice to have a bit of fun, Lord knows it's lacking in your presence, and besides it's more likely that the pressure placed on the *brainstem* as a result of the cerebral oedema caused the coma, not the condition in isolation.' She stopped abruptly, glaring at him hotly. There was a moment of stunned silence, before she made an apology.

'I'm sorry, I spoke in the heat of the moment; I didn't mean what I said.'

Doctor Brodie placed down his carefully wrapped package and sat beside her. He seemed to dismiss her insult and apology alike.

'Where the hell did you learn about neurology?' he asked.

She shrugged. 'School I guess,' she said.

Doctor Brodie's eyes scanned her intently. 'Tell me what you know about a cerebral oedema?'

Jacks looked at him quizzically, wondering why he was so interested in what she had said. She sighed in annoyance; when it became obvious that he wanted her to answer him, she took a breath and spoke matter-of-factly as though he was stupid for asking.

'Damage to the brain may show itself in a secondary response to the primary injury,' she said. 'The brain begins to swell causing the intracranial pressure to rise. If the condition persists, then it may place pressure on the brainstem, which when damaged, results in loss of consciousness, as this is the part of us that controls consciousness. If the condition persists, the body's vital functions will be affected. The only chance in recovery is if the rise in intracranial pressure can be successfully treated.

'Why did you ask? I would hope that you'd know the rudiments of neurology even if it's not your field of practice.'

'What would a patient be given who was suffering from such a condition, Jacks?' the doctor asked, completely ignoring her last comment.

She frowned, unable to fathom his odd behaviour and spoke slowly with an expression that seemed to say, *"get me the hell away from this weirdo!"*

'Hyperventilating drugs could control the intracranial pressure, thus getting rid of as much Carbon Dioxide as possible. To reduce brain swelling, you could consider administering dexamethasone phosphate, initially as an intravenous injection followed by intramuscular injection every six hours for up to ten days. Alternatively, you could administer a rapid intravenous infusion of Mannitol.

'Why are you asking me these questions, Doctor Brodie?'

He looked a million miles away, his thoughts lost in a pool of growing suspicion. He shook himself suddenly and gave half a smile. 'I was just curious as to the extent of your medical knowledge. It seems that you remember something else now, yes?'

Jacks shrugged. 'Yeah I guess so. I must have done biology at school then ... probably failed that as well.'

Doctor Brodie made no comment. His eyes were so penetrating that they made her feel uneasy.

'What's in the package?' she ventured, eager to change the subject.

His features softened. 'A present for you,' he said, handing it to her.

She beamed and ripped off the brown paper to reveal a leather-bound book with gold leaf lettering. A slow grin spread across her face.

'The Complete Works of Shakespeare!' she exclaimed. 'Thank-you, it's wonderful.' She opened the front cover and read the inscription. 'A little something to help you remember, L K Brodie.'

'I'm glad you like it,' he said.

'What does the L K stand for?' she asked, with a grin.

Doctor Brodie's eyes rolled as he answered.

'Lawrence Kyle, but please if you're planning to be on first name terms then at least call me Kyle; I hate Lawrence; only my grandmother calls me Lawrence. One day I'll get 'round to having it changed.'

'Ooohhh vanity,' Jacks remarked, as she thumbed through a few pages of the gift.

'I tried to contact your mother yesterday,' the doctor said, changing the subject to a more serious note.

Jacks looked up from her book in surprise. 'What did she have to say?'

'I phoned her several times, but got no reply. I left a message on her answering machine, asking if we could meet to discuss your health. There are a few questions I have for her,' he ended, as if to himself.

'You and me both,' Jacks cut in. 'So I take it that she never rung you back.'

'No, and I don't think she's listened to her messages yet; the hold music seems to go on for a full symphony.'

'Don't you think it strange that a cleaning lady would have an answer machine, doctor?'

Doctor Brodie looked at her as he spoke. 'This is the twenty-first century, Jacks; such contraptions don't require justification. Stop trying to read something into nothing, Sherlock.'

Jacks watched him closely as he seemed lost in

thought. His pale blue eyes drifted like clouds in a summer sky, his golden hair fell across his face as his head bowed forward in serious contemplation. Jacks had never dared observe him so closely before and felt embarrassed for doing so now.

'Kyle?' she asked, the name sounding strange to her.

He glanced up instantly.

'How long do you think I shall be here?'

She caught a flicker of emotion attack his features, it lasted for a fraction of a second and Jacks could not interpret its meaning.

'It is one of the reasons I am chiefly concerned with speaking to your mother,' he replied. 'There are several worries I have of course—your anger and confusion, your vision yesterday that you were reluctant to reveal to me. You have very little memory and you cannot walk unaided—not yet anyway. However, I feel that you are no longer a threat to anyone. Certainly, since your arrival at St Clemens, you've displayed no violent tendencies; this may be due to your medication, which is another worry I have. If I start to wean you off, will you be able to cope or will you revert to your former state? As to giving you an approximation, I cannot say. We must complete your physio of course, but I think the next important step is for your family to help fill in those blanks you have. Only when you remember who you are, will we be able to tell how great the damage you sustained is endangering your sanity.

'It is good that you have accepted the truth of your situation. As I said, that was vital if any recovery is to be made. I am extremely pleased that it happened so quickly; you seemed so convinced of your mind's creation, that I wasn't sure whether we could bring you back at all.' His face brightened into a friendly smile. 'So if your mother agrees, I think that very soon you will be able to be cared for at home.'

Despite his smile, Jacks noticed a sadness in the depth of his eyes; it intrigued her. The news failed to make her happy as she thought it would. A deep unhappiness and sense of unease was growing within her. Her confusion choked her like so many strangling weeds. The entire bizarre situation was taking its toll; life had become one huge surreal mess.

'Why so glum?' Doctor Brodie asked. 'I thought you'd be over the moon at the chance to escape here.'

Jacks shrugged. 'I'm not saying I like this place or anything—far from it, it's just that this is the only life I know; everything else confuses and scares me. I *do* want to leave here,' she paused shaking her head, her face filling with desperation. 'I just wish I could remember.' Her fingers massaged her temples in the fashion of a charlatan psychic.

'Every-so-often I get this feeling like there's some revelation escaping me. It's like something on the corner of my vision, that when I turn to face, it's gone, and then I'm not sure whether I imagined the feeling to begin with.' She buried her face in her hands. 'Have you ever forgotten anything that you knew to be so cataclysmically important, but you couldn't retrieve it from your mind? It's as though it's locked tightly away; part of me won't allow me to remember.' She looked up sighing.

Doctor Brodie smiled warmly. 'I know how frustrating this is for you, Jacks,' he said, 'but believe me it will get easier; you've got to try to stop being so hard on yourself, the memories will come back and the sense of forgetting something will phase out as memories return. When the feeling you describe starts to distress you, try to remember that it's purely a condition that will get better over time.'

'Kyle, I know it sounds strange ... but it feels as though it's *me* who is holding the memories back; I won't *allow* myself to remember.'

Doctor Brodie seemed to contemplate her words, but whatever entered his thoughts he did not feel compelled to disclose.

'Jacqueline,' he said.

Her eyes flashed dangerously, but he ignored the look and continued.

'How are you coping having Andy around? I

mean it must be an added strain. I've been thinking about having him replaced.'

Jacks glared, wondering whether he was in jest. 'I like Andy,' she said. 'I don't want him replaced.'

'But he looks identical to a fictitious phantom who must only serve to haunt and confuse your feelings ...'

'Are you trying to imply that I'm in love with him? He may *look* like Claude, but I can assure you I have accepted that he is not. Any feelings I may have for him, will be for him and not Claude, is that clear? I enjoy being with him and I've made vast progress during our sessions together, and if I *do* have feelings for him it's none of your goddamned business!' Her face reddened and she marvelled at her sudden hostility.

Doctor Kyle Brodie bowed his head despondently. 'I was only thinking of you,' he said. 'I wasn't attempting to intrude on your privacy. I just don't want to see you get hurt.' He trailed off, realising he was making the situation worse than it had to be.

At that moment, the door swung open and Nurse Cadeaux entered with a trolley.

'Anyone for tea?' she said, beaming, seeming to ignore the heavy silence about her. She did not wait for a reply, but rather began to serve two cups and placed a handful of biscuits on a plate.

'I've just seen your physio' Jacks; he's soooo

nice.'

Doctor Brodie turned away and gritted his teeth. 'And what's so nice about him?' he said, with alarming coolness.

Nurse Cadeaux seated herself next to Jacks and began munching a Tim Tam. Her blatant disregard for etiquette in the presence of the doctor made Jacks smile broadly.

'Oooh I don't know exactly. He's so cheerful and he has lovely eyes and that hair of his, well he's really good looking, don't you agree, Jacks?'

Jacks bit her tongue in attempt to prevent a reply that would really annoy Kyle.

'Yes, his hair is er … very nice … well styled,' she ended awkwardly and shrugged.

Doctor Brodie turned, his jaws still clenching. Nurse Cadeaux, on seeing his stony features, rose from the bed, grabbed another biscuit and bade adieu. Jacks laughed quietly as the woman skipped out of the room, rattling the trolley before her. She stifled the smile on seeing the doctor's sullen expression.

Picking up a biscuit, she dunked it into her steaming cup of tea and nibbled thoughtfully, wondering how to break the silence.

'She's really nice, isn't she? Nurse Cadeaux I mean,' Jacks said, while sipping her tea. She felt like Eliza Doolittle, having to restrict subjects to the weather.

'Frivolous,' was the reply.

'Oh come on now. What is this problem you have with people having fun?'

His looks challenged her firmly. 'This is supposed to be a hospital, not a play-pen,' he replied.

Jacks laughed incredulously, unable to believe how pig-headed he was being.

'For God's sake, chill out, Kyle. You're only jealous.'

He winced and drew back defensively. 'What the hell have I got to be jealous about?'

'Because you never allow yourself any enjoyment.'

'Of course I do; just because I don't frolic about causing possible danger to my patients doesn't mean ...'

'WHAT! What are you talking about? How the hell can you tell me that Nurse Cadeaux is putting me in harm's way?'

He stared past her briefly, as if searching for an answer.

'For one thing, she gave you hot tea,' he said. 'If you spilt it, you could scald yourself, besides the caffeine in it might react with your medication.

'Oh come now, doctor,' she snapped, 'what you really want to say is that she shouldn't have served a hot drink to a nut-ball like me, because I might use it as a weapon.'

His mouth opened as if he was going to speak and closed again, his face settling into a frown. Jacks continued to drink her tea in annoyed silence. Doctor Brodie stared at her for a moment, his gaze dropping to her hands as she raised the cup to her parting lips. He laughed suddenly and she turned toward him with an indignant stare.

'Why on earth do you drink your tea like that?' he asked.

She failed to understand. Glancing down at the teacup, she noticed the little finger of her right hand was stuck out at a ninety-degree angle. She pouted and placed the cup back on its saucer.

'When I told you to lighten up, I didn't mean for you to take the piss out of me,' she tutted, and turned away. Her mouth twisted as she attempted to hold back her smile.

Kyle guffawed, and she, unable to contain herself, let out a chuckle and tutted again.

'Well aren't you the little princess then,' he blurted out, as he got his breath back.

Jacks froze. Goose pimples shot down her limbs. The words seemed to bounce around in her mind like a stray Ping-Pong ball. She looked at him, fearful and expectant.

'Jacks, are you all right?' he asked.

The feeling left her as suddenly as it had arrived and she breathed deeply. 'I ... what you said, someone has said it to me before. 'I can't remember; I know it's important, but I can't ...' She slumped.

'Hey it's okay,' he said, rubbing her shoulder.

She tried to displace herself, unwilling to get emotional. 'Your tea will get cold,' she said.

The doctor withdrew, pausing for a moment before drinking his tea. She looked at him and again saw him distant from his surroundings. She pushed the plate of biscuits toward him and caught a glimpse of a smile returning to his features.

'Thank-you,' he said.

'Will you be taking me outdoors today?' she asked.

'I'm afraid not; we're about out of time, perhaps tomorrow.'

Jacks could not help but feel a little vexed at being made to feel like merely part of his day's work; at times she forgot that he had a job to do and she was just part of that.

'I shall look forward to it,' she said. 'Before you go, can I ask you something?'

He looked at her, his eyes sharp as diamonds.

'Anything,' he replied.

Jacks squirmed, knowing how bizarre it would sound.

'You know when Nurse Cadeaux came in to calm me down in the night, after Meg tried to kill herself?'

He nodded.

'How did she know I was in distress? You haven't got cameras fitted in here, have you?' She added the final comment light-heartedly in effort to conceal how serious her question was.

'I assumed you rang the bell,' he replied, a little bewildered.

'But I can't even reach the bell, I'm not strong enough.'

'Did you call out for help?'

Jacks shook her head.

'Why do want to know?' he asked.

'I know you think that I'm being weird, but could you try and find out for me, please?'

The doctor got to his feet. 'Sure, I'll let you know tomorrow,' he said.

She gave a half smile as he left her.

Her fingers savoured the touch of the book cover, before carefully opening it again and searching for Hamlet. Picking up her cup of tea, she began to read; familiar with each line as her eye perused it ...

Standing on the battlements of Elsinore Castle, Jacks marvelled at how easily she had drifted to sleep.

The enclosing darkness emitted silence and the icy wind chilled her bones. She wandered soundlessly through the night, a feeling of dread growing steadily upon her. The pale moon illuminated the masonry with an eerie glow.

Through the silence, sound found its voice again. There was a rush of footsteps and a maddening cry.

'Look my Lord Hamlet, see where he walks. Tis very like your Father and yet unlike.'

Jacks gazed past Horatio and saw the ghostly figure approach. The men fled as Jacks advanced to meet it. The man wore a long black coat, which went down to his ankles. A sadness seemed to envelop him, hanging like a dark aura. As he leaned over the wall, surveying his Kingdom, Jacks was struck dumb. She could not think how to approach the regal spirit.

'Er, excuse me,' she said, knowing how inappropriate her words were to the setting of the dream.

The man stood, turning slowly about; it was Patrick. His terrifying face caused her to take a step backward, but she lost her footing and fell. There was a blinding light and the castle walls seem to disintegrate before her eyes.

'Remember,' Patrick rasped.

The door to her room swung open just as the cup of tea fell from her hand and smashed upon the floor.

The room had seemed to interchange from monochrome to colour as easily as if someone had flicked a switch. Patrick was gone and she was sat up in bed, having managed to fall asleep with a drink in her hand. The kindly face of Nurse

Cadeaux approached.

'What's wrong, Jacks? What was all that racket in here a minute ago? It sounded as though you had people with you.'

Some time passed before Jacks was able to gather her wits.

'What did you hear exactly?' she asked.

Nurse Cadeaux picked up the broken pieces of teacup and placed them on the tray. She used a few of the napkins to mop up the mess.

'It sounded as though a man shouted, but I suppose it was you yelling in your sleep. You know you should have put this back onto the tray if you felt drowsy. You could get me into trouble if anyone finds out.'

'Sorry,' Jacks said, wondering if that had not already been the case and Doctor Brodie had decided to bully her. 'I don't remember falling asleep at all; in fact I don't remember waking up either.'

Nurse Cadeaux looked hard at her. 'You were daydreaming I expect,' she said.

Jacks sagged. 'You mean hallucinating,' she said, miserable at the thought that it might be true. Lost in thought, she stared ahead considering the latest manifestation. *Remember,* she thought. *Remember what? Remember the past I suppose.* Her eyes came into focus and saw Nurse Cadeaux gazing anxiously down at her. She shivered suddenly, her mind racing.

'Your uniform!' she exclaimed. 'It's white!'

The nurse was clearly puzzled. 'Yes,' she agreed slowly.

Jacks paid no heed to the perplexed face of the woman. 'He said "remember", but he didn't mean the past because he knows I can't remember it, he meant my vision. The vision holds the key to unlocking memory.'

She was clearly excited and Nurse Cadeaux listened carefully, as if trying to memorise Jacks' ravings to play back to the doctor.

'Your uniform is white,' Jacks continued, 'but in my vision the nurses wore blue; it was highlighted by the blood to draw my attention to it. In the hospital I was in before, the nurses wore blue. I didn't know I'd been moved, but my subconscious was saying, haven't you noticed the nurses have changed uniforms? It made me question the ward and thus I discovered that I'd been brought *here*.'

Nurse Cadeaux sat beside her and placed her hands on Jacks' upper arms. 'Jacks slow down,' she said. 'You're not making any sense to me; what vision are you talking about?'

Jacks explained the events of the previous day and Nurse Cadeaux nodded patiently.

'I think you should have a talk with Doctor Brodie; you may be onto something. Dream imagery can often help identify points in your past and present, about your feelings and anxieties. He's the dream expert though, so he can probably tell you what it all signifies.'

Jacks lay back against her pillows, feeling immensely satisfied with her discovery. She tried to calm her excitement in order to remember further details. There was a knock at the door and a man entered with a meal for her. She glanced up smiling, a smile that faded considerably on recognising Bob, who had been with John when they had restrained her.

'Hello Bob, I thought you were on leave.' Nurse Cadeaux said. Her voice had an edge to it and lacked its usual sincerity.

Observing as much, Jacks wondered why her friend disliked him.

'I'm back,' Bob said shortly, smiling as he placed a tray of food in front of Jacks. 'I'll take this away, shall I?'

His smile made Jacks shiver; it was cold and cruel. His stature, although the same size as John, looked more athletic. John was like a big teddy bear, slow and gentle, whereas Bob struck Jacks as being calculating and vindictive. She hoped she was reading too much into her analysis.

'How are you feeling now, Bob?' Nurse Cadeaux asked. It seemed she asked the question, merely to make conversation as he cleared away the tea things.

Jacks caught a glint in his eye. He looked at the broken cup and then at her and raised both his eyebrows in a snide manner.

'Oh I'm fine,' he said, 'fit as an ox now that my ribs are mended.' His glance shifted to Jacks and he smiled a razor smile.

Jacks failed to react. She was actually frightened of him, knowing in her heart that her assumptions were correct. She read it in his face, but also in the way Nurse Cadeaux reacted to him. He walked slowly out of the room and the tension noticeably lifted. Jacks turned to the nurse with a worried expression.

'He seems more psychotic than most of the inmates,' she joked, but her voice wavered.

Nurse Cadeaux gazed awkwardly into her lap. 'Don't worry; you won't have to see him. He works on the ground floor. John is our muscle up here and I'm responsible for bringing you your meals.'

Jacks gazed down at the plate of tagliatelle and decided she had lost her appetite, figuring that he had spat in it—or worse.

'He's not supposed to be up here,' Nurse Cadeaux added.

'Well that didn't seem to stop him,' said Jacks, feeling the nurse's former reassurance slip away like leaves on a breeze.

Nurse Cadeaux shook herself. 'Heh, what are

you looking so nervous about?' she attempted

'Because anyone who can interrupt that obstinately cheerful nature of yours has got to be one mean dude, and considering I was the one who broke his ribs I don't think he's going to want to be my pen-pal from ground floor to fourth, do you?'

The nurse gave a half laugh. 'Don't worry, Jacks; Bob might be a bit of a bastard, but he wouldn't dare do anything to hurt you. I probably shouldn't have said that though, it's not very professional, is it?'

Jacks chuckled. 'Since when do you care about obeying rules?'

'Gee thanks,' she pouted.

'Oh come now, if you fitted in to what this hospital calls professional, you wouldn't be so goddamned smiley and cheerful.'

The nurse's face brightened on realising the intended compliment. 'Everyone's cheerful here,' she said. 'We're paid to be.'

'No, *you* are cheerful and it's not because you're paid to be, but because that is the way you are. *Their* smiles are as sincere as a statement issued from Jack the Ripper saying that he is really a nice guy, just a tad misunderstood. So if being professional means being a miserable, tight-arsed, ladder climbing bitch, I'd rather have you as my nurse any day.'

'Jacks, that is not true, they're nice people and

most of them *do* care. Different people express themselves in different ways.'

'See, there you go, being nice again,' Jacks said. 'Still I guess I was a little harsh.'

'Your dinner's probably cold by now.'

Jacks pushed it away. 'I don't want it,' she said. 'This'll do me fine.' She picked up an apple, polished it thoroughly on her nightclothes and bit into it.

Nurse Cadeaux shook her head. 'You've hardly eaten a thing all day; aren't you hungry?'

Jacks considered how to answer; she was famished, but if she told the nurse the real reason for her not wanting the meal, she was in danger of seeming paranoid, and yet if she lied, she would probably not eat again until the morning. Luckily, her stomach groaned the answer for her. Nurse Cadeaux laughed.

'I'll see if I can find you something else, perhaps something that Bob hasn't touched,' she said knowingly.

Jacks smirked. 'You're too clever. They'll promote you before too long, you mark my words.'

'Jacks, I marked them very well and if I was promoted that would make me a ladder-climbing bitch, no thanks, I think I'll give it a miss,' she said, giggling as she left, tray in hand.

Jacks' thoughts drifted back to Patrick's words. *Remember.*

Opposites, she considered. *There were a lot of opposites; the woman who had lovingly cared for her bear, destroyed and devoured it; Bertha who was aggressive was reduced to a quivering wreck. What could it mean?*

The return of Nurse Cadeaux disturbed her thoughts.

'Will soup do? It's all we had left.'

Jacks nodded and smiled. No sooner had the bowl of soup been placed in front of her, she began to consume it like a starving animal.

'Thank-you,' she said, as she scraped the last morsel from the bowl.

'I brought you some tranquillisers to help you sleep.'

Jacks eyed them suspiciously, considering what possible good they could do.

Chapter Eight

"All life is only a set of pictures in the brain, among which there is no difference betwixt those born of real things and those born of inward dreamings, and no cause to value the one above the other."

H. P. Lovecraft

Jacks lay running through some of the exercises Andy had taught her while waiting for the tablets to take effect. Her eyelids felt heavy and she drifted...

She was sitting on a pew, leaning forward — bored. Her extravagant hat felt heavy on her head and several overhanging feathers obstructed her view. Someone nudged her from the left and she sat up, scowling. Seated beside her was Patrick, signalling with a serious face toward the altar. She smiled snidely and turned.

Trudi and Claude were getting married. Jacks suffered a moment's confusion while she considered that the situation was not as it should be. Looking about her, she saw row upon row of well-dressed congregation members, none of whom she recognised. She could not see her mother and wondered why she was not present at Trudi's wedding. Patrick nudged her again; she turned sharply and stuck her tongue out at him. He went cross-eyed and they sat for a few moments, competing with each other at who could make the most ridiculous face.

One of the choirboys giggled and the vicar glared over at him. Patrick and Jacks gazed forward innocently.

The bells pealed and the wedding procession made its exit. Patrick walked solemnly to the rear.

Outside the church, a storm of confetti whirled. Trudi smiled—obviously proud of her catch, but Claude's attention was not on his bride at all; he stared directly at Jacks, until her answering scowl caused him to look away.

Patrick stepped up to him.

'Congratulations, old chum,' he said.

Jacks walked away, through the people, through the gate, and up the hill.

'That wasn't very polite,' Patrick's voice called from behind her.

'I don't know why you dragged me to his stupid wedding anyway,' Jacks said. 'You know I can't stand him.'

'He's my friend, besides who else would I bring?'

Jacks removed her hat, which was beginning to annoy her, and thrust it at Patrick.

'Why don't you get yourself a girlfriend?' she said. 'You are ridiculous; you have every woman imaginable after you and yet you insist on remaining single. I'm waiting for the day you decide to tell us all you're gay. Honestly Patrick, you're so far back in the closet that you're practically in Narnia.'

Patrick threw away the hat and made a dash toward her. She turned and ran down the hill, her hair streaming behind her. Her shoes impeded her speed and he soon caught her; sweeping her into his arms, he swung her around as if she weighed no more than a child.

'Jacks, you know I'm not gay. The only reason I've no girlfriend, my dear, is because they're all after my money, and none of them know how to have any fun.'

They lay on the grass and threw daises at each other for a while. Glancing up, Jacks saw Patrick on the hill, gazing down at them. He wore a long black coat; his face was deathly white. As he beckoned to her, she glanced back to the other Patrick, frozen in time, his smile fixed for all eternity—content.

She stood and walked toward the figure on the hill. The day had darkened somewhat and the previously clear skies, threatened rain. Looking down, she noticed that the congregation had departed. The church appeared deserted, wind damaged and neglected. Several of the head stones in the yard had cracked from where they had fallen and lay covered with moss and lichen.

She faced Patrick; his features displayed effort as he tried to tell her something. Emotion began to well up inside her as she saw so clearly the contrast between the happy, fun-loving and carefree Patrick, to the dead one, unable to communicate what he felt most important. For the first time, she could remember what he really meant to her; she loved him dearly. Looking up at him, she began to cry.

'Oh Patrick, why did you die? I miss you so

much. I need you; I don't understand any of this. I just want things to be the way they were, even if I don't remember the past, I know that we were happy.' She could not say any more; her tears overwhelmed her.

Patrick reached out and withdrew almost immediately, but Jacks failed to see his look of anguish through her flood of tears.

It seemed hours that she stood there, wallowing in self-pity. When she finally wiped the tears from her eyes, Patrick was gone. She heaved a huge sigh and sat down, letting the cool grass caress her. Wrapping her arms about her legs like a self-defensive child, she listened as the wind whispered softly in her ears. It told her to run.

'But I can't run,' she protested aloud. 'I'm bedridden!'

The voice laughed softly.

Ahead, a woman enter the abandoned church; Jacks could not be sure, but it looked like Meg. She scrambled to her feet and approached the crumbling building. The door was off its hinges and Jacks had to step awkwardly over it to get inside.

Hazy daylight shone in a beam through the broken stain-glass window, highlighting a heavy layer of dust. The sound of Jacks' shoes clattered loudly toward the figure at the altar. The woman seemed to be praying.

'Meg, is that you?' Jacks almost whispered, but her voice still sounded bellowing in the quiet of the ancient building. The women turned; it was indeed Meg. She looked shocked and worried to see Jacks.

'What's wrong, Meg?' Her eye caught a movement and she glanced upward to meet it.

Where the giant crucifix had hung, there was now a man who Jacks assumed to be Meg's late husband, garrotted and swinging gently in a phantom breeze. Jacks stared, horrified.

'He was my God,' Meg said. 'I worshipped him and he did *this* to me.'

Jacks was unsure whether Meg was referring to the Almighty or her husband. She jumped sharply as the dust-ridden organ sounded. Young voices began to sing in the choir pit. Jacks saw three young girls and knew instantly that they had been the victims of Meg's husband.

'Hush little baby, don't say a word,' they sang.

Jacks felt a sickness in the base of her stomach.

'Don't worry, you're not my type,' mocked the dead man's voice.

Meg said nothing, but rather, seemed to be sniffing the air. Jacks could smell it too.

Fire.

The church was burning.

She heard the sound of angry voices crescendo over the crackle of the flames. Jacks retreated as tongues of fire leapt up to meet her. Beyond the door, an incensed mob awaited, to keep her from escape.

'Run Jacks, run!' said the voice of the wind.

'I can't; I'm bedridden!' she cried.

The crowd laughed. Through the smoke and flames that licked up to consume her, Jacks caught sight of Patrick on the hill, silhouetted against a swollen moon.

It was Nurse Cadeaux who awakened Jacks from her raving. A while passed before she could convince herself that she could not smell burning.

'I think I'm going to have a word with Doctor Brodie about your medication,' the nurse said. 'I can't have you going on like this.

'I'm okay,' Jacks said, none too convincingly.

'I knew I shouldn't have let you sleep this long. You'll have to hurry up now, if you're to be ready for Andy.'

Jacks wolfed down her breakfast and had a speedy wash.

'Doctor Brodie said I was to tell you how I knew you were in distress the other night, Jacks.'

Jacks' head jerked up. 'Yes?' she said eagerly.

'It's a bit strange you wanting to know.'

'I was just curious,' Jacks said, trying to sound casual.

'You rang the bell, as well you know.'

Jacks' heart thumped. 'I can't reach the bell,' she

said, and demonstrated by attempting to do so.

The nurse appeared puzzled. 'Maybe somebody moved it,' she suggested.

'They haven't,' Jacks replied. 'So how do you account for it?'

The nurse shrugged. 'I haven't the foggiest. How do *you* account for it?'

Jacks looked away awkwardly. She could not tell the woman what she had seen, so she shrugged back.

'Well it's a mystery then I guess. Perhaps all that lying around in bed has allowed you to develop telekinetic powers,' the nurse said, joking.

Jacks did not laugh.

The door opened.

'Morning ladies,' sang the cheerful voice of Andy. 'Your carriage awaits, milady,' he chirped, signalling to the wheelchair.

'Well, I'll leave you to it,' said the nurse, as she made for the door.

'You can join us if you like,' Andy said cheekily. 'The more the merrier, or if that's not your style perhaps I might fit you in this 'avo for a private session.'

'Oh go on with you; you're terrible,' said Nurse Cadeaux. She blushed on her exit

'It looks as though it's just you and me then, gorgeous,' Andy said.

'Do you flirt with every woman you meet,

Andy?' Jacks enquired as he began to lift her.

He paused, his face close to hers.

'Why? Are you jealous?' he asked.

'Hardly,' she said.

A cloud passed quickly across his features, but Jacks barely perceived it. She was remembering the voice that had told her to run. Her legs filled suddenly with a burst of strength and she stood for a moment without aid. *'But I'm bedridden,'* another voice seemed to say and she slumped again. Andy looked at her strangely.

'You seem to be getting stronger,' he remarked.

'Yeah I guess so,' she said wearily, as he helped her into the chair.

Outside, another fine day awaited them. A gentle breeze rustled the leaves in the trees. Jacks gazed up at the sun as it filtered through the branches, glinting off the mass of green, and breathed in the scent of the Eucalypts.

'Is that the best you can do?' Andy's voice muttered.

'Sorry,' Jacks said distantly, and continued her leg-lifts.

'I think I might start you on a walking frame today,' he said, 'saves me having to chauffeur you everywhere.'

He lay back and Jacks gave him a snide look before drifting off again. Flashbacks of her dream were making it difficult to concentrate for very long. The appearance of Patrick as a living being had shaken her up. She had retained all the feeling about him established during the dream, but she could not remember anything tangible about him.

'What's got into you today?' Andy asked.

She sat up and shook herself out of her deep brooding. 'Nothing really, I just had a bad nightmare and I can't get it out of my mind.'

'You couldn't have been dreaming about me then, or else your girlie face would have gone all pink,' he said, teasing.

He watched her intently and Jacks was unsure how to react. She *had* dreamed about him—or rather his doppelganger, but she felt reluctant to reveal that to him.'

'So what did you see that upset you so much?'

'I can't remember clearly,' she lied. 'I just remember being trapped in a fire and almost burning to death,' she told him, hoping to satisfy his curiosity.

'Smokin',' he joked, and punched her lightly in the arm.

The lack of amusement on her face caused his smile to fade.

'Lighten up, Jacks,' he laughed, as he followed up on his pun.

Jacks rolled her eyes and shook her head. 'Why do I even bother to talk to you, you clown.'

He drew in close to her and gazed into her eyes

mischievously.

'Because you adore me and you know how dull life would be without me around to excite you.'

She tutted. 'Can't you be serious for more than two minutes?'

Another much larger shadow enveloped her own, and the voice of Bob startled her.

'Here's that Zimmer frame you wanted,' he said.

Jacks froze. Andy noticed her reaction and frowned.

'Thank-you,' he said, 'you can take the wheelchair away now.'

Bob walked around and picked up the 'chair in one hand, folding it with ease. Turning, he saw Jacks' eyes upon him.

'Morning,' he said, smiling his razor smile.

'Good morning,' she replied quietly, the feeling of intimidation robbing her of any volume.

He walked away.

'Come on then, Missy,' Andy said. 'Let's get you walking.'

He helped her to stand and she gripped the frame. She stood a long while rooted to the spot, believing that she would fall if she took a step. Gradually, her confidence began to grow and she stepped cautiously forward. With each step, her legs felt stronger.

'Run Jacks, run!'

Hearing the words in her mind, made her more determined.

'Do you think that you can make it all the way back?' Andy asked.

'I'll give it a darn good try,' she replied.

It took over an hour for Jacks to arrive back at her room, by which time she was exhausted. She clambered into bed with minimal aid, lay back with a relieved sigh and closed her eyes.

'Goodbye Jacks,' Andy said, picking up one of her limp arms and kissing her hand.

Jacks smiled, but her eyes remained shut. 'Bye Andy,' she murmured. She fell asleep before the door even closed, and she slept peacefully.

On awaking, the smiling face of Doctor Brodie came into focus.

'Hello Sleeping Beauty,' he greeted warmly.

Jacks blinked. 'How long have I been asleep?' she asked, with a yawn.

'About three hours, but you looked so tranquil I was reluctant to wake you.'

Jacks noticed that his hair had been cut quite drastically.

'It looks nice,' she commented, sitting up.

'What does?' he asked, in a way that convinced Jacks that he knew exactly what she was talking about.

'The new haircut; it suits you.'

'Thanks,' he replied.

Pulling a pen from his breast pocket, he produced a couple of note-pads from his inside his suit. His actions were simultaneous, making Jacks think he looked like a magician, trying to be slight of hand and she resisted the urge to chuckle.

'We have quite a bit to discuss today you and I,' he said.

'Did you manage to contact my mother?'

'No, I'm afraid not, but I have written to her and I will try ringing again. She still hasn't picked up her messages though. If I don't hear from her by the end of the week I shall pay a personal visit, all right?'

Jacks smiled and nodded, wondering how long there was until the end of the week; she had no idea what day it was.

'I hear you had another nightmare last night. Nurse Cadeaux wants me to change your prescription. So tell me, Jacks, have you actually been taking the medication I've prescribed or have you just been pretending to?'

Jacks gaped. 'Of course I've been taking it! Why the hell wouldn't I?'

The doctor's face did not move a muscle. 'If you had been taking your pills you wouldn't be having any dreams because the tablets I have prescribed you suppress paradoxical sleep, therefore *preventing* you from dreaming.'

'I *have* been taking them,' she protested. 'It's not my fault they're having the wrong side effect.'

'I am willing to give the benefit of the doubt here—even if it is highly illogical. I will take you off your present medication and see if that has any effect. Now, Nurse Cadeaux told me that you think your dreams have hidden meaning. I would like to explore the possibility.'

The manner in which he spoke made Jacks feel stupid. She wanted to tell him to stuff his help and go away, but realised it was too important to let foolish pride stand in the way.

'What I would like you to do,' he continued, 'is write down in this journal everything you remember about your dreams of late, and from now on, you will keep a dream diary in which you will record your dreams as you awake. Firstly, however, I want to hear about what you saw in the garden that day as you seem to deem it so important.'

Jacks was uneasy, and reluctant to speak, but knew it was the only way he could interpret. He scribbled down notes as she reiterated the vision and compared the people with their existing counterparts.

'You think that Bertha and the girl are direct opposites,' he said. 'That is quite common in dream imagery, although we must remember that you weren't actually asleep at the time. These things could mean that you are hiding behind a mask when you are feeling vulnerable; destruction of the teddy bear could show your own frustration to your predicament, the fact that she eats the bear could show that you feel that your childhood has been devoured. You think that the blood was thrown to tell you to look at the differences between uniforms, but blood has many symbolisms of its own—success, love, family—there are so many interpretations; it could of course simply be a residual effect of Meg's accident though, could it not?

'The starched uniform could show rigidity, military, strict rules. I have to say the treatment of the child in your vision concerns me, it could point toward you having had an abortion at one time, although there's no mention of such a procedure in your records. The woman quoted Macbeth, which may have been the sole reason for the presence of the dead baby. Going to extremes to prove a point and show how strong you can be, is a direct reflection of your own stubborn personality. When the woman asked you if you've ever wanted children of your own, she was making you think about your future, something which you haven't been doing as you've been too concerned with regaining your past.

'As to the comment, "They're all a little mad

here you know." I find this quite amusing; it sounds like something one would expect the Mad Hatter to say, in which case you would be Alice, trapped in your own Wonderland, where everything is strange to you and you're a dimension away from the world that you knew.

'The doctor who kissed your hand, I also found amusing, not least because he happens to be an old friend of mine. He may have lavished you with attention in your mind to make up for how disgruntled you felt at his aloof behaviour when you met.

'Finally, there was the quote, "Do not forget this visitation is but to whet your blunted purpose." If I remember correctly it's the ghost of Hamlet's father, who speaks the line later in the play, when Hamlet is supposedly mad, and it is uncertain whether or not he will act out the revenge he committed himself to in the beginning. It could mean that you must remember your past and that you're here so that you may do so. But if we took you as being Hamlet ...'

Jacks froze and made a sound in her throat quite unintentionally.

'Are you all right?' Doctor Brodie asked.

She shook her head and made a face that said she felt silly.

'It's nothing really,' she said. 'It's just that I dreamed I was Hamlet yesterday afternoon. At least I thought it was a dream, but I don't remember falling asleep.'

'Don't look so worried, Jacks. You were probably on the edge of sleep. This is what we call the hypnogogic state, when we lose cortical vigilance and vivid dreams can seem real. But because it's the initial stage of sleep, you probably thought that you were still awake.'

'But how do you explain Nurse Cadeaux hearing a man's voice in my room?'

He stared hard at her.

'Are you now trying to tell me that you think it was real?' he asked.

She pouted. 'No. But I do know that there's some really strange things happening and I think it's about time I told you.'

His eyebrows shot up. 'Indeed?' he said, 'I would say it was long overdue.'

'Who pressed the bell when I was in distress? Tell me that.'

'Jacks, if you were that distressed you could have found the strength to get to it yourself; you're not crippled, just weak. A surge of adrenaline occurring during your fright would probably have been enough to give you the strength you needed.'

'But it wasn't me,' she protested.

'Then who was it, Jacks?'

She fell silent, feeling silly and awkward, and although she desperately wanted to talk, she felt so heavy, the surging eyes of ridicule upon her.

'Jacks, why won't you talk to me?' Kyle urged. 'That is what I'm here for after all. It will do no good to let this continue to eat at you.'

'Patrick,' she mumbled.

'Sorry, what did you say?' he asked, leaning in.

'I said it was Patrick!'

'And who is that?'

Jacks instantly regretted having spoken, convinced that Doctor Kyle Brodie would think Patrick an imaginary friend and that she was nuttier than a beech tree.

'He was my friend, but he died,' she explained. 'I keep seeing him; it's like he's always there, just on the edge of sight. I dream about him a lot. He was even in my vision, but I didn't tell you; he was the one who opened the door and beckoned me to enter the ward. He was the ghost in my Hamlet dream too, and told me to remember, which helped me to realise that the nurses wore different coloured uniforms. He appears mostly just before I wake up.'

The doctor listened intently, absorbing the information like a sponge. 'He is what is known as a hypnopompic hallucination, and can seem very real to you. I have to say, I still find it amazing that you're able to dream at all, let alone envision things so vividly. Can you remember anything at all about Patrick that you can tell me, Jacks?'

'Only that I miss him very much.'

A reassuring hand was placed on her arm, and she breathed the tension away heavily so not to cry.

'That would explain why you see him such a lot.'

Jacks shrugged unhappily. 'I guess so,' she agreed. 'So I was making magical mountains out of minuscule molehills, was I?'

Kyle let out a short laugh. 'Something like that.'

She bowed her head and he brushed her hair back gently to see her face.

'Just because there was no supernatural explanation, doesn't mean all that you have told me is not important,' he said. 'I think you were definitely onto something with your dream interpretation idea, so will you keep this diary for me and we'll go over it together, all right?'

She smiled and nodded in agreement.

'I hear that you've been talking to Meg.'

'You don't mind, do you?' she said. 'It's just that I thought it might help me get over my fright, besides I was worried about her.' She shifted position, realising they had resumed their doctor patient chat.

'I think that it's a good idea, and I hear that she has been doing marvellously for the past couple of days, so I don't know what magic you performed ...'

'We just talked,' Jacks explained, 'or rather she

did most of the talking. She told me why she's here. I think it's the most tragic thing I've ever heard.'

Doctor Brodie gave her a look of intense astonishment.

'She actually *told* you what happened to her!' he said.

She shrugged. 'What is so amazing about that?'

The doctor blew air through his pursed lips. 'You mean apart from the fact that she's never done it in the whole nine years that she's been here,' he said. 'We've managed to get dribs and drabs of information from her, but the story in her file came mostly from the police report and good old speculation. It's probably accurate enough, but it hardly disguises the fact that something amazing has transpired between the two of you. She has, for the very first time *ever*, laid herself bare. Do you realise how important that is, if any recovery is to be made? I should go and speak with her.' He bit the corner of his mouth thoughtfully.

Jacks shook her head while pursing her lips, in a gesture of knowing disbelief. 'Just listen to yourself, Kyle,' she said. 'The failed scientist that now finally expects to succeed in that which he considered a hopeless pipe dream. Why don't you ask Meg to write a book! To be honest, I think it is a more likely chance than her having to take the pains to re-live her experience over and over again for the entertainment of ambitious doctors.'

His face was puzzled and Jacks attempted to elaborate.

'If she's never spoken to a doctor about her experience before, what makes you think that she will do so now? She probably has a great distrust of men, so that rules out her speaking to *you* for starters; as for a female member of staff, she's very perceptive, she's not going to subject herself to suffering and ridicule so that someone can be considered a success in their job. She doesn't want to be a subject of experimentation—she just wants to be at peace.'

'Jacks, how do you expect that she'll ever find peace without coming to terms with what has happened to her?'

'Kyle, I don't think you understand Meg at all. She accepted her situation the moment the fire was lit. The thing she can't comprehend is why she was saved from the peace she sought, only to suffer in torment. It is the truth that allows her to exist at all; it is the only piece of her former identity she will now recall. That is probably why she told me not to fear the truth. She said, "sometimes it's all we have."

'The fact that she told *me* her tale is not really so amazing in retrospect. She'd discovered the hurt that she'd caused me and felt guilty. Meg is not a monster; she doesn't want to cause harm to other people. The fact that I was hurt in pursuit of her goal meant, in her eyes, that she owed me something in return. The only prized possession she feels she has is the truth.'

Jacks' heart felt heavy at the thought of Meg, finding it incredible how the woman had coped with the suffering and guilt for so many years. *She is an innocent victim of her husband's crimes,* she thought, *and she was the one who suffered most of all.*

She gave a heavy sigh and wished there was something she could do to help Meg. It was the reason she forgave the doctor his eagerness. She knew he felt the same way, but what he could not accept was that her only salvation was death.

'Jacks, you are incredible,' Kyle said. 'Perhaps I should see about finding you a place on the staff. You've determined more useful information about Meg from a single conversation than was deduced in years of therapy.'

She scowled, certain that he was being sarcastic.

'I'm serious,' he said. 'You have an amazing grasp of her situation.'

'But that's hardly going to help Meg, is it? The only joy in understanding her plight is so a neat little case solved can be placed on her file. "It's not our fault she couldn't be cured. She didn't want to be cured,"' Jacks mocked.

Doctor Brodie rose from his chair and sat beside her on the bed. 'Meg is very lucky to have you as her friend,' he said.

Her stomach fluttered as his eyes pierced into her. She felt unable to make any reply, but rather, absorbed his features. Embarrassment soon consumed her and her gaze fell to the bed-sheets.

'You weren't sitting here for three hours while I slept, were you?' she asked.

The doctor, surprised at the change of subject said, 'No. I went away and came back. I'd only been sat with you a few minutes before you awoke, although why you were so tired to begin with, I'm sure I don't know.'

Jacks pointed toward the Zimmer frame.

'Oh he's got you walking, has he?'

'Yes, *Andy* made me walk from the far end of the main garden.' She emphasised Andy's name, annoyed at Kyle for not having used it to begin with.

'You mean to tell me he made you walk all that way!' The doctor's voice lowered with contempt. 'Of all the irresponsible, reproachable and utterly brainless things to do. You're supposed to build up gradually to these things, not wear yourself out. What was he thinking?' His eyes glared with scornful disdain.

'I did it though,' she said. She sounded wounded at his thinking her so incapable.

He saw the hurt in her eyes and he held her shoulders firmly.

'I'm not getting at *you*,' he said. 'I'm really proud of your progress, but you mustn't try to do too much too soon; it could do more harm than good at this stage; you do see that, don't you?'

Jacks shrugged. She failed to concede his point. It seemed to her that he'd dismissed her progress, and that every time she so much as mentioned Andy's name, he flew off the handle. She refused to look at him.

'I'm sorry,' he said, withdrawing. 'I didn't mean to upset you. Perhaps I should go. I'll leave you to rest.'

She made no sound as he walked out of the room. She was annoyed at him without good reason, she knew. *I know he's only acting up out of concern,* she thought, *but I don't like his interfering.*

After her stubborn temper had cooled somewhat, her thoughts strayed to Kyle's interpretation of her vision. It made a lot of sense, but did not actually unlock any doors to the past as she hoped it would. Jacks felt there was something he missed—something vital. She poured a glass of water and sipped at it thoughtfully going over several hypotheses in her mind, each theory as ridiculous as the next.

'Sorry, you didn't seem to hear me knocking.'

Jacks was startled by the voice of Meg at the door. 'Gosh I'm sorry,' she said. 'I was miles away. Please come in.'

Jacks noticed that Meg was limping slightly, but decided not to mention it, thinking that if Meg wanted to talk about it, she would.

'How are you feeling today, Jacks?' Meg asked, in a curious manner. She looked about her as if the walls had ears.

'Fine I guess,' Jacks replied, 'how are you?'

Meg did not answer at first; her eyes fixed on Jacks and a strange light was in them.

'I've come to warn you,' she said at last.

Jacks shifted uncomfortably. 'I'm sorry?' she said.

'You have to understand that I stayed for you. You've had me worried. But I have no choice now; I don't think I'll be here too much longer, Jacks. I want to help you though, if I can.'

'Meg you're not planning another suicide, are you?' Jacks asked, with concern.

Meg gave a low laugh, which chilled Jacks to the core of her being.

'You're the first person in these long years who has given me something to live for, through no choice of your own, mind. Now I am the one who has no choice; just when I feel the need to remain, I find it is time for me to depart; such are the cruel twists of fate.

'Tell me, why did you run from me in the glade?'

Jacks shivered, her voice filling with

apprehension. 'Meg, what are you talking about?' she asked.

'Did my appearance frighten you? You scared *me*, I can tell you. You ran though, before I could speak with you. You ran and tripped over a fallen tree. There was a lake of blood. Do you know of that which I speak now?'

Jacks' eyes widened as she remembered the hideous nightmare. 'But how could you know ...'

Meg broke in, her voice so clear that it would have put a nightingale to shame.

'I have seen what you have seen; I have been where you have been. As I stood at the gates of death, I saw you there and recognised you. You seemed unreal somehow and yet I knew it was really you. Your image only appeared ghost-like because you do not belong there.

'I have seen you many times since and what worries me most is that your image has been each time, getting stronger and clearer. You do not seem a stranger to that plane, which disturbs me greatly. You have visited many times before, but you don't belong there, *remember that;* the stronger your presence there becomes, the greater danger you will be in. Your friend must know that and he should have taken better care.'

Jacks was unsure whether she was actually hearing Meg's words or if she had fallen asleep again; what the woman said was so surreal, that she found it difficult to believe in Meg's reality.

'What friend?' she stammered.

Meg's voice was profit-like and melodramatic. Had the situation been different and Jacks been party merely as a voyeur, she may have found it amusing. However, things as they were, made her feel like screaming.

'The man I see,' Meg continued, 'each time he is there, watching over you—the man in black; his hair is dark and flecked with grey, his eyes, pools of deep sapphire, so dark that they too appear black on first glance. However, I have looked closely into his eyes. He is trying to communicate with you, and the only way he can do it is to draw you into *his* existence ... foolish.' She tutted. 'Very dangerous.'

'Patrick!' Jacks exclaimed, tears stinging her eyes. 'This isn't real, is it? I am dreaming, aren't I?'

'Jacks, I am here,' Meg said. 'I am real. You see? He selfishly drags you off so often that you cannot determine reality any longer. You must not lose sight of it; that is imperative. Always keep one eye on reality, and do not allow yourself to completely trust the man in black; remember, he will not be the man you knew; his purpose might be quite different to what you imagine.'

'He's helping me to seek the truth,' Jacks snivelled, 'sometimes it's all we have, you said so yourself; I agree, but I have no truth, I have *nothing*, and I want my life back!'

'There are many ways to discover truths,' said Meg. 'It is not necessary to place yourself into deadly peril in order to attain it. You have the answers, but they are not making sense. Try to unravel them yourself; don't rely on a shadow to do it for you.'

Jacks stopped crying. 'Meg, how is it that you saw me and what is the place to which I go?'

'I was about to cross over,' Meg replied. 'I saw Death and he revealed to me the realm of screaming malice, where the dead watch and wait. Restless thoughts of retribution, twisting, growing, digesting painfully their revenge until it can be executed, or else the perturbed spirits remain forever to exist with their hate and sorrow.

'Imagine what will happen to you when you establish a firm enough presence there; yes, you will be able to communicate with your friend, but at what cost? They will know you to be a living being.

'Imagine the sound of a million screaming souls running through your skull, transferring their sadistic and twisted ideas of hate and revenge, many of which have developed for centuries. You cannot begin to understand the sickening atrocities that their countless years of existence can contrive. Could your tiny mind contain such horrors without succumbing to the madness? The crazed voices of the tormented will want you to pursue their ideas of vengeance or resent your living blood and so seek to spill it.

'You see, Jacks, it was *you* who brought me back from death, fearing for your sanity, but more importantly—your very soul.

'I don't know how he's managed to take you there or why, but you have to put an end to it. Remember, he is there for a reason and could be using you for his own secret purpose.'

'Don't all the dead go there, Meg?'

'No, that is just one plane which is close to ours, one of which I am sure there are many.'

'Meg, why did *you* go there? What bitter act of revenge do you wish to carry out?' Jacks asked weakly.

'I wanted to see my husband. He awaits me there I know. He wants to see my suffering, but thanks to you, I will never give him the satisfaction, and he will never be able to leave that place, which is a cleansing thought in itself. He will remain trapped there forever, left to regret his vindictiveness, and hating me as I free my past and myself of him.

'Jacks, I know you're finding this difficult to take in, but for your own sake, save yourself before it's too late.'

The door burst open and the menacing outline of Bob appeared. He walked over to Meg and wrenched her arm violently.

'You fucking bitch,' he growled, 'who said you could make house-calls?'

'Leave her alone,' Jacks shouted.

Bob kicked Meg in the leg; it was when she fell to the floor that Jacks noticed the ugly bruising she was now convinced he had caused. He stood over her and leaned in, his foul breath making her heave.

'One more word from you, you fucking whore, and you'll be writing a suicide note too. Now shut it!

'Right, you mad child-killing bitch—on your feet.' He dragged Meg up by the hair.

She did not even flinch.

'You're going to walk calmly back to your room without a sound,' he ordered. 'If you say *anything*, then the whore over there will bleed for it. LET'S GO!'

Jacks body shook uncontrollably. Her heart pounded with such force, it felt as though it would erupt from her chest. She gasped for air and fell into a dead faint.

Chapter Nine

For in that sleep of death what dreams may come,
When we have shuffled off this mortal coil

William Shakespeare

The familiar surrounding of darkness broke her fall. She sat suspended in nothingness, listening to the voices in her head.

'Run Jacks, run!'

'Never fear the truth. Sometimes it's all we have.'

'Look my Lord Hamlet, see where he walks. Tis very like your Father and yet unlike.'

'He's my friend, besides who else would I bring?'

'Run Jacks, run!'

'Hush little baby don't you cry, papa's gonna sing you a lullaby.'

'Do not forget this visitation is but to whet thy almost blunted purpose.'

'How lovely to see you again, I barely recognised you.'

'Just when I feel the need to remain, I find it is time for me to leave.'

She felt a sudden sense of panic, fearing for her friend. From the depths of her unconscious, she forced herself into waking. There was a pain in her arm, and the face of Bob came into focus. She opened her mouth in effort to scream for help, but the drug he had injected was taking effect too quickly. She wanted to bite his tongue off as it entered her mouth, but her body was paralysed. Her eyelids closed.

'Your ass is mine, you fucking whore,' he said, his foul breath poisoning her nostrils.

The last thing she felt as sleep took her was two

of his clammy fingers being forcibly inserted into her vagina.

Sitting up, Jacks found herself before a great lake. She screamed a silent scream in the frustration of knowing that her body was being violated and there was not a damn thing she could do about it.

Behind her stretched empty meadows, where long grasses swayed gently into a distance of seeming infinity. On the far side of the lake, a dark wood loomed menacingly; it seemed that thousands of tangled, deformed trees cramped like legions, reaching out their gnarled branches and twisted roots, toward the edge of the water.

She wanted to cry. The events of the day had been worse than any glimpse of the nightmare world of which Meg had warned her. She cast her eyes across the calm blue waters and caught sight of Patrick stepping out from the dark beneath the trees. He beckoned to her, but she did not move. She had marked Meg's warning and made no attempt to approach him. The tears began to fall.

Patrick took a step forward, but the water lashed out toward him, threatening. He retreated. She did not see; she wished with all her heart for him to be by her side, despite Meg's terrifying words. Glancing up briefly, she saw that he was gone. A hand rested on her shoulder and she swivelled 'round startled to discover that he was knelt beside her. She threw her arms around him and wept into his breast. His arms were hesitant before they wrapped about her, grateful for the warmth she gave him.

'It's all right,' he said. 'I am here, I'm here.'

His voice was deep and resonant, carrying such an air of authority that Jacks' spine tingled at the sound of it. Her tear-streaked face met his, bewildered.

'You can talk,' she spluttered. She was afraid, remembering what Meg had said about the danger of reaching coherence in his world. 'But Meg said I'm not to talk to you; she told me it's dangerous.'

Patrick drew her hair behind her ears and caressed her face, smiling.

'That is true,' he said, 'but I knew of no other way in which to communicate with you and the state you were in before … well, you were willing to pass over to me. Do not worry though, my dearest; you're not there now. *You* have brought me to you; that is something that only you can do, which is why I have not been able to do so before. I am in *your* world now, or rather the place to which you travel when you dream. See how close the two planes exist. There lies my world across the water, and often now have you travelled there to meet me.'

'But how did *I* bring you here?' Jacks asked, looking suspiciously about her.

'That is something you must discover if you are no longer willing to cross the void. Jacks, I must tell you something.'

She looked at him expectantly

'Your friend has just passed over. She had a painful death, but she is at peace now.'

'Meg,' whispered Jacks, her eyes brimming with fresh tears. 'She knew she was going to die. It was that horrible man, he ...'

She stopped, unable to tell Patrick what he had done to her; he seemed to know already, without the use of words. His eyes hardened like steel and his jaw tightened. He looked like an angry god, terrifying, yet glorious to behold. Jacks reached her hand out to his and his features immediately softened as he took it—tiny it seemed in his own, and he kissed it lovingly.

'It will be all right, Jacks,' he said.

'Patrick!' Jacks jumped, realising how caught up she had been in the wonderful moment, remembering the urgency of speaking with him. 'What have I forgotten?' she asked.

Patrick's face darkened. He opened his mouth to speak. There was a sound from the lake and the water slapped dangerously onto the bank.

'Jacks, I'm so sorry; I cannot tell you. It's not that I don't want to. It's you; I am in your mind now if you like, and it is *you* who is blocking out the past. I have to abide by the rules which this domain places upon me.' He looked uneasily toward the water's edge again.

Jacks frowned with concern. 'But why am I doing this to myself, Patrick?'

He knew. She could see it in his tortured eyes, but he was unable to speak. She nodded in understanding and laid her head against his chest again.

They embraced each other still when the sun had set, the moon had risen, and the stars twinkled their brilliance in the velvet of night. Both were aware of the deeper darkness, across the lake, where the stars did not venture. The sun rose again with a golden dawn and still they clung quietly to one another.

It was nearing noon, by estimation, when Jacks finally broke the silence.

'Patrick, I'm in danger, aren't I? From Bob.'

The water rose and a droplet fell on the bank with a spark and a fizz, as though the whole lake was electrified. Jacks gawped in horror, realising there was something else that Patrick could not tell her, and yet somewhere deep in the depths of her mixed up mind, she already knew.

'Jacks you *are* in danger, yes possibly from Bob, but there are many dangers.'

The water bubbled, growing dangerously turbulent. Patrick's image did the same just before he disappeared. Jacks looked hurriedly about her, but there was no sign of him. The water resumed its calm state. Peering across the lake, she was just in time to see the man in black walking off into the trees.

'Come on, Jacks, what the hell is wrong with you?' Nurse Cadeaux said, with a sense of panic.

Jacks' eyes opened reluctantly, gradually adjusting to the light of the room. Andy was present and observed her closely. Nurse Cadeaux's face filled with concern.

'Jacks, you've been asleep for about eighteen or nineteen hours. We've been worried sick.' She stroked Jacks' hair back and passed her a glass of water.

Jacks eased herself into sitting position, receiving the water gratefully. Her mind started to focus again and she remembered Bob. She hoped she had dreamed what he had done to her, but feeling the bruising on her inner thighs, from where he had pawed at her, she knew that her hopes were in vain. Clutching her ribs, she vomited over the bed.

The nurse ran to fetch something to clean up the mess. Andy stripped the bedclothes and then sat down, placing his arm about her. She leaned into him, grateful of the support. Suddenly she started and looked up at him, expecting to see Patrick.

Andy smiled. 'You okay?' he asked.

She sagged. 'I'll be better when my mother phones Doctor Brodie and I can get the hell out of here.'

'Is he expecting her to ring?'

'Yes,' she said shakily. 'he's been trying to get in touch with her for days.'

Andy passed her the water again to rinse and a bowl to spit. Nurse Cadeaux entered with gloves and a wet flannel. She passed the cloth to Jacks with a concerned smile and took away the soiled sheets.

'You know, when Doctor Brodie had a go at me yesterday,' Andy said, 'I thought he was being a jerk. I never realised that walk would do this to you.'

'He told you off yesterday?' Jacks glowered. 'He had no bloody right!'

He sniggered at her retaliation.

'For your information,' she said, 'I did not sleep so long because I was exhausted. I was ...'

The door opened and Bob entered, followed by Nurse Cadeaux carrying clean bedding. He did not so much as glance at Jacks, but gave a friendly nod to Andy whilst holding the door open for the nurse, then he left.

The colour drained from Jacks' face.

'What is it?' Andy asked. 'What were you going to say?'

'It doesn't matter,' she mumbled quietly. 'I've forgotten.'

Andy and the nurse exchanged brief glances.

'I'm going now, Jacks. There's no way you're well enough for the mile run I had in store for you today.'

'Thanks Andy.' Jacks said, managing an exhausted smile.

'No problem, gorgeous.' He kissed her firmly on the forehead and left.

'I don't know,' Nurse Cadeaux said, 'look at the state of you. What would you say to a nice bath?'

The word was food to the starving.

'I'd love one if I'm allowed,' Jacks replied. 'A sponge bath is all very well and good, but it's no substitute for the real thing.'

'Well come on then. Do you want to try and walk with your frame or shall I fetch a wheelchair?'

'I'll walk,' Jacks said, with a determined grin.

The nurse smiled back. It was then that Jacks noticed the redness about her friend's eyes; she appeared as if she had been up all night or had been weeping—perhaps both. Her disposition was cheerful enough, so Jacks concluded that she was in need of sleep.

In the bathroom, Jacks stared long in the mirror. Her face was a stranger to her. She could not remember having seen an image of herself before.

She was beautiful; her large silver green eyes were emphasised by long black lashes, set in a flawless white face, framed perfectly by her long black hair. Her high cheekbones gave her face an alluring quality.

The mirror steamed as the bath water rose higher and she began to undress. Nurse Cadeaux turned off the taps and offered her help, but Jacks refused aid. The nurse showed her the bell to press if she needed anything.

The door closed and Jacks supported herself with the wall as she removed her pyjama bottoms. Black bruising patterned the tops of her thighs, spreading outward like a child's finger painting. She felt sickened again and wondered exactly what Bob had done to her while she slept, grateful for the chance to cleanse herself in the bath.

Using the support bars, she lowered herself gradually into the steaming water, pulled the shower curtain across, and sighed loudly. Despite the mild scent of disinfectant, the bath was so relaxing, that her limbs felt as though they would melt with pure pleasure. She lay back, the water reaching just above her breasts. Closing her eyes, she breathed deeply. The sound of a dripping tap came suddenly to the forefront of her attention and her eyes flickered open, annoyed by the disturbance.

Neither tap was dripping, so she assumed that

the sound came from the taps in the sink. Raising her hand to the shower curtain, she froze. The room had darkened, but the tiles glowed white and cold. Jacks could see a figure—a darkened shadow behind the plastic curtain. She wrenched it across in one swift movement.

There was no one there.

The tiles continued to illuminate the darkness with their surreal light and she closed her eyes once more, attempting to block them out.

In her mind's eye, a face began to form; it was Andy, or Claude. Jacks lay back as she seemed to feel a soft caress on her throat and face. She sighed, enjoying the sensation. Her mind strayed to the penetrating gaze of Doctor Brodie, and she smiled. *He is certainly handsome,* she considered.

Invisible fingers ran down her throat then gripped suddenly in a tight throttlehold, and pushed. There was the beginnings of a scream, just before she was shoved beneath the water. She could hear herself thrashing about and her scream reached her ears as a watery gargle. She saw the figure of a man standing over her, but his features distorted through the turbulent water. The hands dispersed as quickly as they had appeared and Jacks emerged choking and spluttering. A dark figure stepped out of the corner. It was Patrick. He threw a towel at her to cover her, as if her nakedness offended him.

'Beware your friend,' he said.

Jacks hand made contact with the panic button, the room filled with light and Patrick faded.

When Nurse Cadeaux arrived, she assumed that Jacks had fallen asleep in the bath. She hastily dried her and slipped a bathrobe onto her trembling body.

Jacks breath came in short gasps. 'Patrick!' she wheezed, but it was all she would say.

John arrived and carried her back to her room. They wrapped her shaking form in blankets and the nurse sat beside her, holding her hand. Still, Jacks refused to speak. She figured the attempt on her life could not have been real, but had been Patrick's way of telling her to be wary of Doctor Brodie.

A nurse entered and Jacks recognised her as being the woman who had told her the year when she had begged her to, in what seemed a very long time ago.

'John you're needed,' she said.

Jacks stared at her and the nurse hastened to be away from those searching eyes.

'2011,' Jacks rasped.

Doctor Brodie entered as the nurse made her hasty retreat. He was wearing his outdoor coat as if he had just arrived to work; his hair was uncombed and his eyes red and puffy. He rushed to Jacks' side, but Patrick's demonstration was still vivid in her mind and she withdrew from him, shaking her head, her breath noticeably quicker.

The doctor seemed shocked by her reaction to him and looked sharply at Nurse Cadeaux.

'What the hell is going on?' he demanded. 'I was told that she nearly drowned. Why weren't you watching her?'

'Please doctor, shouting at me is not going to help Jacks, so please refrain from doing so until we're out of earshot.'

He ran his stressed hands through his matted hair. 'Go and fetch me a sedative, nurse,' he ordered.

'Doctor,' she ventured quietly. 'I'm sorry, but I don't think it's a good idea to leave you with Jacks. Look at her; she's *terrified* of you.

He winced, realising she was correct and left the room quietly; had he been a dog, his tail would most certainly have been between his legs.

Jacks was vaguely aware of her surroundings. She was drowning; dark waters surrounded her mind and threatened to drag her into the depths of her screaming subconscious. She tried desperately to focus on the figure of Nurse Cadeaux.

'Patrick,' she wheezed again.

'Who is Patrick, Jacks?' the nurse asked gently.

'He's her friend,' interjected the cool voice of the doctor as he approached again.

Jacks heard his voice and again tried to calm

her turbulent mind. The fear for her life and the feeling of drowning were what she suppressed first. Then she heard the haunting words of Patrick, *'Beware your friend.'* Beads of perspiration ran down her strained features as she forced her eyes to look toward the doctor. The pain in her head was agonising as she tried to focus on the alarm bells ringing in her mind.

'2011,' she said, through gritted teeth.

She saw the syringe as it approached her arm; the fear and anger inside seemed to shrink into a dense sphere deep within her, issuing forth into a blood-curdling scream. She knocked the syringe from his hand. Both doctor and nurse were taken aback by the disturbing sound. Jacks, however, was thinking clearer. She grabbed the doctor by his collar.

'I don't want a sedative,' she managed to say. 'Listen to me ... Patrick isn't dead!'

Doctor Brodie stared blankly at her.

'Kyle *please,* you have to find him.' Her voice metamorphosed from its initial harsh tone, to a desperate pleading as she fought for self-control.

'Jacks, are you all right?' The voice was Nurse Cadeaux's.

Jacks held the eyes of Doctor Brodie for a second, then released him and lay back against her pillows with a frustrated sigh. The nurse stroked her head gently and seemed to breathe out her tension in a long slow breath.

'I'm sorry,' she whispered. 'I couldn't bring myself back. I'll be all right now though.'

She glanced at the doctor, who looked down, seeming to carry a great burden on his shoulders. He appeared exhausted. Jacks stared weakly at him, feeling guilty for what she had put him through; her demand seemed no longer so urgent. She needed to see his smiling face before she could request his aid again. Glancing at both her companions, she deemed the doctor to be in the worst state. She beckoned the nurse with her index finger.

'Do think it would be a good idea to fetch the doctor a cup of tea? He looks like he needs one,' she whispered quietly in the nurse's ear.

Nurse Cadeaux sat up, looked Jacks directly in the eye and smiled a relieved and understanding smile. She rose quietly and made a silent retreat from the room. The doctor stared after her strangely and then risked a glance to Jacks. Her eyes filled with concern and she sat up again.

'Kyle, I'm so sorry for the way I behaved. I was scared, but I'm all right,' she felt her words were foolish and inappropriate. 'He can't be there you see because …' she trailed off realising again that it was not the right time to speak of her discovery.

She reached out and laid a hand on his shoulder. He looked at her; tears were in his eyes.

Jacks was unsure how to react or in what way it was appropriate to behave in such a situation.

'Kyle, it's all right,' she said. Shifting awkwardly forward, she placed her hand on his back, rubbing it gently. He turned his head away and wiped all trace of emotion from his eyes.

'This isn't right,' he muttered under his breath.

His body stiffened and Jacks withdrew her hand nervously. His voice became calm and controlled.

'Don't mind me, Jacks,' he said. 'I've had a bad night that's all. I think it's about time that I went home and got some sleep.'

She could not help but feel hurt by his sudden nonchalance.

'I thought you'd only just arrived,' she said.

'No, I've been here all night. I was about to go home when ...'

'When you were told about the state I was in,' she said abruptly. 'Well next time you'll know better than to check on me, won't you? You can go straight home to bed.'

The door opened and Nurse Cadeaux entered with a cup of tea.

'Jacks thought you might need this,' she said.

The young doctor's face took on mild surprise and the beginnings of a smile lifted the corner of his frowning lips.

'Thank-you,' he said, glancing at Jacks who was

staring hotly in another direction.

'Well, if everything's okay now, I'd best be getting on,' Nurse Cadeaux said, and left.

There was silence as the doctor sipped his tea and Jacks sulked. She risked a glance to him and noticed that he was mocking the way in which she held her tea.

'That's not funny,' she said, secretly glad that things were getting back to normal.

Kyle chuckled mischievously and placed down the remainder of the drink.

'You look awful,' she remarked. 'Why did you have to stay overnight?'

His features darkened and he remained silent on the matter.

'Meg died last night, didn't she?' Jacks said. 'Is that what you're so upset about?'

The doctor's eyes darted upwards. 'Who the hell told you? Is that why you were behaving in such a manner? I told everyone that I would break the news to you, and then only when I felt you were ready.' He was ranting, as if only half-angry by what he had expressed; the rest of the emotion was obviously pinned to events of the previous night.

'It was Meg herself who told me,' Jacks said. 'She told me yesterday afternoon.'

Kyle's eyes hardened with a cold glare, his nostrils and jaws clenched in controlled anger.

'Are you telling me that you knew she was going to die and you didn't even try to save her? You condoned her death? You allowed her to end her own life.' He looked disappointed and disgusted.

Jacks felt like crying at his reaction to her. 'Doctor Brodie, you've got it all wrong; she didn't kill herself,' Jacks spluttered desperately, recalling the terrible events preceding Meg's death. 'It was Bob. He murdered her.'

The doctor's face was cold and hard; obviously disbelieving her statement.

'It's true, Kyle. She came to me and told me that her life was in danger; she said she was going to die and that she had no choice; she didn't want to go now as she had finally found a reason to stay alive, at least for a while longer. I didn't understand what she meant until Bob came in and beat her up. Then I knew; I knew he was going to kill her. You've got to believe me. I saw him do it. He kicked her in the legs, grabbed her wounded wrists and pulled her up by thc hair.'

Her last comment seemed to strike a chord, and the stone stare dropped from the doctor's face.

'Jacks,' he said, 'if you believed Meg was in danger, why did you not let one of us know?' His voice was softer and the coldness had left it completely.

'He drugged me. I slept through the whole

thing. Ask Nurse Cadeaux, she'll tell you, they couldn't wake me up.'

She held out her arm allowing the doctor to see the tiny puncture mark left from the needle. His face reddened.

'It's true, Kyle; she didn't want to die. I wanted to help, and I would have done if I could.'

His head bowed as he remembered what he had seen. 'But Jacks, it was suicide,' he said. 'She used a razor blade, just as she did the last time.'

'Tell me what happened to her.'

'No Jacks, I don't want to upset you. You have made a very serious allegation, which I will have to report.'

'But you don't believe me, do you?'

'Jacks, you never actually saw him kill her, did you? All I have to go on is the words of a woman who has been trying to end her life for years. Why would she suddenly have a change of heart?'

Jacks looked down, unable to tell him the insane words of Meg.

'Bob assaulted me,' she said.

'*HE WHAT!* Is that how you got the bruising around your neck?'

Jacks was puzzled, then nervous realisation struck. 'No that was when I nearly drowned this morning.' She decided to continue quickly so as not to be questioned on that particular incident. She felt embarrassed about what she had to say and found it difficult to find the words.

'He sexually assaulted me, doctor.'

The indignity she felt at that moment was almost too much to bear. The doctor was clearly shocked, but not in a way that convinced Jacks he believed her.

'What do you think he did to you, Jacks?'

She squirmed, her face flushed with shame and anger. 'He put his tongue in my mouth and he ... he put his fingers into my vagina. He may have done other things too, but the sedative knocked me out.'

'Jacks, I'm not saying I don't believe you, so try not to get angry, okay? But if he gave you a sedative, it is possible that you dreamed or imagined what he did to you, especially considering your track record of morbid dreams of late. If a report was made of this allegation, the only thing that would be considered substantial evidence is the unauthorised administering of a sedative.'

Jacks pulled the blankets across the bed and delicately peeled open her robe to reveal the bruising on her thighs.

'Would this count as substantial evidence?' she asked.

His eyes hardened at the sight that met them. He began to rise.

'I'll kill him,' he hissed.

Jacks made a grab for his arm, startled by his violent response.

'Kyle please,' she said, 'that won't solve anything. Would this be considered proof of assault?'

'It's conclusive enough for me.'

He continued to pull away, but Jacks held him back. He looked older—burdened by a weight beyond his years. Finally, he stopped struggling and slumped in his seat.

'If I made an official report of the assault, is it possible that he could remain an employee here?' she asked.

'If he's found "not-guilty" then yes he would be, but, Jacks you have to try; you can't let him get away with it. He'll not dare approach you again.'

'Kyle, have you not looked into that man's eyes? He's a killer. As soon as he discovers my allegation, he will murder me like he did Meg and he'll get away with it. Who in their right mind would believe the testimony of a crazy woman such as me anyhow?'

'I do,' he said, 'and now that you've told me, I can't believe that you expect me to sit back and say nothing.'

'That's exactly what I expect, because if you don't, you'll be signing my death warrant, as surely as if you'd killed me yourself.'

'I shall have him arrested.'

'Kyle, listen to yourself. What evidence can you produce to prove that either crime has been committed, other than my ramblings? Besides, you were right; we can't be sure that he was responsible for Meg's death, although I know in my heart that he is. You yourself would be in danger of losing your position for taking my side against Bob, although I am very glad that you believe me; I didn't know whether you would. All I can ask is that you keep him away from me. He's not supposed to be on this floor anyhow.'

Doctor Brodie nodded thoughtfully as Jacks replaced the covers.

'I know this probably isn't the time to bring this up,' she said, 'but it's about Patrick.'

'You said he isn't dead.' His voice sounded distant.

'Well he can't be,' Jacks explained, 'he died during my coma, so how would I know about his death?'

Doctor Brodie's eyes cleared to reveal their usual sharpness. 'I see, so you dreamed of his death.'

'Yes, and all these silly dreams and hallucinations, they're not real; I see that now, they can't be. Well not that I really thought they were, not until Meg's warning, but she was wrong. Patrick's alive, and I need to see him.'

'And you want *me* to try and track him down,

yes?'

'My mother should know where he is.'

'Ah yes, your illusive mother,' he sighed. His eyes seemed to close involuntarily.

'Kyle, you need to get some rest. I'm sorry for keeping you here.'

He smiled. 'I'm reluctant to leave you,' he said, 'perhaps I should stay.'

'And what aid could you bring to me in this state? Go home!'

'Very well,' he agreed, rising wearily. 'I'll get one of the nurses to keep checking on you though.'

'I'll be fine; you just worry about yourself.'

He smiled again and was gone.

Jacks lay back, excited at the thought of reuniting with Patrick.

How could I have been so foolish? All this time I thought he was dead, and he can't be. Why did the thought not strike me earlier? All these visions were to make me remember him. He's not dead.

Her thoughts strayed to the words of Meg and she felt sorry for her. The woman's words had seemed so convincing at the time that Jacks had been quite willing to accept them, which worried her. It was quite plausible that Meg could have killed herself; she had tried before.

Perhaps it was my own twisted psychosis that had made Bob such a hideous villain, she thought. *Doctor Brodie could have been right, I was so heavily drugged, how could I remember clearly any such abuse? But then again, why did he sedate me at all? Considering Meg's mad story, it is possible it had sent me off the rails without even realising it.*

Such thoughts began to build a logical framework in her muddled mind. A dull pain had been growing steadily in her neck, strong enough to pull her away from her thought process. She flinched as her fingers touched lightly, the bruising about her throat. The wall of rationality came crashing down as soon as it had been built.

How could I have marks on my neck? she wondered. *I didn't do it to myself ... did I?*

She began to weep, not knowing what to think or believe any longer. All she knew was that she was in a mental institution and she decided that she must have been placed into care for good reason. She cried freely and curled into foetal position, wrapping the blankets snugly about her body for comfort.

Chapter Ten

I had almost forgot the taste of fears.
The time has been my senses would have cooled
To hear a night-shriek, and my fell of hair
Would at a dismal treatise rouse and stir
As life were in't. I have supped full with horrors:
Direness, familiar to my slaughterous thoughts,
Cannot once start me.

William Shakespeare

When the nurse entered with a meal, she found that Jacks had not moved at all. The woman managed to make her sit up, but it took great effort. Jacks ate silently, refusing conversation and ignoring the conflict in her mind, opting rather for a numb vegetative state where she could no longer be of harm to herself or to others. The nurse continued to speak to her as if they were actually conversing with each other, in the expert way only medical staff can achieve.

Jacks continued to stare blankly ahead, allowing her mind to think of nothing except the comfort of her bed. Even her ears ceased to hear after a while, and her eyes remained focused on her blanket; every fibre magnified, filling her mind.

That night, when sleep took her, she saw the lake again; she remained focused on the water, unable to see her own world, or that from which the dream figure of Patrick was apt to appear.

She watched the water, a gentle rippling void between two dimensions she had forgotten about by means of repression. All night she gazed silently at the calm waters and no other vision troubled her.

A light pierced her eyes, causing her to blink. She had not even realised she was awake. She lay flat on a stretcher bed, being wheeled out of what looked like an operating theatre. Struggling for a moment, she tried to regain the image of the lake, but it had left her. She became aware of her senses beginning to function again.

Sight, sound, touch …

'How long has she been like this, Kyle?'

'About a day in all,' came the familiar voice of Doctor Brodie. 'I didn't see what option I had; she's totally non-responsive.'

'We'll, get the results to you as soon as possible; don't worry. Craig, will you take Miss Chase back to her room please.'

'I'll give you a hand with her, Craig,' Doctor Brodie said.

'Right you are, doc,' the young man replied.

Jacks saw ceiling lights flicker as they entered the familiar talking lift.

'Doc, she's blinking,' Craig's voice said, excited at his discovery.

The face of Doctor Brodie entered Jacks' line of sight, and she smiled.

He breathed a sigh of relief. 'Thank God,' he said, laughing. 'Can you hear me, Jacks?'

She felt unable to speak, but nodded her head slightly.

'Fourth floor,' the lift said, and they pulled the trolley out and made their way rapidly back to the room. The doctor helped Craig lift her from the trolley to the bed and then poured her a glass of water.

'I thought we'd lost you there, Jacks,' he said.

She gulped down the water, relishing it as it

lubricated her vocal cords. Nurse Cadeaux entered looking glum, but on seeing Jacks sat up and drinking, she clapped her hands together, laughing.

'What happened?' she squealed with delight. 'How did you bring her back?'

'She did it on her own,' Doctor Brodie said. 'Craig noticed her blinking.'

Craig beamed, feeling as proud of his observation as if he had been the cause of her return.

'Okay you two, off you go, I'd like to examine my patient.'

Nurse Cadeaux nodded and smiled. She held the door for Craig as he wheeled the trolley out. As she left, she stopped to turn and wink at Jacks. Doctor Brodie took his patient's pulse and stuck a thermometer in her mouth.

'How are you feeling?' he asked.

'Weird,' was all that she could say. She was wondering why he was doing the nurse's job.

'Wha' 'appened?' she asked awkwardly, trying not to drop the thermometer.'

He removed it, gazing at it for a moment before placing it back into his pocket, appearing satisfied. He then took out a pen torch and shone it in her eyes.

'Look at me,' he said, as she squinted.

A tingling sensation began to overwhelm her as she stared back at him.

'You'd become non-responsive—another coma if you like, but not as deep as your previous one. Your eyes were open but you were not reacting to external stimuli.' The light switched to the other eye. 'I don't suppose that it occurred to the EN what was happening to you; some of the patients here are so fried that it could have seemed perfectly normal to her.

'I took you up for a CT scan. The damage may not have been as bad as I feared, considering that you've decided to join us again, but we shall have to see. It may be necessary for us to operate, but fingers crossed that it was something minor.'

He took out a stethoscope and inserted the earpieces. Jacks opened her robe slightly, her heart pounding as he placed the instrument to her chest. She tried in vain to calm herself, but every time he moved his hand, her heart fluttered even more.

His eyebrow rose slightly. 'Your heartbeat is a little irregular,' he said.

Jacks' face reddened. 'I'm not surprised; it's in shock. That thing's bloody freezing!'

He looked at her briefly then placed the instrument away.

'Do you know, since you arrived here, I can't think of one day without a dramatic event occurring, usually directly involving yourself.'

'It's no wonder I ended up mental then, is it?' she snapped.

'Don't say things like that!'

'Well it's true; I see things that aren't there. I manage to drive people to their death through my insane notions. My mind is completely fucked up, and while I fought desperately to convince everyone of my sanity, I managed to fuck a few of *them* up along the way. I don't know what to think or believe any more, or to feel,' she ended by looking at him, forcing to the back of her mind what she really wanted to express.

He returned her gaze.

'I spoke to your mother this morning,' he said. 'The reason she didn't get in touch is because she's been out of the country; she was visiting your godmother back in England, who has been very poorly of late apparently.'

'*England*, how did she afford to get over there?'

'I don't know, Jacks, but she did tell me who was paying the bill for this place.'

Jacks gazed expectantly.

'The man who knocked you over. Apparently he felt so guilty over the pain he'd caused you and your family, that he offered to pay your medical expenses in aid of a full recovery; he even chose this hospital.'

Jacks stared incredulously. 'Oh I see,' she said, in a tone far from sincere. 'So where's Trudi? Why has she not been to see me?'

'She's still in England. Apparently, you are very

close to your godmother. Your mother said it would break her heart if she knew the state you were in. She's planning on flying out again soon to be with her.'

Jacks' face contorted. 'But what about me?' she asked. 'Why hasn't she been to see me? She hasn't even phoned to find out how I'm doing. I suppose this means that I won't be going home.'

'I'm sorry,' he said. 'I have to say, I don't understand your mother's behaviour at all.'

Jacks was still for a moment, lost in silent contemplation. 'What about Patrick?' she asked. 'Did you find out where he is?'

The doctor's face frowned and he spoke delicately. 'Jacks, your mother didn't know anyone called Patrick. She said she knew all your friends, and there couldn't have been anyone special, as you didn't go out very often. The only Patrick she knew of was the family dog, to whom she said you were very close.'

'The family dog!' Jacks looked horrified. 'That's not true; she's lying. He does exist, he does, and I've seen him … why is she lying?'

Doctor Brodie seated himself closer. 'Jacks it is possible that your love for the family pet could have transformed during your coma to that of a human. You've said yourself that Patrick doesn't talk. Perhaps that's because he can't; he never could.'

She gave an ill-tempered scowl. 'He *can* talk,' she said, 'we spoke the other night, and I had another dream, it was though I was dreaming of the past. He exists, doctor and he's not a bloody dog!'

'Jacks, you're talking as though your dreams are real. Is that what you truly believe?'

She slouched sullenly. 'I told you I don't know what I believe,' she said. 'My dreams *feel* real to me; Meg told me that they are. She gave me a warning; she'd even met Patrick. How could she have known what she did, if they were not real?'

'I think you heard what you wanted to hear,' Doctor Brodie said. 'You cannot honestly expect me, as a doctor, to tell you that you are justified in your beliefs.'

She composed herself before issuing a reply. 'No, but I hoped as a *friend* that you might have at least entertained the possibility, but I can see now I was mistaken.'

'Please don't be like that,' he said. 'I've told you that I believe your dreams to be important. I've given you a notebook, for you to make a record of them, so that we may analyse them together. However, remember this, Jacks ... I was with you when you had one of your visions; I didn't see anything. You didn't go anywhere, you simply switched off for a few seconds while your mind flashed an array of images at you.'

'You don't believe in an eternal soul or higher consciousness do you, doctor?' Jacks asked. 'No of course not, because if you did we wouldn't be arguing now. My body may have remained an empty vessel, but where was *I*? I was enticed into an astral plane where I met Patrick who showed me things that were to help me understand.' She stopped, her words sounding so ridiculous that she could not believe they had actually had the nerve to escape her lips. 'I want to be well again, Kyle,' she said, as she lay back and closed her eyes.

He leaned in close and whispered to her.

'You will be,' he said.

There was a tap at the door and the doctor sat upright at lightening speed. Jacks eyes opened wearily. A man Jacks had not seen before entered, looking concerned. In his hand he held a conspicuous brown file. On seeing the man's expression, Doctor Brodie rose from his seat.

'I thought you should take a look at these right away, Kyle,' the man said.

Doctor Brodie's face went pale with worry. Jacks frowned, confused to what the commotion was about. She watched as he rose from his seat and indicated the door. The man left and Doctor Brodie faced Jacks.

'About the other problem,' he said. 'I've sorted it, so don't worry.' He left.

Jacks wondered at his odd behaviour.

Considering for a moment his parting words, she concluded that he must have been referring to Bob, and became anxious to know what had occurred between them.

A little while after the intriguing exit of Kyle Brodie, Nurse Cadeaux entered, food in hand.

'Hiya,' she greeted. 'I thought you'd probably be hungry.'

Jacks beamed and received the meal gladly.

'So what's going on now then?' the nurse asked.

'What do you mean?' Jacks said, as she broke off a piece of bread.

'Doctor Brodie's on the phone and he's having a right go at someone about you.'

Jacks was puzzled. 'I really couldn't say.' She smiled at the nurse. 'I do believe you're digging for gossip; are you not?'

'Moi?' she said, in mock offence, then grinned. 'Of course I am, but it seems that I won't find out anything from you ... so how's your dream therapy going?'

Jacks winced. 'Sore subject; I've made a bit of a prat out of myself with my crazy notions. I don't know what possessed me to take Meg seriously in the first place.'

Nurse Cadeaux fidgeted uncomfortably.

'It's all right,' Jacks said. 'I know Meg is dead, but what you could tell me is what happened to her?'

The woman's brow furrowed. 'Jacks I'm not allowed to tell you that. Why are you so curious about poor old Meg all the time? It's morbid you know. You should just let her rest in peace.'

Jacks felt ashamed of her lack of feeling and continued to eat in silence. They could hear quite clearly, the voice of Doctor Brodie, as he argued outside the room.

'I think I'd better try and calm him down; he'll disturb the other patients,' Nurse Cadeaux said.

The door burst open and Doctor Brodie stormed in brandishing a hot temper. His face was flushed and the familiar vein of tension protruded from his forehead.

'Nurse,' his voice strained, 'I would be most grateful if you could leave us for a few moments please.'

Nurse Cadeaux stood calmly and walked toward the door, then turning she said pertly, 'Well whatever you want to discuss can't be much of a secret considering your public broadcast just now.' She went cross-eyed at Jacks before walking out.

Jacks laughed.

Doctor Brodie paced over to her, a brown folder in his hand. She placed her tray aside, gazing at him in anticipation.

'You are Jacqueline Chase, are you not?' he asked.

Jacks looked around briefly, wondering whether it was a trick question. 'You know that I am,' she said.

'That doesn't answer my question. Are you Jacqueline Chase? Can you answer me in complete surety with a positive reply?'

Her head started to swim, the room span for a moment and she fought for a sense of equilibrium over the crazy carousel that had taken control of her senses.

'What's wrong, Kyle? What's going on?' she asked.

'Can you tell me in all honesty that you are Jacqueline Chase?'

... *She looked down at her bloody knees and sulked. Her uniform was torn and soiled. She wiped the mud from her face with her sleeve. Painfully, she gathered her schoolbooks together and placed them in her satchel. They had written the word scratta across the canvas. She sniffed as she got to her feet and began limping home, humiliated* ...

Two girls screamed as they hugged one another. She stared at the envelope weakly, her hands trembling. Carefully she ripped open the top and slid the paper out.

FAIL, FAIL, FAIL, FAIL ...

'The cleaning firm said they would be willing to take you on, but you've got to stop being so slovenly, I don't want you showing me up.'...

'Don't tell me what to do; you're nothing but a pathetic failure ...'

Doctor Brodie shook her abruptly. 'Jacks, answer me goddamnit!' he said.

Tears stung her eyes as the memories flashed before them. 'Yes of course I'm Jacqueline Chase,' she snivelled quietly, as she recalled the flashbacks. 'I remember ...' she stuttered.

The doctor gripped her arms tightly, in a manner demanding full attention.

'Do you remember being Jacqueline Chase? Yes or no?' he said.

Jacks squirmed. He was frightening and confusing her. She recalled past events, during which she assumed to be Jacqueline, but she could not actually establish a memory in which her full name had been used. Her face contorted in confusion. She wasn't clear on anything. Her memories were so disturbing that she began to wish that the past wasn't real.

Is that it? she thought. *Could that be the reason my mind withholds vitally important memory? I simply do not want to realise what a pathetic excuse for a human being I am.*

'I don't know,' she cried.

He released her from his pincer-like grip. Choosing to ignore her emotional display, he proceeded in removing the contents of the folder.

'I want you to look at these,' he said, his voice

noticeably softer, but fighting to keep its abrupt edge. He walked around the side of the bed and passed her the first X-ray film and a CT scan.

She wiped away her tears, feeling silly at such a response. Shifting around uncomfortably, she held the scan up, squinting. Doctor Brodie's eyes fixed on her.

'Well what do you see?' he asked.

'A mess,' Jacks replied.

The doctor seemed to relax a little.

'The point of impact was here,' she pointed.

The doctor tensed like a bowstring, his eyes narrowing.

'It appears that the victim was struck with a heavy object.'

'Like a car,' he suggested.

'No, I don't think the damage was caused during a car accident. Look at the lesion here, it's too localised; it looks as though the person was struck around the head with a small, but weighty object. A car is more likely to cause wider spread damage, of course it does depend on the speed of the vehicle at the time of impact.'

Doctor Brodie's hands began to tremble, but Jacks failed to notice, she continued to examine the films with avid interest.

'You say the person is a victim,' Kyle said, 'do you think they were murdered?'

'I'd say so.' She nodded. 'To get a localised

depressed skull fracture would not occur during a fall to the ground, and although a traffic accident would produce the necessary power to sustain the damage, the wounds are different; in a car accident it is more typical to see radiating injuries.'

'So you would conclude this person is dead,' the doctor said. 'I want to be sure on that.'

'I would say so. Look at the damage to the brain and the intracranial haemorrhaging. In my opinion, such is an injury is not survivable. Who is it anyhow?' she asked excitedly.

Doctor Brodie paused, as if for effect. 'Her name is Jacqueline Chase.'

Her eyes widened in sheer horror, the doctor's previous question making sense to her at last.

'According to your records,' he said, 'this was taken the night of the accident.'

She shook her head desperately, feeling cold and clammy. 'But I'm right,' she said. 'That was not caused by any car accident … and I … I couldn't have survived, no one could.' She could not think straight; she passed the CT scan and X-ray to Kyle with shaking hands, not wanting to consider any more. She wanted to shut down again, but did not know how.

'Jacks, everything you have told me is true. I suspected as much. The radiologist I had check it out, knew that, but what I want to know is, how did you? How could a kid who I've been led to believe is, frankly, a bit thick, have known that? Computerised Tomography is not the sort of thing that is studied on the curriculum.'

Dizziness swirled in her confused mind. According to the results in front of her, she was dead. Only one person in a million could have survived such an injury. Now he was questioning her knowledge. *How do I know where I picked it up from?* she thought. *If it wasn't biology class, then it must have been a book or TV. What's the big deal? What does he mean I'm thick?...*

'Don't tell me what to do. You're nothing but a pathetic failure ...'

And so I am, she thought. *That is why I'm here, but an injury like that would have caused extensive and probably permanent brain damage, which would explain the entire crazy situation. There is no secret waiting to be unlocked. It's my own damaged brain preventing me regaining memory. Hell, most of my memory probably doesn't exist anymore. There is no Patrick; he probably is the family dog after all. Why is Kyle making such a big deal? He is probably about to inform me that I need an operation, or that I'm going to die after all. I don't care anymore.*

Doctor Brodie watched her reaction; he saw her self-pitying expression and realised that she had misunderstood. He handed her the second set of films.

'These are the X-ray and scan we performed on

you earlier,' he said. 'I want you to look at them.'

It was a while before she would take them from him. Holding one up, she stared, searching for a tumour or damage that would decide her fate. She blinked hard. Her eyes narrowed slightly; turning her attention back to Kyle she stuttered, 'I don't understand. There's no fracture pattern on this at all. Look at the a-p view; the frontal sinus pattern is different. It's a completely different skull. Has there been some sort of mix up?'

'Jacks, I've been on the phone for hours. I've checked and rechecked. These were taken from the skull of Jacqueline Chase,' he said, indicating the first set of results; picking up the second scan and waving it in front of her face he said, 'This is you. As you expertly pointed out, you and Jacqueline Chase are not the same person.'

Her mouth opened and closed a few times before the anger issued forth. 'Then who the hell am I?' she said.

Kyle placed the films carefully back into the folder. 'I don't know, Jacks,' he said, 'but let me point out a few things to you. Firstly, as you've probably noted, you've sustained no damage to your cranium. There is no evidence to suggest you suffered an injury of any kind from a traffic accident, the accident that was supposed to have induced a coma; so why the hell are you here? Your medical records are completely inaccurate, and the only explanation I can see, is that they have been deliberately falsified.

'Why would your mother lie to us? Even if your name does turn out to be Jacqueline Chase, she knows that you weren't involved in that accident, so why are you here? The man who ran you down is paying for your treatment, except that you weren't run over, so that was another lie.

'What I mistook momentarily, for you trying to be a smart-arse, turns out to be a genuine medical knowledge of a specialist field. You've proven to have a certain level of intelligence, something that your mother took pains to convince me you didn't possess.

'You told me that your memories were unreal somehow. You've had these suspicions about your mother that you can't account for. I think your subconscious has been trying to tell you that there's something wrong all along, and I refused to listen to you. You are here to be treated for mental illness and I assumed that your confusion and suspicion was due to your condition. Now, I want to know what is going on!'

The revelation hit her like a wave of drunkenness and for a moment, she suffered a sensory overload. She could not possibly take any more in. It was some time before she calmed herself enough to speak.

'I never liked it when you called me Jacqueline,'

she said, 'now I guess I know why. I'm not Jacqueline Chase. I know it in my heart, Kyle.'

Peace settled about the room, rather like the calm after a storm.

'Who have you told about all this?' Jacks asked suddenly.

'No one,' he replied. 'The neurosurgeon knows about the results of the scans as does the radiologist, but I never told anyone about my suspicions. Why?'

'I'd keep them to yourself if I were you. We don't know exactly what is going on here. Besides, if something happened to you I'd probably be stuck here forever.' She attempted a smile. 'Nobody else will be crazy enough to believe all this.'

'I'm going to find out what's going on,' he said. 'Don't worry; I'll be careful.' He gathered the folder and squeezed her hand. 'I'm sorry for not being here for you sooner.'

'Kyle, I didn't know for sure whether anything was actually wrong sooner, so how could you? But, I thank you. I'm glad to know you're on my side.'

'I always have been you know,' he said, with a smile, 'you just never realised it before.' He drew away suddenly and rose to his feet. 'Anyway, I'm going to see what I can dig up. Keep your chin up; we may have you out of here before too long.' Through his smile, his face looked troubled.

'Be careful,' she said, as the door closed behind

him.

Finally things are beginning to make a little sense, she thought, *or at least I'm starting to ask the right questions, like who the hell am I? Are the memories I have actually real? If they're not then how did they get into my mind? I wasn't involved in the accident written in my records. Was I even in a coma? If not, why can I not remember anything?*

'Run Jacks, run!' she heard the words clearly in her cluttered head. She shivered suddenly and looked up. Bob stared at her through the window. She felt her body start.

'Run Jacks, run.' She heard the voice again.

Bob slinked in like a scavenging hyena, stalking up to her and laughing while he made ready to tear her to pieces, and woe betide anyone who stood in his way.

Jacks could not speak as he approached. She was certainly more mobile now and so summoned up all her courage and reached for the bell.

He was beside her within a second, bell in hand. He moved it higher and wound it around the reading lamp. Picking up the book on her bedside table, he thumbed through it. She gritted her teeth and glared like a resentful child as he pawed over her property. The roots in his bleached blonde hair were showing through, and he had been under a sun-bed recently; he had a fake skin tone that convinced Jacks that he did not tan naturally. Jacks thought he looked ridiculous. She would have laughed at him had she not known how dangerous he could be.

His eyes lingered on the inscription written by Kyle. 'How quaint,' he said, 'but I aint too fond of triangles.' He snapped the book shut and leaned into her. She could smell the halitosis, despite the fact that he was sucking on a mint.

'Did you enjoy what I did to you?' he asked. 'Yeah you did. You enjoyed it that much you told him about it, didn't you? You were hoping he'd do it to you too, weren't you, whore?'

Jacks saw the emptiness behind his pale blue eyes and it terrified her. She opened her mouth to scream, but his hand shot out and grabbed her by the throat, squeezing. The bruising there still pained her and she realised with horror that he would leave no distinguishing marks, as he was pressing on the original wounds.

No evidence.

He hissed in her ear.

'Your doctor friend thinks he's a real tough guy. Well he aint here now, so I guess he's going to miss all the fun.'

Jacks gurgled, her nails cut into his hands; he failed to even notice. She struggled, punching out at his hideous face. He let go suddenly, more as if he decided to, rather than she had been able to inflict any damage upon him. She gasped for breath, her face purple.

'It's a shame about poor Nurse Cadeaux,' Bob said. 'She came down with food poisoning. Oops, that's where I dropped that Ipecacuanha; let me see now, John has got the week off, Nurse Cadeaux is sick, Nurse Wong clocks off at six and I'm sure she will not be willing to do the night shift. If only she could find someone who is able to do it for her. There's always me of course. I know it's not my floor, but I know the routine. "Go on home and put your feet up, Erica, I don't mind; I didn't have any plans anyhow."'

The man is completely insane, Jacks thought. She could not move; she could barely even breathe after he had half throttled her.

'So I guess it's just me and you tonight then, whore,' he said. 'There won't be any time for games. You spoilt that by being a kiss and tell. After tonight though, you'll not be talking to anyone again.' He grinned, his crooked teeth mocking her helplessness.

He did not look back as he left the room and so failed to see Jacks struggling to her knees, coughing and spluttering as she attempted to free her trachea to receive a full intake of air. She took the bell in her hand, but paused. *If I press it now,* she thought, *Bob will no doubt rush straight back in and disconnect it— and me. I have to get the senior nurse's attention before the woman leaves at six. What time is it now? Four, Half four maybe, perhaps later. I'll have to leave it a while, and then take the risk.*

Perhaps Bob is bluffing. No, his eyes clearly displayed his intent. I must get the nurse's attention somehow, but if I leave it too late to ring the bell, I might miss her; I can't be sure of the time now by any means.

Her hands trembled violently. She felt a lump in her throat and swallowed hard, but it remained—remained to serve as a reminder of how weak she was, how pathetic. *No this won't do at all,* she thought. *Pull yourself together, Jacks. If I ring the bell, Bob will most probably be listening out for it, I have to think of a different plan …*

'Run Jacks, run.'

My legs are certainly stronger; perhaps I can hobble out of here. All I need to do, is get to another floor and ask for help …

No, that's no good either; I'm a mental patient, who's going to believe me? I'll have to escape, but where will I go? One thing at a time, Jacks, let's concentrate on getting off the ward first. If only I knew where Kyle went. She wished he had not left. *Why did he confront Bob? I warned him what the consequences would be.*

Jacks struggled to her feet, Patrick's words playing on her mind. *'Beware your friend.' He could have planned this,* she considered. *Oh, this is stupid; why would Doctor Brodie want me dead?* She shook herself free from her paranoia and considered the Zimmer frame for a moment.

Too conspicuous.

She could only barely walk without its aid. She held the wall to her right, for support, and made her way around the outside of the room toward the door.

On reaching the far side, the door swung open. Jacks froze, petrified, unable to breathe. No one entered, but someone was looking in. Jacks felt sure she would be sick, believing it to be Bob. *But what if it's Nurse Wong?* she considered. Rooted to the spot, she was unable to decide her course of action, convinced that she was going to faint again.

She tried to breathe quietly, but the noise she made seemed deafening; the strain was too great for her. She bit her lip to prevent herself from crying out, but she could not stop the sound, letting out a tiny whimper drawn from sheer terror and anticipation of her own death. The cry was loud enough for the man at the door to hear.

He stepped in.

She collapsed, not fainting, but simply unable to function any longer.

It was Andy. He ran to her side. On seeing him, she held his arms and gasped for breath.

'Oh my God, thank-you, oh Andy,' she cried.

'What the hell's going on, Jacks?' he asked.

She clung tightly to him, there being no way he was going to leave the room, at least not unless he took her with him. She tried to calm herself, knowing that she would sound insane whatever she said, but she had no intention of throwing more fuel on the fire than was needed.

'Andy please, you have to help me. You have to get me out of here!' she pleaded.

The look that met her was not encouraging. His face, usually so jovial, seemed hardened.

'I certainly will not,' he said, 'now get back into bed.'

'Please,' she almost screamed, allowing her emotions get the better of her. Her reaction shocked him.

'Jacks, why do you want to leave? What's wrong with you?'

'It's Bob; he's going to kill me. He poisoned Nurse Cadeaux so he would be put in charge of the night shift, and he's going to kill me, the same way he did Meg, so it looks like a suicide.'

She spoke so quickly that Andy seemed to have trouble keeping up.

'Jacks, no one is going to kill you, now let me help you back to bed.'

She snatched her hand away. 'Nooo,' she cried. 'If you don't help me then I'll die; I'm not lying! Andy please, please.' Her hysterics calmed to simple weeping.

His hands pushed her hair back and he held her head firmly. She looked at him with tearful eyes.

'He's not going to lay a finger on you, do you understand?' he said. 'I'll kill him if he tries.'

She eyed him suspiciously, convinced it was a trick to get her to go back to her bed like a good little crazy bird.

'You believe me?' she tested.

His hand slipped under her bent legs and his other around her back. His face strained for a moment as he lifted her off the floor.

'Do you trust me, Jacks?' he asked.

'Yes,' she risked, confused.

He lowered her to the bed.

'Then believe me when I say that this; Bob will not harm a single hair on your pretty head. Okay?'

She was convinced he didn't believe her. Her eyes pleaded with him, begged him, but he was closed to her. He began to walk away.

'Andy please, don't leave me,' she cried, 'please.'

He smiled thinly. 'I have work to do, gorgeous; as much as I'd like to stay chatting to you, I'm afraid I can't.' He blew her a kiss and was gone.

Her one ray of hope extinguished as soon as it had been kindled and she was back to square one. *He's not going to help,* she thought. *I'll have to do it alone.* She felt a heat begin to burn inside her. Her anger rose. *How could he abandon me like that? The bastard.*

The heat made her body tingle with rage. She was sick of the fear, sick of people treating her like a second-class citizen.

With a grunt, she forced herself to her feet and began the journey toward the door again, determination and indignation carrying her forward. Her hand reached out, steady, and she turned the handle.

It was locked.

Chapter Eleven

Help me find the way again,
The path is lost to me,
Let me know loves splendour,
Please, no more pain and agony.

Unlock my cage and
Free my soul,
Let me fly to you.
I will be yours completely
If your love is true.

Nooo, Jacks thought. *Why is it locked? Of course, Andy probably thought the crazy bitch needs containing.* She breathed heavily, seeking to control the rage she felt. Cautiously, she looked through the window in the door; the corridor appeared empty. She reconsidered her options. She could ring the bell, but that would probably bring Bob; she could break the glass in the door and attempt to unlock it by reaching down. *Who am I kidding?* she thought. *There is no way I'm agile enough.* She turned and looked hard at the only other possible exit.

The window.

She was on the fourth floor, and knew that she would be unable to escape, but she could attempt to alert someone. Her legs felt tired and useless. Using the wall for support again, she made her way back toward the window. Two new problems arose; there was no way to open it; they had been designed to prevent suicide by jumping. She wondered if she could smash it, but still there was the issue what she would do then. She could see no one below. The grounds seemed to stretch for miles. There was no one, absolutely no one.

CLICK.

The door swung open and Bob made his slimy entrance. 'Are you thinking of doing my job for me?' he said. 'How very considerate.'

Death was inevitable, that she knew, yet she had ceased to be frightened by the odious excuse for a man. She hated him, and she hated herself for having been so afraid.

'How did you do it, Bob?' she demanded. 'How did you kill Meg?' Her voice was cold as ice. Bob's face lost its satisfaction; her fear was gone, and it was that which had excited him.

'I didn't do it,' he said, 'she did. I made her cut herself up and she did precisely what I wanted because she wanted to save *you*. I think in her fucked up mind, she thought that you were one of those kids she slaughtered.'

Jacks' fists clenched tightly showing the white of her knuckles. 'Meg was no killer,' she hissed. 'The only murderer I know is you!'

He ignored her attack and continued relishing each detail, in the way a bard would stir hearts with tales of heroic adventures. 'She cut off four of her fingers and placed them about the room. I made her remove her hair, rather fitting I thought. That's what they used to do to lunatics in asylums. They'd sell their hair to wig makers. Nowadays scum like you get treated like fuckin' royalty.'

Jacks' lip curled in a snarl; she wanted him dead. She had never felt such a violent and negative emotion before. In real terms, she knew that she did not stand a chance, but hoped at least to mark him before he put an end to her life. *It might be enough for people to ask questions*, she thought. *He might not get away with it.*

'You're the one who should be locked up, Bob,' she said. 'You're a bloody psychopath! In fact, you don't even deserve the title; you'd wear it like a crown. You're a fucking joke. You get off on your authority and the fear and pain you inflict. You're a fat, hideous piece of shit. Even I, a helpless mental patient, was too much a woman for you, weren't I? MY GOD YOU HAD TO KNOCK ME OUT FIRST! Let me see, could that be because the size of your penis is laughable? That's the truth of the matter isn't it, you murdering bastard? The women laughed at you and eventually you gave up and decided to find your thrills elsewhere.

'How tragic. How heartbreaking. How utterly pathetic!'

He moved into action quicker than she had anticipated. She blocked his oncoming blow with her arm, but his other fist crashed into her stomach with an incredible force. She never imagined he was so strong and as she fell to the ground, unable to move through the pain, it felt as though her intestines had ruptured. She lay sprawled on the floor, trying to cover her head, her eyes half closed.

There was a yell and he stopped hitting her. The pain was excruciating and she opened her bleary eyes, fighting the urge to vomit. Andy had hauled Bob away, and they grappled one another. As her eyes began to close, she saw Andy land a punch on Bob. She wondered how long Andy would hold out, figuring he couldn't be much of a match for Bob's brute strength.

May as well close my eyes and die now, Jacks thought. *Save myself a lot of pain.* Her eyes opened one last time to see Andy knee Bob in the groin, then darkness came and she saw no more.

A gentle rain fell invisibly about her. She stood in the glare from an unseen streetlight. The pain was gone. Everything was gone. The sound of a car engine became apparent. She turned to see a blue Volkswagen pull up, out of which stepped Bob—*the ghost of Christmas present.* He removed a handful of money from his inside pocket and began to count it, a look of satisfaction on his face.

A gradual pressure on Jacks' shoulders was building, as if the air itself was solidifying there. The process seemed so slow that it was a while before it became evident that two hands rested upon her.

'Jacks,' whispered a familiar voice, as the strong hands swivelled her around to face him.

Patrick: The ghost of Christmas past.

He drew her to him and held her silently.

'Patrick,' she said, 'you don't exist. You're just a physical embodiment of the insecurity I have or, or something like that.'

He let go of her, his eyes so dense they were like two black holes—doomed pathways to another world. The footsteps of Bob approached and Patrick turned her sharply to face him. Bending, he whispered breathlessly in her ear.

'You must get him to walk into that alley, but you must remain in the pool of light, Jacks. Don't be frightened of him; he's never going to hurt you again.'

His voice was irresistible; she would have felt compelled to do as he told her at that moment, even if it had meant plunging to her death. She noticed the alley to her left. No light fell there; it was like a gaping hole of nothingness.

'What the fuck is going on, you little whore?'

Jacks saw the stormy face of the 'ghost of Christmas present' approach, but the giant was no more; smaller he seemed, almost insignificant.

'How did you get out, bitch?' Bob demanded. 'I'll kick your fuckin' head in.'

Jacks could not decide how to lure him into the alley. He was before her—his fists lashing out like a bad-tempered ape. She stepped backward, glancing into the alley, searching for a sign from Patrick. Bob turned as if he thought she was looking at someone and she sprung into action. She lunged forward and shoved him into the blackness.

The opaque dark consumed him completely and he disappeared. She stood for a moment, expectant, waiting for him to emerge.

Nothing.

The invisible rain fell about her once more, but it was the only sound she heard.

Nothing.

She stepped cautiously forward and peered into the alley opening.

Nothing.

She was no longer certain it was an alley at all. She saw no walls, as a light of some sort would have reflected off them; it was simply black.

Looking down, she noticed that the pool of light in which she stood, cut off sharply at the edge of the opening. She stood at that brink and could no longer heed Patrick's demand. Taking a deep breath in anticipation, she stepped forward into the dark.

The moment she passed over the threshold, she heard a low laughter echoing off the walls, which seemed to be bathed in a dull, phosphorescent light.

The ghost of Christmas present meets the ghost of Christmas past, she thought.

Patrick had his back to Jacks, his long dark coat silhouetted like wings of night. Bob backed away, pleading. The whole alley seemed to pulsate and groan as if it were alive.

Bob screamed. A scream that lasted the whole while he was ripped apart piece by piece, even after his vocal cords were removed. Jacks watched in horror, unable now to turn away, as an unseen force mangled the flesh; muscles and ligaments lacerated apart, like the meat off a bone in the mouth of a hungry carnivore.

He has to be dead by now, she thought. *Anyone would be.* Yet, she knew he was not; somehow, he remained alive, even as his beating heart was wrenched away and his remains were stripped to the bones, which splintered and split asunder, until the complete set of bodily components that had been Bob, fell to the ground in an orderly squelch. His screams continued until Patrick's laugh consumed them.

Jacks felt the pain in her stomach, enhanced by the sickness that afflicted her. She staggered toward the light—the pain increasing. Patrick, suddenly aware of her, pivoted to see her retreat.

'Jacks, wait, JACKS,' he cried.

'Jacks … Jacks!'

Her eyes fluttered open; her stomach continued to burn with the agony of Bob's attack. Andy's face smiled down at her. She struggled to sit up, and glanced nervously about. There was no sign of Bob. Andy had saved her. Suddenly, the closeness of death overwhelmed her and she sobbed hysterically, throwing her arms about him.

I'm still alive, she thought. *By some miracle Andy came back and saved me.*

He sat stroking her hair, his face buried next to

hers and he inhaled, as if capturing the scent of her aura. She felt goose pimples ride up her legs at his sign of intimacy. Looking up at him, her eyes were awash with tears. He reached out his hand as the water swelled, and removed it gently on his finger. His hands drew her hair back, dragging it sensuously down her cheek.

'I told you I wouldn't let him hurt you,' he said.

She blinked away another round of tears and his mouth was on hers, drawing her closer. She returned his kiss, her mind debating why. *It's good to be alive,* she thought, *nice to have support and appreciation; it's the excitement of the experience.*

In moments, she drew away from him, feeling embarrassed. As he continued to stroke her hair, Jacks felt unsure how to proceed; she tried to push the kiss to the back of her mind, as though it never really happened. He saw the expression on her face and drew away.

'Jacks, I apologise,' he said. 'I didn't mean to offend you. I kissed you in the heat of the moment. I'm sorry if the idea now repulses you.'

'Andy, it's not that,' she said. 'You're a very attractive man, but this isn't right.' She decided to pull away from the subject of the kiss, as it made her feel uncomfortable. 'Someone has just tried to kill me; don't you think we need to inform the authorities?'

His voice was cold and slow as he made his

reply. 'You are quite right of course. Let me help you back to bed, then I shall go and ring the police.'

'Thank-you, Andy.' Jacks took his hand as he pulled her up. 'You saved my life,' she said nervously.

Andy bowed low in his old boyish manner, seeming to dismiss her former rejection. 'Glad to be of assistance,' he said.

She clambered back into bed and he pulled the sheets up.

'What happened to Bob?' she asked. 'How did you manage to stop him?'

'Strength isn't everything in a fight you know. Besides, once he realised his game was up, he was most eager to depart.'

He saw her face cloud over.

'Don't worry,' he said, 'he's not coming back.'

'But how do you know? How can you be sure?' Her thoughts returned to her hideous dream, realising that anything could have happened while she was unconscious. 'You didn't kill him, did you?'

'Of course not!' He laughed. 'What do think I am?'

'A hero,' she replied, and relaxed a little.

Andy leaned over and unwound the panic button, placing it in Jacks' hand.

'I've got a phone-call to make. Ring if you need me, okay?'

She nodded and smiled as he left. Placing the bell carefully beside her, she huffed angrily. She felt stupid for not having pushed Andy away when he made his advance and she was furious with him, as she felt he had taken advantage of her while she was in emotional turmoil.

Have I any right to be furious with the man I owe my life to? she thought. *When it comes down to it, I'm plain embarrassed at having been reduced to an utter state of helplessness—yet again.*

The pain in her stomach was calming—nothing more than a dull ache. Images of the ferocious destruction of Bob returned to her mind with fresh fury.

'Patrick,' she said aloud.

Is he real or not? she wondered. *Probably not. He's just a side effect of those bloody antidepressants. However, if he is real, what then? If the visits he paid me actually happened, then Bob is dead; his body will never be discovered.* She knew she should have found that thought comforting, but despite the fact she clearly remembered wanting him dead, she felt sorry and sickened by his gruesome fate.

An image appeared in her mind; she imagined the Police searching for Bob. He would never be found. Andy would be questioned.

"Strange how he never packed anything to take. His car is still parked in the hospital grounds, so he didn't even drive out of here ... strange."

Patrick isn't real! she thought. *But what if he is?*

'ANDY,' she yelled, and reached for the panic button.

He was at her side in moments.

'What's wrong? What is it?' he gasped.

'You haven't phoned the Police yet, have you?'

'I was about to,' he said.

'Well for God's sake don't, not yet.'

He eyed her suspiciously.

'Does Bob drive a blue Volkswagen, Andy?' she snapped. 'Does he?'

'I wouldn't know,' he replied.

She sighed and tried a different angle. 'I know this is going to sound strange, but you can't phone the Police, because I think he's dead, and if I'm right then you'll get the blame. We've got to keep quiet about it.'

'Jacks, I didn't kill him,' he insisted.

'I never said that you did. If you ring down and ask if he's left the building, I'll bet they say he hasn't, nor will he … ever. His blue Volkswagen will be parked outside, and *he* will never be found.'

Andy leaned forward, looking out of the window, down four floors to the brightly lit parking lot.

'What makes you think he's dead?' he asked, with a frown.

Jacks wanted the support of someone who seemed to believe her implicitly, but she held her tongue, not knowing how to tell him.

'I don't know,' she said, 'but I've got a feeling and if I'm right then you'll probably get the blame. I know it sounds weird, but you have to trust me. You have to leave here, go home, and pretend tonight never happened.'

'Jacks, you're freaking me out here, but you're my friend and I trust and respect you. I am going to do what you ask. I won't phone the Police, and I will go home, but the whole ward will be left unattended and I will lose my job if anyone realises I abandoned you all.'

'Just go, Andy,' she said. 'Most of the patients have probably been knocked out for the night anyhow.'

'You are being totally weird, but,' he kissed her forehead, 'I still adore you. Night gorgeous.' He strode out of the door.

If Bob was still alive, Jacks was alone, with nothing but the Complete Works of Shakespeare to protect her. *But I'm not wrong,* she thought. *I saw Andy's face when he looked into the car park. It was obvious that he spotted the car I described. Of course, it is possible that I noticed the vehicle on one of my visits to the great outdoors, but why would my mind want to associate the car with Bob? Because my mind is screwy.*

No, it isn't that. Bob is dead. I know it as sure, as if I killed him myself. Her jaw dropped slightly. *I did kill him, or as good as. I wanted him dead. Patrick had no power over him until he entered that alleyway. I pushed him into that place; he would have never volunteered to enter. I caused his death; he would not have died if it hadn't been for me.*

'Don't blame yourself, Jacks,' murmured Patrick's voice from beside her ear; he was, however, stood at the foot of her bed.

'You're not real,' she said.

He gave an ironic smile. 'If I'm not real, then Bob is not dead, and you have nothing to feel guilty about.'

'My mother said that you are the family pet.'

He laughed dramatically. 'Your *mother* said that, and how very right she was.'

'Stop playing stupid games, Patrick! Tell me what I want to know.'

His smile faded at her reproach.

'I told you; it is *you* that doesn't allow yourself to hear the truth. There is nothing I can do.'

A maddening glare passed over her features and she grinned fiendishly. 'So you can't tell me here. Let's go to *your* place, shall we.' She struggled to her knees and crawled to the end of the bed. 'I don't want you here, Patrick!' she screeched. 'You are to leave.'

His eyes widened and he began to fade. She dived forward, clutching at his fleeting image as she fell.

Spinning, spinning.

The sun made her eyes smart, but she remained looking at it all the same, just to see how long she could go without blinking.

Spinning, spinning.

In a circle, they kept going around and around, the clouds and the sun. She blinked, her eyes watered and she sat up, feeling wobbly.

Spinning, spinning.

The roundabout sped. She giggled with delight as the boy stopped pushing and jumped on beside her. His young face was familiar as an old pair of shoes, yet she could not place him.

'What do you want to be when you grow up?' she said, brimming with childish admiration.

'I don't know,' he shrugged, 'an adult I guess.'

Jacks giggled and threw her child feet over the edge of the roundabout, enjoying the air resistance push against them.

The roundabout began to slow. Her legs seemed longer. She looked at the boy and saw that he was ageing. By the time the roundabout stopped, it was plain that the boy had been Patrick. She sat in awe and wonder at the transformation. She had known the little boy's face, not because she now knew him to be Patrick, but because she recognised him as he was *then*.

She knew the place too; she had played there as a child, but more recently, she had dreamed of it, surrounded by a sea of blood.

'Remember,' was all Patrick would say.

'Remember what?' she demanded. 'I've followed you here, despite the danger and you're still not telling me anything.'

The sky darkened in an instant. Thunderclaps rent the air and a heavy rain poured out of the midnight sky. Patrick turned and leaned on the castle wall, surveying his kingdom.

'Look my Lord Hamlet, see where he comes again.

Thunder rolled overhead.

'Tis very like your Father and yet unlike,' Horatio cried through the storm.

Patrick turned. The rain soaked through Jacks' clothes and made moving difficult. The water drenched her hair, half blinding her as she approached.

Another streak of lightning flashed, very close this time, during which Jacks saw the doctor kissing her hand; she observed closely the look in his eye.

'Remember.'

Jacks saw Patrick dimly through the sheets of rain. He was not getting wet.

'Oh my God' she exclaimed
'PATRICK!'

And she remembered.

Chapter Twelve

Darkness,
Emptiness,
The silent screams of a breaking heart.
Pain,
Loneliness,
The tormented wails of a haunted soul.
Falling,
Falling,
Will there be a return from the void surrounding?
Without help,
Without hope,
Life will never be the same again.

The morning sun shone brightly outside the window in Jacks' room. The crouched over figure of Doctor Brodie sat on her bed, his head in his hands. There was an unnerving transparency to his outline, as though he was but a reflection of reality.

Her first attempt to speak was unsuccessful; she felt out of sync somehow. She became aware of the sound of dripping, as water ran from her drenched garments and pattered onto the floor.

'Kyle,' she uttered, steadying herself at last.

He failed to hear her at first, as if her voice to him was no more than a breeze, mocking her memory. He turned slowly and jumped to his feet on seeing her wet and shivering.

'Where? How? What happened to you?' he asked.

'So, cold,' she stammered, through chattering teeth.

Her soaking form crumpled to the bed like an overused dishcloth and Kyle removed his coat, wrapping it around her.

'What's going on, Jacks?' he asked. 'Where have you been? I've been worried sick.'

A thin veil seemed to cloud her eyes. She failed to respond, barely perceiving his words. He slid beside her, hoping to gain her attention.

'Does this have anything to do with Bob? He's gone missing; he abandoned the ward last night.'

Silence.

'Did he take you away?' He put a hand on her arm in effort to gain her attention. 'Where have you been?'

Her mouth opened slowly and a guttural sound ensued. 'I've been to London to see the queen.' She gave a low chuckle, which broke into a deep-throated laugh, a sound that was somewhat unsettling to the ear, being empty and hollow enough to disturb the most indomitable of characters.

Without warning, she threw herself into Kyle's arms, her laughter metamorphosing into deafening sobs. Doctor Brodie said nothing at first. He cradled her, rocking her gently in effort to soothe her. Gradually, the sobbing ceased and she snivelled softly, her hold on him relaxing. He retreated, his eyes all questions as he observed the wet hair sprawled across her face and the tiny drops of water that fell into her lap.

'Jacks, come on,' he said, 'we must get you into some dry clothes before you catch a chill.'

He made his way to the door and the crying grew louder in volume. He stopped, turning, his eyes all concern.

'Well how about you at least slip into your dressing gown then? Come on, get yourself undressed.' He passed her the robe and then turned his back.

Under normal circumstances, she would have undoubtedly found his behaviour amusing. It was absurd that a doctor be embarrassed about nudity, or at least respect someone's privacy in such a manner.

Jacks continued to cry as she let her nightdress fall to the floor into a small puddle of water that had formed at her feet. She slipped the dressing gown on and began to shuffle silently toward the window. The sun blazed and warmed her damp skin, causing her to blink in the dazzle.

Doctor Brodie ignored the clothes and approached.

'I'm sorry about the mess,' she said. 'I was caught in a storm.' Her voice sounded remote.

He rested his hands firmly on her shoulders.

'Jacks,' he said, 'there hasn't been a storm; we didn't even have rain. Now look at me.'

He pulled her around, her eyes focused on him once again, no longer distant. Her lashes looked thicker as her tears clumped them together and the green of her eyes was like grass, jewelled with autumn dew.

'Where have you been?' he demanded. 'Do you know where Bob is?'

She gulped, as if the words were too difficult to speak. She did not dare to blink; observing even the tiniest reaction from him was crucial. She needed to know that she could trust him. Patrick's words still plagued her thoughts.

'He's dead,' she replied. 'He tried to kill me, but Andy saved me.'

'Beware your friend.'

'Oh my God,' he said.

She felt his grip tighten.

'So Andy killed him!'

His scrutinising eyes were intensely threatening, doing nothing to alleviate the fear she felt.

'No he didn't,' she protested. 'He saved my life, but he didn't murder Bob.' She began to wish she had kept her mouth shut.

'Did Andy take you away?' he asked.

'No, and neither did Bob. I never even left the room.'

His bewilderment was plain, but Jacks did not feel like explaining herself. She was tired— exhausted.

Drawing away from him, she hobbled back to her bed. He stood for a moment, as if she was still before him, as his body fought to catch up with his mind. Slowly he turned; Jacks had drawn the covers up to her neck, as if to protect herself from blustery winds. She stared fixedly before her, silent as the grave.

He approached and sat beside her on the bed.

'Jacks, why won't you speak to me? Why won't you tell me what happened or where you have been?'

Looking at him suddenly, her eyes penetrated his, searching, questioning. She failed to find any signs that she had reason to distrust him. His pupils seemed to expand slightly—his irises dancing like baubles at Christmas, but his gaping pupils inviting her to gaze within; she felt goose pimples shoot down the backs of her arms and she blinked. *I want to trust him,* she thought, *but I'm not telepathic.* She stared hard at him, trying without success to determine what lay behind those windows of the soul.

'Would you know of any reason why Patrick warned me to be wary of you?' she asked.

His form tensed, feeling he was getting nowhere, like a teacher whose students are so unruly that he cannot even take the register.

'Patrick again,' he huffed. 'Jacks, will you stop evading my questions. I am serious. I want to know where you've been.'

'I've been with Patrick,' Jacks said icily. 'My question was in deadly earnest and you just evaded, not me.'

There was a definite change in her voice; she sounded stronger, harder and not at all prepared to take any of his doctor patient power-trip bullshit. He stood his ground, however, and yet gave in to her at the same time.

'Jacks, Patrick does not exist, he's part of your

psyche, he may even be an extra personality, I've yet to discover. But if you feel alarm bells have been going off, warning you against me, there need not be a sinister explanation; it may just be your natural distrust of men; you're frightened by the intimacy of our relationship.' His face blushed slightly, as if he had not meant to phrase his words in such a way and attempted to elaborate. 'The doctor patient relationship in this type of establishment can be a very close one, but you can trust me; it's against my code of ethics to betray your confidence.' His voice stuttered and he eventually trailed off.

She picked up on a whole other meaning while he had waffled. Looking into his eyes again, they seemed like inviting pools, into which she could fall ... or drown. A heat surged through her body; her heart beat so loudly that the sound echoed in her ears; accompanied by the sound of her breathing.

Is that what Patrick meant? she wondered. *He might have been aware of my feelings and wanted to put me on my guard; Kyle is a doctor after all and could never return my affections; he's already said so — 'code of ethics', and yet I see something in his eyes. No, I must be imagining it and yet, he behaved like a jealous lover whenever Andy was around, and the day after Nurse Cadeaux forced me to compliment Andy's hair, Kyle got himself a haircut ... now I'm really thinking like the teenager I'm supposed to be.*

She continued to gaze into in his eyes; they sparkled so much, it was as though they were the epicentres generating the electricity that seemed to be flowing between them.

There's no time for this now, she told herself. *There are more important matters to hand than those of the heart; that was most likely the nature of Patrick's warning. I can't afford to develop feelings and flitter about like a lovesick teenager. I'm caught in a web of deceit and could be in deadly danger and **that** is what I need to focus my energies on.*

'Patrick's my brother,' she said, at last.

She could feel the tears welling up once again; the frustration of not trying harder, sooner, to understand what he was trying to tell her, for disbelieving and fearing him.

'He's been trying to tell me all along,' she continued, 'I just wasn't tuned in enough to realise. All the clues were there; I remembered him, even though everything else was gone. I remembered how deeply I loved him, but knew that we were not lovers. I saw the playground in which we played as children. In my Hamlet dream, he was shown to me as the ghost. Horatio had said, 'tis very like your father and yet unlike'. He is like my father but isn't; he's my brother.' She cried softly. 'He's my brother and he's dead!'

Jacks gazed up at the calm features of the doctor. His pallor had paled somewhat.

'What, no words of conjecture from the great Doctor Brodie?' she mocked. 'Even if you don't believe that I have visited my brother, you cannot deny that he existed, you see, I *remember* him; the first tangible memories I've had. I remember playing together as children. I remember his horse that I stole because I preferred it to my pony, and how I rode off with it and got lost in the woods. I was so terrified when Patrick found me, hours later, but he didn't scold me; he gave me the horse. I remember him taking the blame when I smashed a Royal Doulton jug, which I wanted to use for my tea party when I was little.

'He always let me win when we fenced together, even though he was a master and I was dreadful at it. I remember his Burberry coat he always liked to wear … and still does.'

The tears came again, and still Doctor Brodie said nothing. He rose and fetched his briefcase, clicked it open and removed some documents. He placed a photograph in front of Jacks. She wiped away her tears and looked at it. It featured a plain looking girl with greasy, black hair. She wore a school uniform and Jacks considered it to be the reason she looked so miserable—nobody likes having a school photograph taken. Her lips were thin and pale and her small green eyes looked glassy and distant.

'Who's that?' she said, after a time.

'Don't you know?' Doctor Brodie's eyebrow raised in a questioning manner. 'Her name is Jacqueline Chase.'

Chapter Thirteen

A candle in the blackness,
A suffocating flame.
Darkness awaits me
And never-ending pain.

No going forward,
No changing the past,
There is no escape,
Death's cornered me at last.

However could I leave?
How could I say goodbye?
But the kindest choice to make
Is to choose to die.

As I sit here in confusion,
Pondering on what might be,
Am I right to end it here?
I am now, that I see.

'That's me?' Jacks questioned in alarm, trying desperately to recall the image of herself in the mirror. Even had the photograph been severely out of date, the two were nothing alike.

'No, this is Jacqueline Chase, not you,' Doctor Brodie said. 'This is who you are supposed to be. This is the girl who lived in a suburb on the other side of the country; she attended a High School some four kilometres from her home. This is the girl who was a little dim and got picked on a lot, who barely scraped any marks on her HSC. This is the girl who went a little off the rails. This is Jacqueline Chase; the girl who was your life story before you discovered it was a fraud. So I take it you don't actually recognise her?'

Jacks shook her head slowly; her eyes fixed on the image of the girl who was supposed to be her. 'I don't understand,' she murmured.

Doctor Brodie's voice changed to a high-pitched female impersonation, which at any other time would have been amusing. '"Let me see now, Jacqueline Chase, yes—she's thin, she's got black hair and green eyes, very pale ..." Now tell me Jacks, how would you describe *your* appearance? Would it be slim, black hair, green eyes, and pale complexion?'

'That description could easily be pinned to Snow White,' she said, 'but it doesn't mean they look anything alike.'

'That's precisely my point. Most people are incompetent when it comes to describing other people. If it came to the crunch and someone was asked to give a description of Jacqueline they could easily be talking about you now, couldn't they?'

'But why? Why am I here? Why have I been made out to be this … wait a minute, you said she was bullied at school. I remember … I was picked on. It's one of those memories that I told you about, it's unclear somehow, unreal, like I read a book and somehow managed to recall the story as my own life. How could Jacqueline's memories be in my head? And where is she now? If I'm her, does that mean she's me?'

Doctor Brodie placed the photograph carefully back into his briefcase. His frown deepened making him appear much older.

'I don't think so, Jacks. Look.' He showed her a medical record of which ended with her present predicament. 'This girl's records have been grafted with yours to make your switch seem more believable; they even changed her blood type to match your own. It was lucky for me that the nurse at her school kept her own files. You have completely different blood groups.

'I managed to speak with her mother; she hasn't seen Jacqueline in about a year. Apparently they had a big argument over some older man she'd been seeing—a rich man, and she ran off with him in the end; she sends postcards every couple of months from different locations.'

'So she could have replaced me then,' Jacks said.

'No, I don't think she's even alive. It would be too risky for whoever is behind this to let her take your place. I think that the only way in which she played your role was in posing for that X-ray. I believe she was killed simply to prove that you were in an accident.'

'But that's horrible, Kyle!' Jacks exclaimed. What makes you think that? How can she have been sending postcards if she's dead?'

'Who said that she wrote them? All that had to be accomplished, is a vaguely similar style of handwriting. Jacks, she can't have taken your place, wherever you are from, she would have to be a similar predicament, wouldn't she? There would be no point to it. I think that you are being kept out of the way for a reason. She would not have been allowed to live. What if she went home? All it would take is for someone to start asking questions and it wouldn't take long to discover that there are two of you.'

Jacks' head was swimming, the words in the medical report blurred before her eyes and she shook the feeling away.

'But who killed her?' she asked. 'Who's behind all this?'

'The rich man perhaps, whoever he is.'

'Kyle, how did you end up there in the first place?'

'I went to see your mother,' he said. 'I was angry and wanted to find out the truth. Although considering what I know now, it probably would have been fatal for me had we met with each other. I found out the address from the telephone number I had been given.

'What I found sent me cold. There was an empty office in an empty building, a solitary answer machine the only thing to be found. That was when I got really worried. I left a lot quieter than I broke in let me tell you. I got the school address from your records and decided that was my next port of call.'

Jacks' lips pursed tightly together. 'I knew all along that she wasn't my mother,' she said. 'I told you that there was something wrong.'

'I know, Jacks, and I wished I had listened to you sooner, but how was I to know? I thought your paranoia was all part of the reason you were here. What I really don't understand is why it's so essential to keep you alive. If someone wanted you out of the way, why not just kill you? We know that they are capable; why go to all the trouble and expense to put you in here? We have to find out exactly who is paying your bill.'

'Are you crazy?' Jacks said. 'If you start asking questions like that again, it shows that you did not accept the first answer; you'll be endangering yourself, besides, I've got a better plan. We are going to pretend everything is normal here. I'm the good little nutball patient and you the caring psychiatrist. Keeping up appearances does not arouse suspicion and keeps us both alive.

'When you leave here today, you will be paying a visit to an old friend of yours, the doctor who works at the hospital that I was transferred from. Patrick *was* trying to tell me things through the dreams all along; the presence of the doctor only became clear to me just before I remembered that Patrick was my brother.

'I've met your friend before, at a party I think. Part of my vision was mixed up with actual memories. He kissed my hand when I met him. When I met him at the hospital he behaved strangely, but back then, I thought he was being rude. I think he *recognised* me; that was why he was staring, that is why he looked at my records, and when he saw a different name to the one he expected, he walked away thinking that he had been mistaken, but he wasn't. He *knows* who I am, and you are going to find out!'

Nurse Wong's face appeared at the window, her sharp eyes peered down her pixie nose, but on seeing Jacks, her mouth gaped.

She entered. 'Jacqueline,' she said, 'how on Earth did you get back into this room without my seeing you?'

Jacks shot a look at Doctor Brodie and glanced at the clothes on the floor. The doctor instinctively placed his briefcase in front of them, and knocked his coat on top.

'I didn't leave this room, Sister,' she squeaked, 'I hid under the bed and must have fallen asleep. Bob came in and started to threaten me. He told me that he'd poisoned Nurse Cadeaux and that he was going to kill me. I tried to get out, to fetch you before you went home, but he locked the door, so I err, hid under the bed.'

The woman's disdainful look had returned. It was difficult to determine whether the nurse believed her or not. She always looked at Jacks as though she was a stain that the woman wanted removed.

'Nurse,' said Doctor Brodie, 'perhaps you could see about getting Jacks some food. Thank-you.'

She glared for a moment in a way that would have put Medusa's stony stare to shame, and then she left, obviously believing such a task below her pay grade.

The doctor picked up his coat and the wet clothes beneath it then took his briefcase in the other hand.

'How *did* you get in here without anyone seeing you, Jacks?' he asked.

Her face looked tired. She felt like an interrogated suspect who has been asked the same question repeatedly, as if the answer would eventually be different.

'I told you,' she said, 'I didn't leave the room.'

The doctor tried to smile. 'I know that trick; it's done with mirrors,' he said light-heartedly, but his face was uneasy. 'I'm going to pay a visit to a friend now. I'll see you as soon as I get back.'

The door opened again and Andy walked in.

'Good Morning Doctor Brodie,' he said. 'What have you there? You appear to be a little wet.'

The doctor gave a smile that actually did not smile, as the water dripped from the clothes onto his brown leather shoes.

'A slight accident with a water jug,' he said. 'If you'll excuse me.' He nodded to Andy and risked a glance back to Jacks, then left.

Jacks stared after him long after he had gone. Andy watched as she sat in quiet contemplation.

'Is there something going on between you two that I need be jealous about?' he asked.

Jacks looked up at him, amazed at the level of frivolity to which he would stoop, especially after the previous night's events.

Jacks sat back on the bench, inhaling the sweet scent of the surrounding flowers. She did not speak to Andy, and he decided not to pursue conversation in his usual boisterous manner. She became aware of his eyes upon her and glancing toward him she saw him watching her closely.

'I've upset you, haven't I?' he said.

She appeared slightly puzzled for a moment; so much had happened, she had almost forgotten that they had kissed.

'I'm sorry for having been so forward,' he continued, 'but I like you—a lot. I guess I had a bit too much testosterone running through my system after that fight. What with the thought of him hurting you, and then you lying there looking so helpless and beautiful; I couldn't help myself. Please forgive me, Jacks.'

She could not help but feel amused by Andy's behaviour. She had always thought that his conduct was due to him wanting to rebel against rules and set procedures, but now it seemed that his brash and flamboyant nature was a smokescreen, to cover his true feelings, disguising the truth with the truth.

'Hello Jacqueline.'

Jacks cringed at the voice of her would-be mother, using a name which was not her own. *What the hell is she doing here?* she thought. She swallowed, trying to calm herself. *I mustn't let her know what I've discovered.*

'Who is this gorgeous woman?' Andy said, back to his usual cocky self.

'Hi mum.' Jacks sounded indifferent, despite the fact that her insides felt as though they were set on spin dry.

The impostor bent down and kissed her on the cheek. Jacks tried desperately not to let her body stiffen with the disgust it felt. *This woman,* she thought, *had something to do with the death of two people, Jacqueline and my brother.* She envisioned herself wringing the woman's neck.

'I should have guessed,' said Andy. 'You look so alike.'

'No we don't,' Jacks snapped. *I'm never going to pull this off,* she thought.

The woman seated herself next to Jacks on the bench and Andy sat in Jacks' wheelchair.

'I'm sorry I haven't been to see you, Jacqueline...'

Blah blah blahdi blah. Jacks switched herself off, thinking of anything to get her mind off the woman ... *Yea, though I walk through the valley of the shadow of death, I will fear no evil: for thou art with me; thy rod and thy staff they comfort me. Thou preparest a table before me in the presence of mine enemies ...*

Was Meg right after all? Have I been placing myself in danger when I visited Patrick? Meg was quite correct about tuning in. Each time, the dreams have been a bit more coherent, not to mention the strange sensation on my recent return. My physical self was transported over; that never happened before, to my knowledge.

'Blah de blah blah godmother in England.'

'Yeah great whatever,' Jacks risked.

'You've not been listening to a word I've been saying, have you?' her impostor mother said.

Jacks could not control herself; she tried biting her tongue, but found it impossible. 'Sorry, 'kind of switched off after hello. It happens quite a bit to me; I am mental after all.' Her eyes challenged the woman, revealing more than she had meant to.

'I hear you've been having strange dreams, about Patrick.' The woman's voice was cool and testing.

Jacks knew that above all, she must react correctly or else it was over. A pressure was building in her head. She knew that Patrick was there; she could feel him. She just hoped that he would forgive her for what she was about to say.

'Yes they were really strange. There was this weird bloke and he never said a word to me in my dreams. Then the doctor explained to me how my sub-con-thingy had turned my pet dog into a man. Since then I've been dreaming of an Irish setter instead. Was Patrick a setter, Mum?'

'Yes dear, he was.'

Lying bitch! Jacks thought. She felt sick, having to make herself sound as thick and crass as the woman sat beside her, and she felt guilty for speaking about her brother in that way, but she had no choice.

The woman appeared satisfied with Jacks' reaction, but she kept glancing behind her as though she could see something. Jacks could not help but glance back too.

Patrick had a booted foot on the arm of the bench and leaned forward listening to the conversation. Jacks, aware of eyes upon her, pretended not to see him.

'What's wrong, mum? Why do you keep looking behind me?'

'I think I've got some grit in my eye,' the woman said. She obviously could not see Patrick, but saw something there, on the corner of her vision.

'Woof woof,' Patrick mocked.

Jacks bit her lip to stifle a laugh and coughed.

'I've been thinking of taking you over to England with me when I go,' said the woman, 'considering you're doing so well.'

Jacks was stunned. Every word was testing her.

'I don't want to go to England, mum.'

'But your godmother wants to see you.'

'I don't even remember her,' Jacks said.

'What about your sister, don't you miss her? Don't you miss me?'

Pass me the sick bucket please! Jacks thought. 'I'd rather you all see me when I'm better. I can't even walk properly yet.'

'That woman was in the car that knocked me down, Jacks,' Patrick's voice breathed in her ear.

Jacks' teeth clenched together as she imagined the sight of her brother crushed under the wheels of the car. *This woman knows who killed my brother,* she thought. *She was directly involved and helped to place me in my prison; she helped take my life away.*

Jacks could neither move nor speak. *I want the truth,* she thought. *I want revenge.* She fought for self-control, realising the woman was there for the simple reason of testing how well the plan was proceeding. If she suspected anything, then Jacks was as good as dead.

'Mum, I'm really hungry,' she said. 'I missed breakfast, and I'm tired. I don't want to seem rude, but I need to rest.'

She began to rise and Andy leapt to his feet, helping her into the wheelchair.

'Kept it warm for you,' he said.

'It was really nice to see you, mum. I would love to go away with you, but when I'm a little better, okay? Thanks for coming.'

Andy was quick to pick up on his cue to wheel her away. Jacks glanced back and saw the woman wave. Behind her, the figure of Patrick towered and waved as well.

At least five hours had passed since Doctor Brodie left her and there was still no word from him. She grew worried; his involvement placed him in danger. *What choice do I have?* she thought. *Still, I'll never forgive myself if something happens to him.*

Her evening meal arrived, delivered by the nurse who had fed her chocolate ice-cream, when she had first been admitted to hospital. The woman's hair had changed somewhat; her long locks, now dyed red, were sheared into a bob. Jacks wondered why she had not seen her in so long.

'Nurse,' she said, 'have you any idea how Nurse Cadeaux is doing?'

The woman gave a brief smile. 'She's better now, Miss Chase, she'll be doing the night shift this evening in fact. Now make sure you eat all of that! I hear you've not had much of an appetite lately,' she said, as she changed the water jug.

When Jacks had finished, she drank the accompanying orange juice down in one gulp. The nurse appeared satisfied and gathered the plate, leaving Jacks with a silent smile. Jacks felt thirsty and leaned over to pour a glass of water.

Another half an hour passed, and Kyle still wasn't back. Jacks wondered if they should have gone to the police after all, but knew if they had done so, they would never know exactly who had been involved. *The bastards would run like rabbits at the sight of a fox,* she thought, *and I need to know; I have to discover who killed Patrick.*

She had so many feelings developing within her—revenge, hate; she wanted them dead. She shocked herself; thoughts like that were so unlike her, but they were present nonetheless.

A solitary bead of perspiration trickled a path down her cheek to her slightly open mouth; she was almost panting. Her lips curled into a smile, as she tasted the salt water. She remembered the taste of it had reminded her of blood. Back then, she had been terrified, now it exhilarated her; she was an animal on the hunt—a ravening wolf.

Run Jacks, run.

Her limbs were seized with a new life and vigour.

Run Jacks, run, and all along I've been able to, haven't I? She snarled a slow smile. *I was never in a coma. My body would never have suffered in the same way. Somehow, they've managed to make my mind believe that I can't walk. Patrick tried to tell me.*

Run Jacks, run.

Her body seemed to twinge as if receiving shock treatment; her tongue groped around her jaws, tasting the sweat again; her breath heaving and her body tense as a bowstring. She was a stalking cat about to pounce. She could smell them—actually *smell* their blood. That is what she wanted—blood. Blood and vengeance.

Another shock ran through her body. She ran her hand through her hair—damp with sweat, trying to gain control.

All these feelings aren't like me, she thought. She felt so hot and peculiar. Eagerly draining the last of the water, she found her mouth remained dry. The strange perception was growing. Her vision seemed out of focus and yet as sharp as razor at the same instant. Time appeared to have slowed and yet seemed too quick for her to catch up with it.

Fear attacked her, choked her like a constrictor's deadly embrace. She had experienced the sensation before, if not so strong, when she had first awoken from the so-called coma.

Alarm bells rang inexorably in her mind, telling her how important it was for her to think clearly and yet they pealed so loudly as to serve to break her limited concentration.

Hospital.

Uniforms.

White and blue uniforms.

But I know I was moved, why is that suddenly so important?

Her eyes closed; it was not darkness that she saw, but white. *This feeling, the burning heat and anger, it was in the other hospital when it last afflicted me.*

The sensation of forgetting grew. Everything she had just brought into her head was fleeting, her mind being raped of memory.

NO.

She fought to hold onto something … anything.

Chocolate ice-cream.

'Chocolate ice-cream. Oh my God,' she repeated the word ten or more times, to give it a heavy enough imprint, therefore allowing it to last a while before being reaped by the ravenous locust of memory.

Chocolate ice-cream.

The nurse who had brought me chocolate ice-cream was from the other hospital!

The thought was going, going, gone.

She felt as if she were losing her mind and she was scared, scared that her memories would be wiped out, erased from her brain and she would become a vegetable.

Is this how they did it?

Did what?

The black patches in the corner of her eyes were growing, searching blindly for each other in order to create darkness absolute.

The sensation of panic left her empty head. She was still conscious and her eyes remained open. Now the only part of her left to take had surfaced, a part of her she would be unable to see under normal circumstances (except perhaps at a glimpse whilst dreaming), her deep subconscious, her id, the darkness within, uninhibited now by the constricts and rules of society and morality; the true self, stripped bare of its conscience.

Had the other part of herself been there, it would have been terrified by what it saw, but it would be her sense of right and wrong causing such fear. She met with what the more enlightened wishes to be at one with—the inner self, the hidden self, the true being. If anyone was ever enlightened enough to reach their destination, they would no longer have a place in civilised society; they would be locked up to deal themselves with the madness of their mind.

An image repeatedly appeared before her, each time growing stronger. For some reason it made Jacks think of a teddy bear.

Is it three circles?

Why a teddy bear? Perhaps I was abused as a child; this is after all where I would have banished any repressed memory. No, it's more like an insignia, a symbol.

The stronger the image appeared, the more Jacks realised how utterly important it was. She felt a sense of urgency, which she had never known before in the whole course of her existence.

It's the meaning of life, she decided. The image remained unclear and Jacks struggled, believing if she could decipher it then she would know everything. Yet still it reminded her of a teddy bear, or even the little battery-powered train she had had as a child, the one that played nursery rhymes; but it did not look like either.

She laughed, and yet knew that no sound had left her mouth. The insignia, the meaning of life …

Made in Taiwan.

The image drew away from her slightly. She had laughed; she had been ironic; she had attempted to reason; parts of her ego still existed and they were trying to break through. She could still see the symbol, but it was retreating. She reached out to it, not with her hand (for her limbs were leaden), but her mind. In her present state, her mind could achieve such feats. It was becoming clearer again.

Three, square, circles.

It was not the paradoxical symbols themselves that were important, but what lay beyond them. Light seemed to flicker at its edges, in a colour Jacks had not experienced before; it was almost violet, and yet nothing like. It was *beyond* colour. Staring unblinking into the shape, thoughts of pyramids entered her head for reasons unknown. She was so near, her body tingling, aware that it would change her life forever—that is, if she survived the experience. She did not care either way, the only thing of importance being, she had to know.

It was gone.

Darkness swallowed it as quickly as a frog licks an unsuspecting insect from the air.

She gaped, despondent, until she became aware of the light again, quivering behind the form of a man, whose long coat outlined by the magical colour made him appear so black that she yearned even more for that which lay beyond him.

'Nooooo,' she shrieked, outraged by her brother's interference.

'Jacks listen to me,' he said. 'You *must* not go there. What you will find is not what you expect. It will destroy your mind utterly. Such knowledge is not for you, or any other living creature, do you understand?'

And it was gone again. Completely

And then there was light; not much, but enough to distinguish dimly the features of her brother, and objects in the room were less black against a blacker backdrop.

'Jacks, you've been drugged, and she's given you an overdose, you have to pull out of it.'

Aphasic for a moment all she could utter was, 'Chocolate ice-cream.'

'Yes Jacks, chocolate ice-cream,' Patrick said. 'The bitch has drugged you, just as she did back then; that's why you attacked those people. You have to try to come back.'

'Was I about to meet God?' she asked, as if in a trance.

He ignored her.

'They must know then … that woman posing as my mother must have been suspicious. I thought I did quite well.'

Her vision was definitely returning. As the room grew brighter, Patrick faded away, until Jacks wondered whether he had actually been there at all. He may have been part of her mind warning her, helping her. It was at such times, she could be inclined to believe Kyle's theory about Patrick, had she not been stood on the battlements of a Danish castle, being heavily rained on the night before.

Feeling returned, and she found that her body still burned. Patrick had removed the blindness from her eyes, but had left the hate in her heart.

She could hear the voice of the bitch nurse outside the room and she scrambled to her feet, reaching instinctively for her book.

The door opened slowly.

'Jacks?' The voice sounded softer, different somehow. The nurse stepped in.

Though Jacks' vision was blurred, she saw the outline of bobbed red hair and swung the Complete Works of Shakespeare full force into the woman's face. The woman fell to the ground with a thud. Jacks could hear her speaking, but could not distinguish the words.

'I'm going to kill you, you fucking bitch!' Jacks heard herself screech.

She kicked the nurse in the ribcage then struck her around the back of the head with the book. The woman cried out and Jacks sprang at her, punching, kicking, clawing her face, determined to tear her apart piece by piece.

Strong arms dragged her back.

'Oh my God,' a voice said, and Nurse Wong ran to the woman's side.

Jacks kicked and struggled, afraid that Wong was going to help the bitch.

'What have you done?' The senior nurse's voice had lost completely, its controlled edge.

'Is she dead?' spoke another voice, a voice that made Jacks' blood run cold.

She froze, turning slowly.

'No, she's still breathing. LET'S GET SOME HELP IN HERE!'

Jacks' eyes met with the hard look of the psycho nurse. She jerked her head back to her victim, the misty veil lifting from her sight. She fell back, unable to breathe. As the tranquilliser took effect, she saw a crowd of medical staff around the bloody heap that was Nurse Cadeaux.

Chapter Fourteen

Time's glory is to calm contending kings,
To unmask falsehood and bring truth to light,
To stamp the seal of time in aged things,
To wake the morn and sentinel the night,
To wrong the wronger till he render right,

William Shakespeare

Jacks awoke to find herself in a dimly lit room. There was no bedside cabinet, no lamp, no chairs, and no window; just her and the bed in a battleship grey room, a murky, forty-Watt light bulb above, and no light-shade. She attempted to rise, but found thick white straps restrained her hands and feet. It was not part of the building likely to be shown to visitors, who were led to believe their cash was being spent on the least painful, most comfortably luxurious treatment their money could buy; imprisonment was not something they tended to promote in their sales manual.

She listened hard, straining to hear any noise beyond the door and struggled to break free of the bonds, but her efforts were in vain. She was parched, but the drug-induced sensation of her mouth feeling like sand had dispersed.

Wondering how long she had been kept in such a state, inevitably, her thoughts arrived to Nurse Cadeaux. She remembered, as if from some horrible nightmare, her friend's face lacerated by her own fingernails.

She looked at them.

At least they cleaned the blood off, she thought.

She felt thoroughly wretched, wishing that she had been able to control herself. *But that's what the drug does isn't it? Its main function is to make me lose control, convincing everyone I'm crazy.*

Overwhelming frustration arose at the thought of the smug nurse standing at the scene of the crime, apathetic to what had occurred.

She knew, Jacks realised. *She knew I'd figured out what's going on, just as my phoney mother knew. My life is over, or soon will be. I'm probably not even in hospital grounds any longer.*

Several clicking sounds chorused at the metal door, and then it swung open to reveal Doctor Brodie, followed by a man of medium height with brown hair. He was dressed in black and appeared rather thespian-like; he did not walk into the room so much as, glide.

Kyle rushed over to Jacks, who cried involuntarily. He immediately set to releasing her from her restraints. As soon as her arms were free, she sat up and awkwardly threw her arms about his neck, sobbing. He returned the embrace forcibly, one arm about her back the other held her head, his fingers buried deep in the black locks of her hair. For a moment, they clung to each other, all thoughts of ethics and propriety gone.

'It's all right, Jacks, it's all right.' He drew away, stroked the hair out of her face and caressed her cheek.

He was dangerously close to her; she could even hear his breathing. His eyes locked on her in the same way hers were on him. She glanced at his slightly parted lips, and then back to those glorious eyes. They leaned in toward each other and her whole being was aflame, but it was a very different experience than caused by the drug.

There was a polite cough and the other man spoke.

'Would you like me to leave?'

The two drew apart in an instant, each blushing in their turn.

'Er, Jacks, allow me to introduce an old friend of mine, this is ...'

The man stepped boldly forward.

'Alberto,' he announced proudly with a fake Italian accent. With a dramatic sweep of his arm, he grabbed Jacks' hand, giving it a series of tiny kisses. 'Ah Chante` Mademoiselle.'

'He's more commonly known as Tim,' Kyle said dryly.

Jacks laughed, and Tim backed off, seeming a little put out, while Doctor Brodie proceeded to release her legs from the remaining bonds. Tim then handed him some items from his briefcase.

'Kyle, have you been told what I did?' Jacks asked. 'I attacked Nurse Cadeaux. Is she all right? I need to know.'

The doctor's face was grave. 'She's going to live, if that is what you mean. Why did you do it?'

Jacks proceeded to explain how the impostor nurse had drugged her and how it had made her react. By the time she had finished her tale, she was weeping again, remembering vividly what she had done to her friend.

'We've got to get you out of here,' Kyle said.

Jacks could not believe what she was about to say.

'But I almost killed someone. If you take me away, won't you be breaking the law? You might lose your position.'

He glanced briefly at Tim, and then placing the documents on the bed, he removed a small syringe from his case.

'I'm going to take a blood sample,' he said. 'It's possible that there'll be some trace of the drug in your system, if so it may show up on a tox' screen and we can use it as evidence; we've gathered quite a bit already.'

As the doctor drew the blood, Jacks picked up the paperwork from the bed. Two photographs were among them.

'It's me!' she cried.

She was wearing a cap and gown and was holding a degree. The other picture was of a group of students of which she assumed she was one.

'These photographs were taken the day you graduated, Jacks,' Doctor Brodie said.

She gaped at the pictures and then at the two men at her side.

'Your name is Jackie Denise Rothschild,' he paused, expecting that the mere mention of her true name would be enough to help her recall. When it became apparent more information was required for such a task, he continued.

'You are twenty-five years of age; you graduated last year, in radiology. While at university you seemed to take an avid interest in the performance arts and you joined the dramatic society, where you excelled in the roles of Lady Macbeth and, perhaps more importantly, Hamlet.'

Jacks had to remind herself to breathe. She was finally hearing what she had wanted to know ever since she woke up in a psychiatric hospital, but it was all so unexpected. After convincing herself several personal facts were not true, she now discovered that they had been very close to the mark after all.

'It was at a ball at your family home,' continued Kyle, ' that you met my friend Eric. The host of that soirée was your brother, Patrick,' he paused, observing her for a moment as if to determine how she was coping. 'Patrick was a medical graduate, like yourself, but gave up medicine to go on to help run the family business, until he met with a tragic car accident just before Christmas last year. He was only thirty when he died. On hearing the news, Jackie, so distraught, said that she needed time away from it all, and flew off to India, to 'save the tigers'.

'On the event of your father's death, the whole estate, the multi-million dollar business, *everything*, now goes to you, his last surviving heir. The inheritance is set up in trust and it is not until your thirtieth birthday that you can take sole control over your inheritance. Apparently, your father wanted to give you time to study before burdening you with heavy responsibility. The will names a small board of trustees and until you come of age, they have control over billions of dollars.

'Once your father dies, they will gain sole control over the money. That is why they are keeping you alive. Once your father dies and it is discovered that you are not in Bengal, but non-compos mentis, control of your money passes over to the board of trustees. As long as you are in here and are certified insane, they will have your money and it will be perfectly legal.'

'But I'm not in here, Jacqueline Chase is.'

'That's true; I suppose it was easier to keep your identity hidden until your father was out of the picture. After that, your duplicate personality could be passed off as part of your condition. After all, whoever is behind this, had enough knowledge and contacts, to land you in here in the first place and the fact that it's costing them so much, is a small investment considering the eventual return.

'At a guess, I'd say we are running out of time. Your father probably doesn't have long to live.

They couldn't kill him too soon after the death of your brother, as it may have aroused suspicion, but my estimate is that, they have been weaving their webs about your father's life, as expertly as they have controlled your own. The people behind this will be trusted, perhaps close friends of your family. They are going to have access to your father and ...'

'Enough! I've heard enough.' Jacks wailed. Her chest felt tight and she fought for air. Her body shook with both fear and anger. 'How did they make me forget? How did they take my whole life away?' she sobbed.

'I think that is where I step in, fair maiden. Kyle thought that you might have been hypnotised. I am a hyp ...'

Was as much as Tim managed to say, before Jacks dived at him and attempted to wring his neck. She snarled like a wild animal, when Doctor Brodie attempted to pull her away; her eyes turned to him, blazing, but despite their ferocious anger, they were empty somehow, as if the human element had been removed. She struck out with her fist. Tim managed to push her away from him and he fell coughing to the floor. Jacks made another spring toward him, but Doctor Brodie grabbed her tightly in a bear hug from behind. She gave a throat-tearing scream and struggled, lashing out with her feet.

'Jacks, listen to me, hear my voice. It's me, Kyle. Come back to me, Jacks. Come back, *please,*' he pleaded.

Her body vibrated with animal energy. Her breath slowed somewhat and he felt her relax in his arms.

'Oh my God,' she cried. 'What happened? What did I do?'

Kyle relinquished his hold on her, and stood up straight, smoothing out his ruffled appearance.

'Tim, I thought I told you not to say anything unless she was restrained.'

Jacks swerved abruptly to face him. Tears stung her eyes.

'It's all right, Jacks; it wasn't your fault,' he said. 'Now you have to trust me, okay? We need to get you back into those restraints.'

She backed away, shaking her head. 'Why?' she asked.

'Because we're going to help you, but we can't do that if you keep attacking us, now can we? And we're not sure exactly what words are used to trigger your violent behaviour.'

Tim got to his feet, the purple tone having left his face. Jacks lay back onto the bed while they strapped her in, feeling strangely like a magician's assistant about to be sawn in two. Tim's face lowered over her and he smiled mischievously.

'Now I have you right where I want you,' he said.

Jacks heart stopped, until Kyle told Tim to stop messing around and be serious.

'Now Jacks, I want you to look directly into my eyes, all right? Thatta girl,' Tim said. 'Do not look away, just stare at my eyes, and listen to the sound of my voice. Look into my eyes and listen to the sound of my voice. You will begin to feel tired, Jacks, Are you feeling tired?'

'Yes.' She answered blankly.

'Can you tell me your name?'

'Jacks,' she replied.

'Can you tell me your full name, Jacks?' he asked.'

Her head swung violently from side to side. 'Noo, I'm not supposed to,' she struggled.

'Jacks, listen to me. Your name is Jackie Rothschild. I want you to remember. You have been given words to commit to memory—special words. Can you tell me what they are?'

'Hypnotism …' Jacks shook her head and struggled violently to break free from her restraints. 'You will not touch him,' she growled, madness in her eyes. Her back arched and she collapsed into the bed, thrashing and pulling.

'Jacks, who do you think we're trying to harm?'

'My father.'

'What other words Jacks, think, concentrate,' Kyle butted in.

Tim shot him a look to quiet him down. 'Jacks, we are not going to harm your father,' he said, 'do you understand?'

Her face filled with anguish and she struggled against believing what the depths of her mind seem to make so clear to her.

'I want you to relax. I want your sleep, to be peaceful. Sleep now.'

The tension lifted from her features and her body sagged.

'Tell me the other words, Jacks.'

'Hypnotherapy, trance, hypnotist,' she said robotically.

'Jacks, when you hear these words, what do you see?'

'You, you are holding a gun to his head,' she droned. 'You say you are going to shoot, but I know that I can stop you. I can move faster than the bullet, I can take you by surprise, and I will kill you.'

The two men exchanged worried glances.

'Whenever you hear these words now, your father will not be in any danger, and you will not need to protect him; you will simply smile. Do you understand?'

'Yes.'

'How long did you spend with the person who spoke to you as I do now, Jacks?'

'From the day of Patrick's funeral, to the day I was placed into the hospital.'

'Five months!' Doctor Brodie exclaimed, in horror.

Tim gave him another warning glance. 'Why were you kept away for that long, Jacks?' he asked.

'Because they wanted to wipe my memory and give me a new one, but Patrick kept talking to me; it made their task more difficult.'

Tim looked to Kyle, who shrugged.

'Jacks, do you know who put you in a trance? Can you give us a name?'

Jacks began to wheeze; her body went rigid as if she was having a fit, and she could not breathe. Doctor Brodie dashed to her side, but Tim held him back.

'It's all right,' he said. 'I don't need to know. You can relax again now. No one is strangling you. Relax, breathe, that's it.' Tim moved away from Jacks and signalled for the doctor to join him.

'I could take her into deep regression, but to be honest it would be dangerous,' he explained. 'Who knows how many fail-safes this sick bastard has managed to implement. He's had five months for Christ's sake! It's a miracle that she has an ounce of sanity remaining after such an extreme bout of mental torture; it must have been hell.

'I've learned of a few cases where my art has been used for criminal purposes, but this is the first time I've experienced one first hand. I feel sick! Whoever did this had to overcome her conscience, which would tell her to kill is wrong, and implant a scenario where killing is acceptable. They would have had to run experiment after experiment. God only knows what horrors she had to endure.'

The doctor's face seemed ashen. His eyes fixed on the floor, dark contemplation filling them.

'Jacks, I'm going to count back from ten,' Tim said. 'When I reach one, I want you to wake up and remember everything that we have discussed. Ten, nine, eight, seven, six, five, four, three, two, one.'

Her eyes blinked and she saw Tim smiling down at her. She breathed heavily, the weight of years lifting from her shoulders.

'Can you let me out of these now please,' she said, rattling the restraints. As she was released, she sprung to her feet and headed for the door. 'Well come on then. We have to save my father.'

'Don't you think that we should ring him first?' Tim asked. 'I mean, if we start running out of here with a certified psycho, no offence of course, then I think we can pretty much assume that whoever's behind all this will get to hear about it. The old guy will have a bullet in the head long before we ever arrive, and you can be sure they'll make it look like a suicide.'

'Do you honestly think that someone with as much capital as my father is going to answer the phone? If whoever answers it, is part of this conspiracy, and Kyle or I asks to speak to him, then my father is as good as dead. We have to think of a way to warn him.'

'Tim, you could drive over there,' Doctor Brodie suggested. 'No one knows who you are.'

'Including my father, he'd probably not even agree to speak to him.'

Jacks snatched up the Dictaphone from Kyle's case and began a heartrending speech to her father. On completing it, the men could see the tears in her eyes.

Tim smiled. 'Good thinking darl',' he said. 'Have you got your mobile, Kyle?'

The doctor nodded.

'Then I'll keep in touch. Adios amigos.' Grabbing the briefcase, Tim made his exit in a cliché manner.

'What do we do now?' Jacks asked.

'Sit and wait I suppose. You okay?'

She smiled. 'I guess so,' she said. 'I'm really thirsty though. Do you think that you could fetch me something to drink?'

'No problem,' he said, jumping to his feet. 'Be back in a sec.'

As he opened the door, she heard a terrible caterwauling outside, as some unfortunate was being taken back to their room. She supposed that the rooms in that section must be soundproofed.

The doctor had not been gone long, when Jacks heard the lock opening. She looked up smiling, and then started slightly on seeing Andy in the doorway.

'Come on, Jacks, let's go,' he said urgently.

'What! Go where?'

'I don't know yet,' Andy replied. 'All I know is that I've got to get you out of here. Doctor Brodie sent me; he's concerned for your safety.'

'Where is he?' she said, trying not to let her trembling become noticeable.

'He's in a full on fistfight with one of the auxiliaries, who incidentally was on his way to see you, to put you to sleep permanently, if you take my meaning. I ran to help him, but he screeched at me telling me to get you to safety, so let's go!'

Jacks sprung to her feet and dashed forward.

'We've got to help him, Andy,' she cried.

'Sure thing, princess, whatever you say. Just let's not get caught in this bottleneck.'

Jacks felt a cold sweat break out. *What did he call me?* she thought. *Princess? He's called me that before, but when?*

He hadn't used that nickname in all the time she'd been there. It was Doctor Brodie who had said it, and the word had triggered off something in her mind. Only then, she couldn't remember what …

'*Care to dance, princess?*'

'*David, I'd rather waltz into the fires of hell than to spend more than ten seconds in the company of a slimy leech such as yourself. Now get out of my way, you horrid man before I call my brother and inform him that you were making lewd advances.*' …

'*I don't know why you dragged me to his stupid wedding anyway; you know I can't stand him.*'

'*He's my friend. Besides, who else would I bring?*'…

'*Whatever this is, whatever you hope to achieve here, you will fail, like you always fail. You are nothing but a drunken, egotistical waste of space. My father will see you rot for this!*'

'*Well aren't you the little princess; you always know it all. I'll teach you …*'…

'*I was never good enough for you was I, princess? Even Patrick thought that. He was my best friend and still he wouldn't let me have you.*'…

'*Beware your friend, Jacks.*'…

'It's you!' Jacks cried. 'It was you all along … *David!*'

A look of apathy crossed his features as he closed the door and stood with his back against it.

Chapter Fifteen

Ophelia: You must sing 'A-down, a-down', and you call him a-down-a. O, how the wheel becomes it! It is the false steward, that stole his master's daughter.

Laertes: This nothing's more than matter.

Ophelia: There's rosemary, that's for remembrance; pray you, love, remember. And there is pansies, that's for thoughts.

Leartes: A document in madness—thoughts and remembrance fitted.

(Hamlet: William Shakespeare)

'Check mate,' David said. 'I must say, Jacks I am utterly amazed how you managed to remember me; but then you were always a remarkable woman, in many ways.'

Her memories flooded back, uncontrollable and painful, the fragments she had preserved, contained in dream imagery that Patrick forced her to relive. She recalled David's wedding. He was married to Trudi, accept Trudi was not her sister, neither was Trudi her name. She had been one of a long line of women only too pleased cater to David's every whim, including Jacqueline Chase.

'You bastard; you killed my brother!' she cried. He was your best friend and you murdered him.'

'What are friends for, if not to help one another? He helped me to realise my dream, and I'm making it come true.'

'I fail to see what Patrick gained from it,' she said.

He smiled wickedly, clearly enjoying himself. 'Well let's see. Patrick gets to rest in peace. He was after all such a tormented soul. He was *obsessed* with you, you ungrateful bitch. He adored you, even more than me I think. Do you not remember all the things he did for you? And you gave him *nothing*. I put the stupid wowser out of his misery. You should have seen his face when he saw that it was *me* behind the wheel, of course once I'd backed over him a few times there wasn't actually much left of his face.'

Jacks howled and leapt toward him. His reaction was startlingly quick and he punched her half-heartedly in the face. Her nose felt as though stung by invisible bees. The blood began to ooze, but Jacks pushed back the pain. David tilted his head, smiling, and reached out to catch a droplet of blood as he had done her tear, back when she had thought him her friend. He raised his finger to his mouth and he unravelled his tongue to lap her blood up like a filthy rodent.

Sickened by his indecent theft, Jacks gave him a swift knee in his genitals. His entire form fell forward, but he retaliated quicker than she would have thought possible, backslapping her with enough force to send her hurtling backward. He leaned back against the door, guarding against her escape and nursing an aching crotch.

'Jacks, there's no way that you can stop me, and there's nowhere for you to run.'

'You did all of this for money. You killed my brother and that girl, and you're going to murder me too, all for money.' Her voice seethed with detest and loathing for the creature that stood before her.

'Well yes,' he said, in a puzzled tone, as if he actually needed another reason. 'And *us* of course; I know that you thought that I wasn't good enough for you before, but you've changed; I've changed you, and for your past mistreatments, I forgive you,' he said, in a patronising tone.

'You're insane,' Jacks hissed, incredulous to the fact that such an unstable man could have created and executed the tremendous plot.

He approached her slowly, stalking … closing.

'Come now, Jacks, you kissed me, or had you forgotten that?'

'You kissed me, you moron!' she raved. 'It's not the same thing.'

'True, but strange, I don't remember hearing any complaints at the time. I was your hero that night; the night I saved you from the clutches of big bad Bob. Actually, I was quite lucky I came in to see you when I did; he really meant to kill you, you know, silly man. However, he was very reasonable once I stuck a few notes under his nose. He played his part beautifully; he should go on the stage. Strange though, he never did collect the rest of his payoff … I wonder why.'

'I told you, he was killed,' Jacks said, trying to curb her temper, which she had lost some time ago. She needed to stall, knowing that Kyle couldn't be far away, if she could just distract David long enough …

'What about your wife?' she said, through gritted teeth.

'You mean your dear sister? Impressive that you can distinguish the truth after what I put you through, although it doesn't matter; I had always intended to return your identity eventually; who better than my loyal wife, to play dear Trudi? Although why you kept calling her that, I never quite determined. I tried to programme her as Sarah. That was the name of Jacqueline's sister, and it concerned me that you insisted on misnaming her.'

'Gertrude was Hamlet's mother,' Jack said coldly. 'She slept with the enemy.'

'I see,' David said, with a laugh, 'and Claude? Ah yes, Claudius—the treacherous king. Your infatuation was an interesting experiment though, don't you think? I wanted you to lose control, to love me and yet love someone who was truly beneath you. In that way you would feel grateful when you realised that I could not only reciprocate your feelings, but also offer you a life worthy of you.

'You should have seen how you reacted when I kept throwing obstacles in your way. You cried yourself to sleep some nights; it was quite moving. You once told me that I had no discipline; well you were wrong; you don't know how difficult it was not to give into you when you begged me to take you in my arms. You knelt at my feet and offered yourself to me, and still I turned you away. I would say that I am the most disciplined man I know. But now there's no more pretending.'

He was some feet away from her. Instinct snapped her into action and she sprinted to the exit. His arm shot out and grabbed her, throwing her to the bed; he was on top of her in a second. She kicked at him, but he dismissed the pain and grinned savagely over her, his fingers finding the split in her robe and entered, fondling her thighs with an excited hand.

She punched him full on in the face. Both his arms grabbed her own and wrestled them above her head, pinning them. She continued to kick with her legs, but he seemed to enjoy each blow as it struck. Straining, she tried to wrench free her arms, but with his entire weight beating down on her, it made little difference.

He had to let go of one of her arms while he strapped the other in. She scratched him, screaming with frustration as he gasped, delighted by the struggle. As she realised her efforts were pointless, her body went limp. He looked at her, a mad light in his eyes. Taking his hands away, he saw that she no longer resisted him. Gently, he lifted her other hand and placed it in the restraint.

She stared blankly forward.

Smiling fiendishly, he peeled open her gown; the sight that met his eager eyes caused him to pause, panting softly. Still Jacks made no move. She seemed trance-like, but he did not care. His hands grabbed her breasts roughly and squeezed them together, toying with them until her nipples grew hard at his touch. He bent over and kissed her neck, then bit it lightly. Working his way down her naked body, he pawed, panted, licked and bit, until he reached her womanhood, there he gasped.

'You don't know how long I've waited for this,' he drooled. 'You gave me my first hard on when you were only eleven.'

He brought his mouth close to her opening and breathed, slobbering onto the sheets, like a dog. Jacks opened her legs, as if welcoming him in. He gave a cry of excitement and sat up, unbuttoning his fly with trembling fingers. His penis burst out, full and erect in his waiting hands and Jacks made her move. This time he was so wrapped up in ecstasy, that he was completely unprepared for her retaliation. She kicked him in his left temple. There was little power behind the impact due to her awkward position, but it was enough to stun him. Her knee drew up to her chest and she rammed her foot down swiftly into his manhood, hitting her target with ease. He screamed, backing away like a beaten puppy.

'You can fuck me if you like, Davie, but it's gonna hurt,' she snarled.

His eyes were tearful and his speech strained as he fought the rising sickness in his abdomen.

'You bitch,' he hissed, 'you're damn right I'm going to fuck you. You're mine; your money's mine, and I'll fuck you till you bleed!'

Jacks laughed. 'You'll have to put some ice on it first, lover boy,' she sneered.

'I'm going to kill you, you fucking bitch,' he hollered.

'Come now, David, all's fair in love and war, and please refrain from using such language around me; I know a dropout such as yourself may not have the widest of vocabularies, but I'm quite certain that you can think of something a little more constructive to say. Now, tell me again how you murdered my brother.'

'Why?' he asked. 'Does it excite you?' He grimaced, as he rose painfully to his feet, nursing his groin.

'No,' Jacks replied, 'because he wants to hear what you have to say.'

'Who does?' David croaked, as he slithered toward her once more. He stopped suddenly, blinking as one of her restraints then the other snapped and she sat up haughtily covering her nakedness. The image of Patrick formed before David's eyes. His hand rested on his sister's shoulder like a grotesque family portrait, silent, still and staring, their eyes filled with murderous intent.

David's lips quivered and he backed away. He opened his mouth, but only a squeak issued forth.

Turning, he fled, his throbbing member still jangling from the open fly.

His terrified hands grabbed the door and yanked it open. The walls seemed to ripple as though the room was merely a reflection in a lake, but he was too terrified to notice. Screams drifted in from the open door, insane and inhuman. His foot took a step out, but he immediately scrambled back, shrinking and stumbling as he saw the nothingness that awaited him.

With a yelp, he slammed the door; the walls quivered more noticeably and backing away, he clutched desperately to the end of the bed, as if he expected the floor to vanish at any moment.

'What's happening?' he screamed.

The power instilled in the place seemed to possess Jacks utterly. All signs of her former compassion were gone, no doubt drifting merrily along in a time where there still existed meadows of green. There, in that place, her own hatred and Patrick's thoughts of revenge, seduced her utterly.

She watched, without feeling, as Patrick approached the pleading form of David. Tears streamed as the man begged for mercy and forgiveness; it was not a place to which such things belonged, however. Patrick gripped him firmly about the collar and hauled him up, until his feet were dangling in the air, then he dropped him. His whole body quaked with fear as Patrick's fingers spread and plunged into his arms, as though they were jelly, burning, searing.

David screamed.

Jacks looked away, not from fear or revulsion, more because she realised that she *should* feel such things. The mutilation of David did not appease the bloodlust she felt; she remained empty and hollow, and the emptiness filled up every second with the rottenness which existed in that place. She realised that Meg had been right. Patrick *had* changed. The brother she knew would never kill; he could not even abide their father fishing. She felt keenly the loss; she had not only lost her brother to death, but chaotic madness.

What was I thinking? she thought. *That the hand of revenge would be dealt and Patrick would be at peace? How very naïve.*

The room seemed to swell and then burst, as if it were no more than a bubble, to reveal the true horrors hidden from her before. She had finally reached the coherence of which she had been warned, but now questioned whether Patrick would protect her from the endless terrors that waited.

It was the smell that first caught her attention; the putrid stench of rotting flesh, the sickly kind of scent that certain orchids can imitate to entice insects for the purpose of consumption. The ground seemed to pulsate as she walked, as though it was alive. Dark patches of dried blood stained here and there, and a fresh trail had formed from where Patrick dragged David.

Human remains were scattered and piled, and Jacks wondered how many people actually visited the place in order to create the extent of the décor. The space was cavern-like, vast beyond imagining. In parts, the darkness seemed tangible, malleable, as though wrought by the night terrors of the living.

Jacks saw dark shapes about her. Moans and screams seemed to pull at her eardrums until she thought she would run mad with the pain and so join the deafening chorus.

Patrick was in the distance and she hurried after him, fearful of the close proximity of the shadowy shapes. A cranking sound ensued, like an ancient torture device resurrected after many centuries of dormancy. A quiet sound of a music box drew her eyes upward and she saw thousands of columns whose dark metal looked like slithering snake skin, each of which was instilled with a life-force of its own, each bearing a different hate, at the summit of which were the bodily remains of beings who had been the object of grudges of the dead.

A wheel turned slowly, a contraption Jacks had seen the like of before, a medieval torture device used during the persecution of witches. At the foot of the snakelike pillar, swayed the resembling figure of a woman, dressed in puritan attire, who Jacks guessed to have been tried and executed for witchcraft, and so sought revenge on her accuser. *But that would have been centuries ago,* she considered. Yet the body was still recognisably human, no putrefying corpse. She gazed into the man's open eyes morbidly fixated for a moment, as he span around and around.

Time had no meaning there, and whether the man was indeed still alive, or simply a shadow of the past; he was destined to remain forever. For in that place, eternity was a reality; it was part of daily existence. There was no escape from the endless suffering for either party; it being a symbiotic fortune that continued into infinity.

Amongst the millions of minds crying out in pain, Jacks distinguished a sound she recognised. It was the scream of Bob; the pieces of his carcass embedded into a revolving contraption, to better display to all, the remains of the kill. Jacks backed away on seeing a solitary eye staring down at her—pleading.

A fold of skin blinked over it and it stared again before revolving out of sight. Patrick stood at the foot of a nearby pillar, seeming to admire his handy work, as David was slowly grated to death, his pain and falling flesh feeding the desire of the pedestal that bore him.

Jacks could feel the cold hand of fear finally catch up with her. It was a sensation that began in the depth of her stomach. It seemed to be triggered by the screams, but pulsated in unison with the ground. She tried to calm her breathing, knowing that she would be lost forever if she panicked.

I've got to get out of here, she thought, *while I still have an ounce of sanity left.* She turned, in order to flee toward the direction in which she had come, hoping to find a way back.

Hundreds of the damned stood on mass, having crept up silently behind—a wall of the dead, blocking her retreat.

'Come now, Jacks, did you honestly think I would let you go?'

She turned and saw Patrick advance.

'You owe me your life,' he said. 'It belongs to me. You and I will be together for blissful eternity. Does that not make you happy?'

She replied carefully, trying desperately to keep control of her terrified mind.

'Patrick, I don't belong here; surely you must see that.'

'Oh but you do,' he said. 'How else would I have achieved this glorious vengeance without you aiding me every step of the way? Look.' He signalled behind her.

She turned, reluctant to face the horrific legion.

'They were impressed by your work and will be only too happy for you to remain and help us continue in ours.'

He drew in close behind her and gently massaged her shoulders. She felt no warmth from the gesture and turned to face the man who had once been her brother, hoping to see some trace of feeling.

'Please Patrick, don't do this,' she whispered. Despite her efforts to hold back the tears, a couple escaped and fell to the ground to be swallowed with a hiss by the evil beneath her feet.

He kissed her lightly on the mouth. His lips were cold and an icy feeling spread across her body.

'No tears, Jackie; I insist,' he said. 'You must let go of your past sentimentalities; you will find no use for them here. Look Jacks, look upon our glorious achievement.'

Jacks *did* look. She saw the rippling skin of thousands of pinnacles and wondered if she was to destroy one, if the soul trapped there would then be free. The ground shuddered a warning beneath her and she smiled slowly, knowing her assumption to be correct.

Patrick held out his hand toward her and she took it, hoping to disguise her trembling fear. They walked amongst the host of the tormented and she thought hard of simple joys in order to hold onto her sanity—eating, drinking, flowers, the sky, Doctor Lawrence Kyle Brodie.

There has to be a way out, she thought. Concentrating hard, she tried to recall everything Meg had told her.

'You are very quiet, my dearest Jacks. What is on your mind?' Patrick asked nonchalantly.

'Apart from "a million screaming souls", nothing at all,' she replied.

She had quoted Meg half in jest, but the humour was absorbed instantly and Patrick stared at her icily. She began to see a vision of Meg in her mind. *Always keep one eye on reality. That is what Meg said,* Jacks thought and it gave her an idea. She envisioned the scene in her mind. She was part of that world now and it did not prove too difficult.

A coverlet of snow settled gently about her. The glistening white veil shrouded the garden's summer glory. The flowers looked beautiful yet disturbing in their frozen state. All was quiet and still; it was as though a moment of time had stopped and been subdued to the cold to keep it intact.

'Why have you brought us here?' Patrick enquired as he paced about, his heavy boots crunching the snow underfoot.

'I think it's beautiful,' Jacks lied, looking about her, searching for a specific thing—her way home.

'Beauty has no place here,' Patrick said.

'And yet it can still exist,' Jacks snapped back. 'I can make it real, just as you did. If I am to remain here, brother, then you cannot deny me beauty.' She shivered, looking down at her bare feet and flimsy robe. She watched as the fabric darkened and grew until she had created a copy of Patrick's garb.

He smiled wryly. 'My dear sister,' he said, 'I'm afraid you have no choice; either way, you will remain.'

Jacks walked purposely to the sunlounger and seated herself, beckoning to Patrick, who approached and stood towering above her.

'Do you recognise this place?' she asked. 'You brought me here some time ago, do you remember?'

He stared at her, his eyes hard. She stood and kissed him quickly on the cheek then stepped away.

'I love you, Patrick,' she said. 'I just want you to know that.'

His eyes narrowed slightly and suspicion filled his twisted mind. He made a grab for her, but too late; she sprinted toward the hospital bed. Before, it had horrified her, now she dived toward it; it was her solace—her saviour. The outraged screech of her dead brother echoed into the darkened room.

Jacks sat for a moment, catching her breath; her body shook violently as she fought to regain synchronism with her surroundings. She found it difficult, feeling as though she was phasing in and out, existing neither on Earth nor in Patrick's dimension. Visions of the horrors she had seen, flickered in a pulsating rhythm before her eyes, keeping in time with the terrible life force present in that chaotic domain.

She staggered through the door and appeared into the hallway, her image still faint and unable to regain solidity. The nurses sat chatting to one another, failing to notice Jacks' wavering form. The lift doors opened to reveal Doctor Brodie, his greyish pallor revealing his deep anxiety.

With horror, Jacks could see that he had not acknowledged her, despite the fact that they were face to face. She shook her head in disbelief as he stepped forward and walked straight through her. A gushing sound rushed through her ears, and for a fraction of a second she heard clearly again, the screaming of the tortured dead. Her mouth opened and a bloodcurdling scream issued forth. The anger, frustration and fear of all that had happened to her, were encapsulated in that cry.

The doctor paused as if he sensed, rather than heard, the sound. As the scream came to a close, she reached forward with gritted teeth, focusing all her attention on her hand and grabbed the doctor by the collar of his jacket, yanking him violently back into the lift. He turned in fright, mumbling a few inaudible words of exclamation. Jacks pressed G on the number pad and the lift began its descent.

Kyle stared at her incredulously.

'Jacks, my God!' he cried. 'Where did you come from? How did you get out of that room?'

Her body still trembled uncontrollably. She reached out, wanting to make sure she was real enough to touch him. She felt the woven wool thread of his coat beneath her fingertips and lurched forward into a desperate embrace. He held her tightly to him and spoke no words.

'*Ground Floor,*' the elevator said.

'We have to get out of here, Kyle,' she urged. 'I don't care where we go, but I'm out of here *now*.'

He began to speak, but she grabbed his hand and dragged him into the foyer` before the words left his mouth. She looked around helplessly and put her hands to her head.

'Jacks, what is it?' he asked.

'I don't know. This just isn't right. Part of me is still there I think and I don't know how to bring it back.'

She ran forward; Doctor Brodie glanced back to reception, the guard smiled and waved at him. The doctor's face contorted when he saw that the man had no eyes. The windows seemed to bulge and swell like a child blowing an enormous bubble.

They ran.

Glancing back, Jacks saw the strained glass pulsating. She lunged left dragging the doctor with her and they fell to the ground just as the front of the building exploded into a million shards. They lay for a moment, catching their breath.

'That's supposed to be unbreakable glass,' Kyle muttered in a dreamlike voice.

'Tell that to the glass,' Jacks said. 'Come on.'

She stood and offered her hand to him; taking it, he jumped to his feet, his eyes shining and glazed.

'Kyle, are you all right? You can't afford to lose it now. You have to stay focused, okay?'

He stepped forward quickly and his lips met hers in a lingering kiss.

Where are my feelings? she wondered. *How long have I wanted to do this? How long have I been in love with him? But there's nothing. Despite the danger, I should feel something.*

He drew away and whispered, 'I love you,' before resuming the kiss with more passion than before.

Why are we not running? she thought. Pushing him away, fear seized her heart and squeezed it with a dreadful warning.

'We have to leave,' she said, 'we have no time for this right now. Patrick's still here; I can feel him. I'll be taken back there unless we can escape. Do you understand anything that I'm saying to you, Kyle?'

He had a foolish grin on his face, entirely inappropriate for the situation. She grabbed his sleeve, pulling him as she headed toward the car park and he tottered behind her like a lost lamb.

'It's strange, ' he said, trance-like, 'but I don't even remember falling asleep.

Jacks stopped abruptly. 'You think you're asleep, Kyle?' she said. 'Do you think you're dreaming?' Her eyes darted about in sheer panic. 'Oh my God. What have I done?'

She gaped up at him wide eyed and he approached, holding her forearms tenderly.

'I'm still there,' she whispered, and bit into her lower lip. 'I didn't make it back. The only piece of reality I managed to hold onto was *you*. I've dragged you in here with me, and you came because of your desire to be with me, oh my God!' She shook her head slowly, not wanting to believe what she knew to be the truth.

The sound of hollow clapping appeared from nowhere and Patrick stepped forth. 'How marvellous, Jacks,' he said. 'How fitting that *he* should be our next.'

Jacks stepped between the two men, outstretching her arms to shield the doctor.

'Stay away,' she demanded. 'You will not touch him. He's going back, Patrick.'

Patrick laughed insanely, a laugh that proved shrill enough to break the illusion. Jacks reached back and squeezed the doctor's hand as the wriggling ground appeared beneath them.

'Close your eyes, Kyle and do *not* open them,' she said.

'Jacks, Jacks,' Patrick said, 'he will not be able to see these delights until I have crucified him on a quia timetporte`.' He signalled to a vacant pillar.

'Oh God help us,' she uttered in despair.

He laughed his tin laugh again. 'God, ha!' he said. 'It may surprise you to discover, my sweet sister, that He does not tend to visit us much here; I cannot think why, we are after all such good Christian souls.'

'The Lord is my shepherd; I shall not want,' Jacks chanted. 'He maketh me to lie down in green pastures: he leadeth me beside the still waters. He restoreth my soul: he leadeth me in the paths of righteousness for his name's sake. Yea, though I walk through the valley of the shadow of death, I will fear no evil ...

Patrick stared at her, his face far from amused by her rebellion.

'It is a shame that you didn't try talking to Him more often,' he said. 'He may have actually listened to you now, but He has forsaken you, as He has the rest of us. Now give the doctor to me and we will destroy his soul together.'

'Patrick, how is it that you are not bound by your revenge?' she asked. 'You've made some sort of bargain, haven't you? You've made a deal so that you don't have to mourn your bitterness and spend eternity at the foot of one of those monstrosities. It's not revenge you seek; there's nothing left to appease accept that thing's lust for suffering and misery. You would rather spend infinity on a murderous spree, slaughtering innocent people than accept the consequences of your vengeful actions.'

'*Our* vengeful actions, Jacks. I could never have dealt my revenge without the aid of my dear sister.'

'You're not my brother,' she seethed, and turning, she slapped Doctor Brodie across the face.

His eyes appeared wounded at the violent action from the woman he loved.

'Wake up, Kyle,' she ordered. 'You have to leave here.'

'Jacks, he's not asleep,' Patrick said, 'you brought him here physically. He will offer himself to a quia timetporte`. Now give him to me.'

Her mind raced, wondering how she could have mustered enough power to accomplish such a feat when it had taken Patrick months to achieve. The snake-like quia timetporte` shuddered and contracted downward; it remained wet and quivering in excited anticipation of its approaching feed on an innocent.

Jacks noticed the figures of the lost souls roaming toward them. Her mind raced through images and memories concerning Patrick, like searching through microfilm. *There was some higher power Patrick was afraid of … the lake,* she thought. *He described it as the void between the two planes, but it's more than that. It managed to hurt him and send him back here. Perhaps it could send us back to our world. Perhaps God hasn't abandoned us after all, and He will lead a path through still waters.*

The ground quaked and Patrick scowled as it changed to dark earth beneath the boughs of twisted trees. Jacks ran forward with Kyle in tow.

'Jump Kyle,' she shouted.

They leapt into the air and Jacks was aware of many things at once—the loud splash of water, a burning sensation and screams, her own and Doctor Brodie's. She saw her hand reach out towards him and felt herself being dragged back.

As he fell from nowhere into the hospital lift, Doctor Brodie saw the hand of Jacks as it retreated back into nothingness and her screams faded.

The pain throbbed from the shock of the water. Looking up, Jacks saw briefly, the figure of the doctor on the opposite bank, his outstretched hand held toward her.

He had escaped.

She collapsed in stinging agony. Patrick swept her roughly into his arms and she knew that he fully intended on offering her to the awaiting evil. She attempted to struggle, but the void had left her weak. Lifting her hand to his face, she caressed his cheek, smiling. He paused for a moment gazing down at her.

'I'm sorry, Jacks,' he said. 'At least this way I get to spend eternity by your side.' He returned her smile, but his eyes were devoid of any real feeling.

The pulsating quickened like an excited heartbeat and Patrick laid Jacks in the bed of the awaiting quia timetporte`; it quivered slightly, yet did not move to grasp her in its eternal embrace.

The touch of its skin was neither cool nor warm, but seemed to be extremes of both at the same time, threatening to burn or freeze whoever made contact. The surface that had seemed snake-like, was in fact hairy, reminiscent of a billion spiders' legs. It had a heavy muscular quality, a single limb from an endlessly vast creature, whose purpose was the digestion of the unwanted.

Jacks could feel it burble and purr beneath her, as it told her what she must do. Patrick gazed in helpless confusion as Jacks rose to her feet.

'It doesn't want me, brother,' she said.

His eyes narrowed slightly as she leaned in and kissed him.

'It wants *you*.'

Without warning, she pushed him and he landed awkwardly, the quia timetporte` constricting immediately, ensnaring him like a flytrap clings to its meal. As it stretched to its full height, Jacks could hear Patrick's growls and cursing, which soon changed to sobs at her betrayal.

She walked away to the sound of her brother's pleading—a new purpose in her insane mind, a job to do—a destiny to fulfil.

Epilogue

The door clicked open.

'How are we today, Kyle?' the nurse asked, without any sign of caring for an answer.

'She spoke to me again,' he said, rattling his restraints. 'She was here.'

'Of course she was, Kyle, now I'm going to give you a little something to help you rest easier.'

He struggled, but it only made the pain more acute as the needle hit its mark.

'She's coming for me,' he whispered, as the drug sent his mind into oblivion.

And he dreamed.

Bibliography

Carter, Rita. *Mapping the Mind*. (Weidenfield & Nicholson, London, 1998)

Gray F.R.S, Henry. *Gray's Anatomy The Classic Collector's Edition* (Galley Press, Leicester, 1988)

Hope, R. Longmore, J. McManus, K. and Wood-Allum, C. *Oxford handbook of Clinical Medicine Fourth Edition*. (Oxford University Press, Oxford, 1998)

Temple, R. *Open to Suggestion*. (The Aquarian Press, London, 1989)

Edt Gregory, R L. *The Oxford Companion to the Mind*. (Oxford University Press, Oxford, 1987)

British Medical Association, Royal Pharmaceutical Society of Great Britain. *British National Formulary 33*. (Pharmaceutical Press, Oxon, 1997)

British Medical Association. Royal Pharmaceutical Society of Great Britain. *British National Formulary 41* (Pharmaceutical Press, Oxon, 2001)

References

The author gratefully recognises the following quotations.

Pages 138/139/141/172/211/276/325
Shakespeare, W. *Hamlet.*

Pages 140/234
Shakespeare, W. *Maceth.*

Page 156, Poe, E A. *Complete Tales and Poems.*

Page 180, Lovecraft, H P. *The Silver Key.*

Pages 296/345, Psalm 23, *Holy Bible, King James Version.*

Page 309, Shakespeare, W. *The Rape of Lucrece.*